Praise for *One Perfect Lie*

"This twisty thriller about high-school secrets and deadly consequences is impossible to put down." —*People*

"Readers can be assured that the author nails the high-school milieu, from athletic rivalries to sexting . . . they're in for one thrilling ride." —*Kirkus Reviews*

"Entertaining . . . This fast-paced read culminates in a daring chase that would play well on the big screen."
—*Publishers Weekly*

"Scottoline slams the plot into reverse at midpoint and accelerates at full speed." —*Library Journal*

"Scottoline is the master of inventive plots and relatable characters." —*HuffPost*

"Engaging . . . a roller-coaster ride."
—*RT Book Reviews*

"Lisa Scottoline has created another highly entertaining story that compels reading to the finish."
—*San Francisco Book Review*

"A definite 'five star' read, Lisa Scottoline has created yet another title you do *not* want to miss!"
—*Suspense Magazine*

"Reading the story is like watching a wild action movie, with thrills and excitement galore."

—*Ashbury Park Press*

"A riveting and emotional story with shocking twists that you won't see coming." —*Fresh Fiction*

"This is Lisa Scottoline at her plotting best."

—*Inside Jersey* magazine

"Scottoline is particularly successful at depicting her teenage characters, and skillfully captures high school with all its pettiness, frustrations, and sexting."

—*Mystery Scene*

"*One Perfect Lie* leaves no doubt that [Scottoline is] an accomplished crafter of tension-filled plot." —NJ.com

Titles by Lisa Scottoline

Rosato & DiNunzio Novels

Feared
Exposed
Damaged
Corrupted
Betrayed
Accused

Rosato & Associates Novels

Think Twice
Lady Killer
Killer Smile
Dead Ringer
Courting Trouble
The Vendetta Defense
Moment of Truth
Mistaken Identity
Rough Justice
Legal Tender
Everywhere That Mary Went

Other Novels

After Anna
One Perfect Lie
Most Wanted
Every Fifteen Minutes
Keep Quiet
Don't Go
Come Home
Save Me
Look Again
Daddy's Girl
Dirty Blonde
Devil's Corner
Running from the Law
Final Appeal

Nonfiction (with Francesca Serritella)

I See Life Through Rosé-Colored Glasses
I Need a Lifeguard Everywhere but the Pool
I've Got Sand in All the Wrong Places
Does This Beach Make Me Look Fat?
Have a Nice Guilt Trip
Meet Me at Emotional Baggage Claim
Best Friends, Occasional Enemies
My Nest Isn't Empty, It Just Has More Closet Space
Why My Third Husband Will Be a Dog

ONE PERFECT LIE

Lisa Scottoline

St. Martin's Paperbacks

This is a work of fiction. All of the characters, organizations, and events portrayed in this novel are either products of the author's imagination or are used fictitiously.

Published in the United States by St. Martin's Paperbacks, an imprint of St. Martin's Publishing Group.

ONE PERFECT LIE

For information, address St. Martin's Publishing Group, 120 Broadway, New York, NY 10271.

www.stmartins.com

Library of Congress Catalog Card Number: 2016053892

ISBN: 978-1-250-25280-7

Our books may be purchased in bulk for promotional, educational, or business use. Please contact your local bookseller or the Macmillan Corporate and Premium Sales Department at 1-800-221-7945, ext. 5442, or by email at MacmillanSpecialMarkets@macmillan.com.

Printed in the United States of America

St. Martin's Press edition / April 2017
St. Martin's Griffin edition / February 2018
St. Martin's Paperbacks edition / February 2020

10 9 8 7 6 5 4 3 2 1

To Shane and Liam, with love

Lying to ourselves is more deeply ingrained
than lying to others.

—Fyodor Dostoyevsky

Chapter One

Chris Brennan was applying for a teaching job at Central Valley High School, but he was a fraud. His resume was fake, and his identity completely phony. So far he'd fooled the personnel director, the assistant principal, and the chairperson of the Social Studies Department. This morning was his final interview, with the principal, Dr. Wendy McElroy. It was make-or-break.

Chris waited in her office, shifting in his chair, though he wasn't nervous. He'd already passed the state and federal criminal-background checks and filed a clear Sexual Misconduct/Abuse Disclosure Form, Child Abuse Clearance Form, and Arrest/Conviction Report & Certification Form. He knew what he was doing. He was perfect, on paper.

He'd scoped out the school and observed the male teachers, so he knew what to wear for the interview—a white oxford shirt, no tie, khaki Dockers, and Bass loafers bought from the outlets in town. He was six-foot-two, 216 pounds, and his wide-set blue eyes, broad cheekbones, and friendly smile qualified him as handsome in a suburban way. His hair was sandy brown, and he'd just gotten it cut at the local Supercuts. Everyone liked a clean-cut guy, and they tended to forget that appearances were deceiving.

His gaze took in Dr. McElroy's office. Sunlight spilled from a panel of windows behind the desk, which was shaped like an L of dark wood, its return stacked with forms, files, and binders labeled **Keystone Exams, Lit & Alg 1**. Stuffed bookshelves and black file cabinets lined the near wall, and on the far one hung framed diplomas from Penn State and West Chester University, a grease-board calendar, and a poster that read DREAM MORE, COMPLAIN LESS. The desk held family photographs, pump bottles of Jergen's and Purell, and unopened correspondence next to a letter opener.

Chris's gaze lingered on the letter opener, its pointed blade gleaming in the sunlight. Out of nowhere, he flashed to a memory. *No!* the man had cried, his last word. Chris had stabbed the man in the throat, then yanked out the knife. Instantly a fan of blood had sprayed onto Chris, from residual pressure in the carotid. The knife must have served as a tamponade until he'd pulled it out, breaking the seal. It had been a rookie mistake, but he was young back then.

"Sorry I'm late," said a voice at the doorway, and Chris rose as Dr. McElroy entered the office on a knee scooter, which held up one of her legs bent at the knee, with a black orthopedic boot on her right foot.

"Hello, Dr. McElroy, I'm Chris Brennan. Need a hand?" Chris rose to help her but she scooted forward, waving him off. She looked like what he'd expected: a middle-aged professional with hooded blue eyes behind wire-rimmed bifocals and with a lean face framed by clipped gray hair and dangling silver earrings. She even had on a dress with a gray-and-pink print. Chris got why women with gray hair dressed in gray things. It looked good.

"Call me Wendy. I know this looks ridiculous. I had bunion surgery, and this is the way I have to get around."

"Does it hurt?"

"Only my dignity. Please sit down." Dr. McElroy rolled the scooter toward her desk with difficulty. The basket in front of the scooter held a tote bag stuffed with a laptop, files, and a quilted floral purse.

Chris sat back down, watching her struggle. He sensed she was proving a point, that she didn't need help, when she clearly did. People were funny. He had researched Dr. McElroy on social media and her faculty webpage, which had a bio and some photos. She'd taught Algebra for twelve years at CVHS and lived in nearby Vandenberg with her husband, David, and their Pembroke Welsh corgi, Bobo. Dr. McElroy's photo on her teacher webpage was from her younger days, like a permanent Throwback Thursday. Bobo's photo was current.

"Now you know why I'm late. It takes forever to get anywhere. I was home recuperating during your other interviews, that's why we're doing this now. Apologies about the inconvenience." Dr. McElroy parked the scooter next to her chair, picked up her purse and tote bag from the basket, and set them noisily on her desk.

"That's okay, it's not a problem."

Dr. McElroy left the scooter, hopped to her chair on one foot, then flopped into the seat. "Well done, me!"

"Agree," Chris said pleasantly.

"Bear with me another moment, please." Dr. McElroy pulled a smartphone from her purse and put it on her desk, then reached inside her tote bag and slid out a manila folder. She looked up at him with a flustered smile.

"So. Chris. Welcome back to Central Valley. I hear you wowed them at your interviews. You have fans here, already."

"Great, it's mutual." Chris flashed a grin. The other teachers liked him, though everything they knew about him was a lie. They didn't even know his real name, which was Curt Abbott. In a week, when it was all over and he was gone, they'd wonder how he'd duped them. There would be shock and resentment. Some would want closure, others would want blood.

"Chris, let's not be formal, let's just talk, since you've done so well at your previous interviews, and as you know, we have to get this position filled, ASAP. Mary Merriman is the teacher you'd be replacing, and of course, we all understood her need to take care of her ailing father." Dr. McElroy sighed. "She's already up in Maine, but reachable by email or phone. She would be happy to help you in any way she can."

Whatever, Chris thought but didn't say. "That's great to know. How nice of her."

"Oh, she's a peach, Mary is. Even at her darkest hour, she's thinking of her students." Dr. McElroy brightened. "If I expedite your paperwork, I can get you in class this Thursday, when the sub leaves. Can you start that soon?"

"Yes, the sooner the better," Chris said, meaning it. He had a lot to do by next Tuesday, which was only a week away, and he couldn't start until he was in place at the school. It gave new meaning to the word *deadline*.

"I must warn you, you have big shoes to fill, in Mary. She's one of our most beloved teachers."

"I'm sure, but I'm up to the task." Chris tried to sound gung ho.

"Still it won't be easy for you, with the spring semester already well under way."

"Again, I can handle it. I spoke with the others about it and I'm up to speed on her syllabus and lesson plans."

"Okay, then." Dr. McElroy opened the manila folder, which contained a printout of Chris's job application, his fake resume, and his other bogus papers. "Chris, for starters, tell me about yourself. Where are you from?"

"Mostly the Midwest, Indiana, but we moved around a lot. My dad was a sales rep for a plumbing-supply company, and his territory kept changing." Chris lied, excellently. In truth, he didn't remember his father or mother. He had grown up in the foster-care system outside of Dayton, Ohio.

Dr. McElroy glanced at the fake resume. "I see you went to Northwest College in Wyoming."

"Yes."

"Hmmm." Dr. McElroy paused. "Most of us went to local Pennsylvania schools. West Chester, Widener, Penn State."

"I understand." Chris had expected as much, which was why he'd picked Northwest College as his fraudulent alma mater. The odds of running into anyone here who had gone to college in Powell, Wyoming, were slim to none.

Dr. McElroy hesitated. "So, do you think you could fit in here?"

"Yes, of course. I fit in anywhere." Chris kept the irony from his tone. He'd already established his false identity with his neighbors, the local Dunkin' Donuts, Friendly's, and Wegman's, his persona as smoothly manufactured as the corporate brands with their bright logos, plastic key tags, and rewards programs.

"Where are you living?"

"I'm renting in a new development nearby. Valley Oaks, do you know it?"

"Yes, it's a nice one," Dr. McElroy answered, as he'd anticipated. Chris had picked Valley Oaks because it was close to the school, though there weren't many other decent choices. Central Valley was a small town in south-central Pennsylvania, known primarily for its outlet shopping. The factory store of every American manufacturer filled strip mall after strip mall, and the bargain-priced sprawl was bisected by the main drag, Central Valley Road. Also on Central Valley Road was Central Valley Dry Cleaners, Central Valley Lockshop, and Central Valley High School, evidence that the town had no imagination, which Chris took as a good sign. Because nobody here could ever imagine what he was up to.

Dr. McElroy lifted a graying eyebrow. "What brings you to Central Valley?"

"I wanted a change of scenery. My parents passed away five years ago, in a crash. A drunk driver hit their car head-on." Chris kept self-pity from his tone. He had taught himself that the key to evoking the sympathy was to not act sorry for yourself.

"Oh no! How horrible." Dr. McElroy's expression softened. "My condolences. I'm so sorry for your loss."

"Thank you." Chris paused for dramatic effect.

"How about the rest of your family? Any brothers or sisters?"

"No, I was an only child. The silver lining is that I'm free to go anywhere I want. I came east because there are more teaching jobs and they're better-paying. Teachers here are rolling in dough, correct?"

Dr. McElroy chuckled, as Chris knew she would. His starting salary would be $55,282. Of course it was unfair that teachers earned less than crooks, but life wasn't fair. If it were, Chris wouldn't be here, pretending to be somebody else.

"Why did you become a teacher, Chris?"

"I know it sounds corny but I love kids. You can really see the influence you have on them. My teachers shaped who I am, and I give them so much credit."

"I feel the same way." Dr. McElroy smiled briefly, then consulted the fake resume again. "You've taught Government before?"

"Yes." Chris was applying to fill the opening in AP Government, as well as the non-AP course Government & Economics and an elective, Criminal Justice, which was ironic. He had fabricated his experience teaching AP Government, familiarized himself with an AP Government textbook, and copied a syllabus from online, since the AP curriculum was nationally standardized. If they wanted to turn the public schools into chain stores, it worked for him.

"So, you enjoy teaching at the secondary level. Why?"

"The kids are so able, so communicative, and you see their personalities begin to form. Their identities, really, are shaping. They become adults." Chris heard the ring of truth in his own words, which helped his believability. He actually *was* interested in identity and the human psyche. Lately he'd been wondering who he was, when he wasn't impersonating someone.

"And why AP Government? What's interesting about AP Government to you?"

"Politics is fascinating, especially these days. It's something that kids see on TV and media, and they want to talk about it. The real issues engage them." Chris knew that *engagement* was a teacher buzzword, like *grit*. He'd picked up terms online, where there were so many teacher blogs, Facebook groups, and Twitter accounts that it seemed like the Internet was what *engaged* teachers.

"You know, Chris, I grew up in Central Valley. Ten years ago, this county was dairyland, but then the outlets came in and took over. They brought jobs, but we still have a mix of old and new, and you see that in town. There's been an Agway and a John Deere dealership for decades, but they're being squeezed out by a Starbucks."

"I see." Chris acted sad, but that worked for him too. He was relying on the fact that people here would be friendly, open-hearted, and above all, trusting.

"There's an unfortunate line between the haves and the have-nots, and it becomes obvious in junior year, which you will be teaching." Dr. McElroy paused. "The kids from the well-to-do families take the SATs and apply to college. The farm kids stay behind unless they get an athletic scholarship."

"Good to know," Chris said, trying to look interested.

"Tell me, how do you communicate with students best?"

"Oh, one-on-one, definitely. Eye-to-eye, there's no substitute. I'm a friendly guy. I want to be accessible to them on email, social media, and such, but I believe in personal contact and mutual respect. That's why I coach, too."

"Oh, my, I forgot." Dr. McElroy frowned, then sifted through her file. "You're applying to fill our vacancy for an assistant baseball coach. Varsity."

"Yes." Chris had never coached before, but he was a naturally gifted athlete. He'd been going to indoor batting cages to get back in shape. His right shoulder ached. "I feel strongly that coaching is teaching, and vice versa. In other words, I'm always teaching, whether it's in the classroom or on the ball field. The setting doesn't matter, that's only about location."

"An insightful way to put it." Dr. McElroy pursed her lips. "As assistant baseball coach, you would report to Coach Hardwick. I must tell you, he doesn't keep assistants very long. His last one, well, moved on and wasn't replaced. Coach Hardwick likes to do it all himself, his own way. And he can be a man of few words."

"I look forward to meeting him." Chris had researched

Coach Hardwick, evidently a well-known jerk. "I'm sure I can work with Coach Hardwick. He's an institution in regional high-school baseball, and the Central Valley Musketeers have one of the finest programs in the state."

"That's true." Dr. McElroy nodded, brightening. "Last year, several players were recruited for Division I and II."

"Yes, I know." Chris had already scouted the team online for his own purposes. He needed to befriend a quiet, insecure boy, most likely a kid with a troubled relationship to his father. Or better yet, a dead father. It was the same profile that a pedophile would use, but Chris was no pervert. His intent was to manipulate the boy, who was only the means to an end.

"So where do you see yourself in five years?"

"Oh, here, in Central Valley," Chris lied.

"Why here, though? Why us?" Dr. McElroy tilted her head, and Chris sensed he had to deliver on his answer.

"I love it here, and the rolling hills of Pennsylvania are a real thing. It's straight-up beautiful. I love the quiet setting and the small-town vibe." Chris leaned over, as if he were about to open his heart, when he wasn't even sure he had one. "But the truth is, I'm hoping to settle down here and raise a family. Central Valley just feels like *home*."

"Well, that sounds wonderful! I must say, you lived up to all of my expectations." Dr. McElroy smiled warmly and closed the file. "Congratulations, Chris, you've got the job! Let me be the first to welcome you to Central Valley High School."

"Terrific!" Chris extended his hand over the desk, flashing his most sincere grin.

It was time to set his plan in motion, commencing with step one.

Step One

Chapter Two

Chris pulled into the Central Valley U-Haul dealership and parked his Jeep, a 2010 black Patriot. He slipped on a ball cap, got out of the car, and looked around. There were no other customers, which was why he'd come midmorning on a drizzly Wednesday. He didn't want any witnesses.

The U-Haul office was an orange-and-brown corrugated cube with a glass storefront, and two security cameras on its roofline aimed at the front door and the parking lot, mounted high enough that Chris's face would be hidden by the brim of his ball cap.

The dealership was smaller than the Ryder and Penske dealerships, but it had a storage facility out back, and the units were temperature- and humidity-controlled, making them the perfect place to store ammonium nitrate fertilizer, which was the main component of homemade IEDs, or improvised explosive devices, like an ANFO bomb.

Chris crossed to the lineup of gleaming white-and-orange pickups, cargo vans, and box trucks in several different lengths. The ten-foot box truck would be large enough to hold the fifty bags of fertilizer and the other equipment. If a ten-footer wasn't available, the fifteen-footer would do, though it was slower and its large size could attract attention.

Chris spotted only one ten-footer parked in the lot. According to the website, it was available next week, but he wasn't leaving anything to chance.

"Hello, sir, I'm Rick." A salesclerk came over in a green polo shirt with a logo patch and khaki pants.

"Hi, I'm Mike Jacobs. Nice to meet you." Chris extended a hand, and Rick shook it with a smile.

"How can I help you today?"

"I'm interested in the ten-footer." Chris gestured to the truck. "Is this the only one you have?"

"Yes. When do you need it?"

"Hmph." Chris paused, for show. "Let me think, today is Wednesday the thirteenth. I need it for Monday of next week, the eighteenth. Is it available?"

"I have to check and get you a rate quote. You know, you can check availability and reserve online with a credit card."

"I saw that, but I didn't want to reserve it online and send my nephew over to pick it up, only to find out that it's not available."

The clerk hesitated. "Did you say your nephew's going to be picking it up?"

"Yes, he'll be the one to come in and get it. I'm only in town for the day. I'll pay for it once I'm sure of my plans."

"How old is he?"

"Seventeen, a high-school junior." Chris didn't elaborate, because he couldn't. Not yet anyway. He'd just gotten the email confirming that he'd been hired and he was on his way to the school-district office, where he'd fill out the remaining forms. He'd start classes tomorrow and he'd have to pick a boy right away.

"Oh, that's a problem. He has to be eighteen to rent one of our box trucks."

Chris blinked. "But I'd be renting it, not him."

"Sorry, but just the same. He can't pick it up for you or drive if he's under eighteen."

"Really?" Chris asked, feigning surprise. Ryder had a minimum age of eighteen and at Penske, it was twenty-one. "But he has a driver's license, and I'll send him in with cash."

"Sorry, I can't help you out. Company rules. It's on the website in the FAQs."

"Rick, can you bend the rules, just this once? I can't come all the way back to Central Valley just to pick up the truck."

"Nope, sorry." The clerk motioned to the trailers at the end of the row. "Can you use a trailer? He'd only have to be sixteen to rent a trailer."

"No, I really need the truck."

"Then I can't help you, sorry. Did you check Zeke's?"

"What's that?" Chris's ears pricked up.

"Oh, you're not from here, that's right. Everybody knows Zeke." The clerk smiled. "He's a Central Valley old-timer. He fixes farm trucks. Actually, he can fix anything. He always has a truck sitting around to sell or rent, and all the locals use him when we don't have availability. I doubt he'd be picky about renting it to a seventeen-year-old. Most of those farm kids been driving since they were thirteen."

"Good to know," Chris said, meaning it. "Where's his shop?"

"Intersection of Brookfield and Glencross, just out of town." The clerk smiled wryly. "It doesn't have a sign but you can't miss it."

Fifteen minutes later, Chris was driving down Brookfield Road, understanding what the clerk had meant by not being able to miss Zeke's. The intersection of Brookfield and Glencross was in the middle of a soybean field, and on one corner was an ancient cinder block garage surrounded by old trucks, rusted tractors, and used farm equipment next to precarious stacks of old tires, bicycles, and random kitchen appliances.

Chris turned into the grimy asphalt lot and parked in front of the garage. He got out of the car, keeping his ball cap on though there were no security cameras. No one else was around, and the only sound was tuneless singing coming from one of the open bays.

"Zeke?" Chris called out, entering the garage, where a grizzled octogenarian in greasy overalls was working on an old Ford pickup on the lift. A cigarette dangled from his mouth, and his glasses had been repaired with a Band-Aid over the bridge.

"Yo."

Chris smiled pleasantly. "Hi, my name's Pat Nickerson. I hear that you might have a truck to let. My nephew's going to pick it up for me because I'm only in town for today. But he's seventeen. Can you work with that?"

"He a good boy?" Zeke's eyes narrowed.

"Yes."

"Then no!" Zeke burst into laughter, which turned into hacking, though he didn't remove the cigarette from his mouth.

Chris smiled. The guy was perfect.

"What kind of truck you need?" Zeke returned to working under the vehicle.

"A box truck, a ten-footer."

"I got two box trucks, a twelve-footer and a big mama."

"The twelve-footer will do. Does it run okay?"

"Oh, you need it to *run*?" Zeke asked, deadpan, then started laughing and hacking again.

Chris smiled, playing along, though he was deadly serious. An unreliable truck would not be the ticket. "So it runs reliably."

"Yes. I'd let you take it for a spin but it's not here. My cousin's usin' it."

"When will it be back? I need my nephew to pick it up next week, on Monday morning."

"No problem. I've got that one and another coming back. This time of year, it's slow, and nobody's been in. I've always got somethin'. You're moving Monday, we'll have it here Sunday night."

"Okay, let me double-check with my nephew to make sure, and I'll get back to you." Chris didn't explain that the truck wasn't for a move. It was for transporting an ANFO bomb that would kill as many people as possible and cause mass destruction. An ANFO bomb was easy to make and safe to assemble. Combine 96 percent ammonium nitrate fertilizer and 6 percent Number 2 fuel oil, diesel fuel, or kerosene in a drum, making a slurry the consistency of wet flour. To make it even more explosive, add nitromethane, a fuel used in motorsports or hobby rockets, readily available. Wire a blasting cap to TNT or a Tovex sausage, fire it with a simple electrical circuit, and drop it in the drum.

"Okay, fella. Call or stop back. My number's in the book. How long you need the truck for?"

"Just the day or two."

"Fine. Seventy-five bucks a day, cash. You gas it up. I'll have it here Monday morning for your nephew. Nine o'clock."

"How can I be sure?"

"Because I said so." Zeke cackled, the cigarette burning close to his lips. "Okay, fella. See ya later."

"See you," Chris said, turning to go. He had so much to do. The bombing was happening on Tuesday. Only six days away.

Kaboom.

Chapter Three

"I'm Mr. Brennan, welcome to AP Government," Chris said on a continuous loop, standing at the threshold to his classroom and greeting the students. They didn't walk so much as shuffle, the girls in their UGGs and the boys in plastic slides.

"*You're* Mr. Brennan? Oh, whoa!" one female student said, flushing in a way that Chris found charming. But he wasn't tempted. The girls weren't his target. The boys were.

Chris kept smiling, greeting the students while he assessed the boys, uniformly sloppy in T-shirts, sweatpants, or school logowear. Some of them met his eye with confidence, so he eliminated them from consideration. Instead he noted the boys who had weak grips, averted their eyes, or had bad acne. Nobody with acne felt good about themselves. At seventeen years old, Chris had hated his skin, his face, and himself.

"I'm Mr. Brennan, hello, how're you doing?" Chris kept saying, as they kept coming. He had combed his class rosters and identified the boys he had both in class and on the baseball team. In this class, there were three—Evan Kostis, Jordan Larkin, and Michael "Raz" Sematov. Chris kept his eyes peeled for Evan, Jordan, or Raz, but they hadn't come yet.

"Whoa!" "Awesome!" "Look!" the students said as they reached their desks, delighted to discover that a surprise snack awaited them. Chris had placed either a soft pretzel, a packet of chocolate cupcakes, or an apple at each seat.

"Mr. Brennan, why the snacks?" one of the boys called out, holding up his cupcakes.

"Why not?" Chris called back, remembering the boy's name from the roster. The kid was Andrew Samins. "I figured you guys could use a treat."

"*Free?*" Samins asked, incredulous. "Wow, thanks!"

"You're welcome." Chris smiled, making a mental note.

"Awesome, thanks!" "Wow!" "Cool!" "Thank you!" the students chorused, the hubbub intensifying as they compared treats, leading inevitably to noisy negotiation over the snacks, which had been his intent. They were guinea pigs in an experiment, they just didn't know it. Their negotiations would give him clues about the boys' personalities: who had power and who didn't, who could be manipulated and who couldn't. Of course, the fights were over the chocolate cupcakes and the soft pretzels. Nobody wanted the apples except for the girls, either that or they settled for them. Chris wanted to see what happened with Evan, Jordan, and Raz.

"But Mr. Brennan," one girl said above the chatter, "we're not supposed to eat in class. It makes crumbs, and mice come. I saw one in the music room before break."

Another girl chimed in, "Also this is a peanut-free classroom, Mr. Brennan. I'm not allergic but some people could be."

"Ladies, the snacks are peanut-free. Dig in, and I'll take the heat." Chris watched the students take their seats. He'd arranged the desks the conventional way, five rows of six desks. He hadn't assigned them specific seating because he wanted to observe the friendships that had already formed.

Chris returned his attention to the hallway and spotted Evan, Jordan, and Raz walking toward him, looking at something on Evan's smartphone. Chris had researched them on social media and knew that Evan Kostis was the most popular, a rich kid with a doctor father, so Evan wasn't his first choice for a pawn. Evan was the handsome one, with brown eyes, a thin nose, and thick black hair that he kept flipping back. He had a winning smile, undoubtedly thanks to orthodonture, and he dressed cool in a red Patagonia vest, Musketeers hoodie, slim jeans, and Timberland boots that looked new.

Next to Evan was Mike Sematov, whose unruly black hair curled to his shoulders. Sematov had bushy eyebrows and round dark eyes, and he was hyper, trying to grab Kostis's phone. Sematov's nickname was Raz, evidently from Rasputin, his Twitter handle was @cRAZy, and his Facebook feed was usually videos of people vomiting or popping zits and abscesses. Sematov was an excellent possibility because his father had passed away in August from pancreatic cancer. It wasn't easy to find a kid with a dead father, and Chris thought Raz might be a winner, unless the boy was too cRAZy.

Chris shifted his attention to another possibility, Jordan Larkin. Jordan was six-foot-one, but his stooped manner made him look awkward, all gangly legs and arms. The boy had a longish face with fine-boned features, but his hazel eyes were set close together and his hair, a nondescript brown, was too short. He dressed inexpensively, in a blue Musketeers Baseball sweatshirt, generic gray sweatpants, and Adidas's knockoff slides. Best of all, Jordan was the son of a single mother, which was almost as good as a dead father.

Chris smiled and extended a hand as the three boys reached the classroom. "I'm Mr. Brennan, gentlemen. Welcome to AP Government. I'll be coaching you guys, too."

Evan was the first to shake Chris's hand, looking him directly in the eye. "Evan Kostis. Ahoy! Welcome on board!"

"Good to meet you, Evan." Chris was about to turn to Jordan just as Sematov thrust his hand forward.

"Mr. Brennan, yo, I'm Mike Sematov but call me Raz. You don't look like Ms. Merriman." Raz smiled goofily.

"Can't fool you!" Chris kept his smile on, making a mental note of the fact that Sematov had offered his nickname and a handshake. The gestures suggested that Raz wanted a connection with him, so maybe there was something Chris could build on. "Raz, go in and pick a desk. Also I put out snacks for everybody."

"Awesome!" Raz's dark eyes lit up, and he ducked inside the classroom.

"Sweet!" Evan bolted after him, leaving Jordan alone with Chris, who extended a hand to the boy.

"You must be Jordan Larkin. Great to meet you."

"Thanks." Jordan shook Chris's hand, breaking eye contact to peek inside the classroom. "Are you for real about snacks? You know, they freak if we eat in the classroom."

"What they don't know won't hurt 'em," Chris said, then added, improvising, "We're celebrating. It's my birthday."

Jordan smiled, surprised. "Oh, jeez. Happy birthday."

"Don't say anything, I don't want to make a fuss."

"Sure." Jordan looked away, and Chris felt he had scored a point, co-opting the boy. Meanwhile Evan and Raz were racing each other to the snacks, and the only empty desks left were the first seats in each row. The remaining snacks were a soft pretzel and two apples.

"I call the pretzel!" Raz bolted toward the desk with the soft pretzel.

"I saw it first!" Evan chased after him, hip-checking Raz to grab the pretzel.

"Dude, yo!" Raz said, mock-outraged.

"Loser says what?" Evan shoved the pretzel in his mouth and claimed the desk, making the class laugh.

"Okay, everybody, let's get started!" Chris closed the classroom door, and the laughter slowly began to subside. Raz slumped into the desk at the head of the row, sulking as he set down his backpack. Jordan took the last empty desk, at the head of the row closest to Chris's desk, then he accepted the apple without complaint. The transaction confirmed to Chris that Evan Kostis was the leader, Raz was a question mark, and Jordan was the follower.

"Class, as I said, my name is Mr. Brennan and I'll be replacing Ms. Merriman. I have her syllabus, and we'll try to pick up where she left off." Chris clapped his hands together to get their attention, since they hadn't settled down. "I'm new in town. I grew up in the Midwest, taught in Wyoming, and I think we're going to have a fine rest of the semester."

"Can you ride horses?" Raz called out, and Chris took it as another attempt to make a connection.

"Yes, I can," Chris answered, which was true. "Anything else you want to know? I'm happy to answer a few questions."

"Are you married?" one of the girls called out.

"No, I'm not," Chris answered to hooting and giggling.

"Are you a dog person or cat person?" asked another girl, the one who worried about peanut allergies. Her name was Sarah Atkinson, Chris knew but didn't let on.

"I like all animals but I don't have any pets right now. I'm not allowed. Last question?"

"Boxers or briefs?" Raz shouted, then burst into laughter, joined by the rest of the class.

"No comment." Chris smiled, then motioned for them to settle down. "All right, let's jump right in. I'm going to assume that you read the materials Ms. Merriman posted on her webpage and I reposted them on mine. That's how I'm going to run this class, too. Government derives its power from the consent of the governed. We also have a social compact, you and I."

The students began pulling out their three-ring binders, spiral-bound notebooks, finding pens and pencils from their backpacks. They weren't allowed to use laptops in class.

"My webpage has the syllabus, the assignments, and the quiz and test schedule. Class participation is a third of your grade." Chris walked to his desk, which contained the Teacher's Edition of their textbook *How Government Works,* the black binder of his notes for class, and a class roster with students' faces, none of whom he cared about except Evan, Jordan, and Raz. He consulted it before he asked the next question. "Mr. Samins, Andrew Samins? Let's start with the readings. What was the first social compact in this country?"

"Uh, I don't know, I'm not sure. I was sick yesterday so I didn't do the homework."

"Okay, you get a free pass, one day only." Chris smiled, like the Cool Teacher. "Anybody else?" A bunch of girls raised their hands, and Chris glanced at his roster. "Sarah Atkinson? Sarah, why don't you tell us?"

"It was the Mayflower Compact."

"Correct, and why was the Mayflower Compact a social contract?"

"Well, the people on the Mayflower decided to get together and they said that they would make an agreement on how they were going to govern themselves."

"Right." Chris noticed Evan and Jordan hunched over their notebooks to take notes. Raz was doodling a picture of a pilgrim. "In 1620, the Mayflower made its way to the Boston area with a hundred and two passengers. On November 11, 1620, forty-one of them—only the men—wrote and signed a document that created a system of self-governance, because they had to start a settlement, plant crops, and harvest them."

Chris could see that Evan and Jordan took more notes, and Raz kept doodling. He continued, "The Mayflower Compact was a first example of popular sovereignty. Does anybody know what popular sovereignty means?"

Sarah's hand shot up again, but Chris pointed to an Asian girl behind her. "Yes, hi, please tell me your name before you answer the question."

"Brittany Lee. Popular sovereignty means that the political authority is with the people, like the citizens, and they can do what they want to the government. They can start one or they can even overthrow one."

"That's right, Brittany. The notion is that individuals have rights, and that the government has power only because it comes from the people." Chris wanted to get to the exercise he had planned, with an ulterior motive. "Now, you were supposed to read the Constitution and the Bill of Rights. These two documents embody what is unique about American government, which is that the Constitution sets the structure of government and the Bill of Rights sets the limitations on government. In other words, the Bill of Rights protects the rights of the individual. Let's do an exercise that will help us think about what it was like to be setting up a government."

Chris moved to the center of the room, and Raz turned the page, hiding his doodle. "Imagine you were one of the founding fathers, the actual people who wrote the Constitution and the Bill of Rights. Which document would you write, if you had the choice? Are you the authority, the person who wants to set up the government and establish rules that everyone can live by? *Or* are you the person who wants to set forth what rights belong to the individuals, so that they can never be taken by the authority?"

Sarah's hand shot up. "Like, do you mean are we Republicans or Democrats?"

"What about the independents?" called a boy in the back. "My brother's an independent!"

Raz turned around. "Your brother's an independent geek!"

Chris shot Raz a warning look, wondering if the boy was too much of a loose cannon for him. "Everybody, stand up, right now."

There were moans, giggles, and chatter as the students rose by their desks, some reluctantly. Evan stood up quickly, and Jordan rose, hunched, without making eye contact with Chris.

"This unit, we're going to write our own Constitution and our own Bill of Rights. We're going to set up the government we would like and then we're going to set limitations on that government. So you need to decide if you want to write our Constitution or our Bill of Rights. Regardless of whatever political party you might be, or your parents might be, I want you to think about this for yourself."

A few students smiled and started talking among themselves.

"Don't do what your friends do. Pretend you were one of the founding fathers. Would you have been one of the people to set up the government or one of the ones to limit government? I'll give you a moment to decide. Close your eyes and think for yourself."

The students closed their eyes, giggling. Evan obeyed, and Jordan bowed his head as if it were a moment of silence. Raz closed one eye, then the other, making faces.

"Okay, the people who want to write the Constitution, walk toward the wall where the door is, with your eyes closed. And the people who want to write the Bill of Rights, walk to the side where the windows are. But don't open your eyes."

The class burst into chatter, and Sarah called out, "How can we walk with our eyes closed? We can't see! We'll bump into the desks!"

"Just do it, Sarah!" Evan called back. "You're not going to die. If you bump into something, go around it."

"Don't worry, I won't let you hurt yourself." Chris watched as the students took hesitant steps, walking with their arms outstretched, jostling each other, bumping into desks and backpacks, chattering and laughing. He kept an eye on Evan, Jordan, and Raz, as they were choosing sides.

"Keep your eyes closed!" Chris called to them. "Constitution or Bill of Rights? Up to you, people!"

There was more giggling, and one of the girls almost ended up walking out the door, but after a few minutes, the students sorted themselves into their noisy sides.

"Okay, everybody open your eyes!" Chris said, having accomplished his mission.

Chapter Four

Chris entered the faculty lounge with his lunch tray, looking for an empty seat. Teachers sat eating at tables of fake-wood veneer with blue bucket chairs. Their animated chatter filled the air, which smelled like an outlet perfume and tomato soup. The lounge was windowless, ringed by oak cabinetry and builder's-grade appliances, with walls painted Musketeer blue. An old blue couch sat against one wall underneath a mirror, and the far wall held a water-cooler with backup water bottles.

Chris headed for a table that still had empty chairs, and one or two teachers flashed him friendly smiles, undoubtedly having gotten the memo with the subject line, **Give CHRIS BRENNAN a Warm Central Valley Welcome!** He'd met some of them in the cafeteria, when they'd introduced themselves and told him that the double-decker grilled cheese was on the menu, evidently a cause for celebration. Chris didn't know if it was harder to fake being a teacher or being jazzed about a sandwich.

There was a table with a few empty seats, at which sat two female teachers in shirtdresses, one with short brown hair and one with long. The one with short hair motioned to him. "Come here!" she called out, smiling. "Join us!"

"We don't bite!" she added.

Chris forced a chuckle, setting down his tray. "Thanks. I'm Chris Brennan. Great to meet you."

"Great to meet you, too. I'm Sue Deion, I teach Calculus." Sue gestured to her friend. "And this is Linda McClusky. She teaches Spanish."

"Nice to meet you, too, Linda." Chris sat down, going through his mental Rolodex. He'd researched Linda McClusky because she also taught eleventh grade. She lived in Bottsburg with her husband, Hugh, a piano teacher, and ran the Central Valley Players, which was performing *Annie* in May. Chris would miss the production.

Sue asked, "So what are you teaching, Chris?"

"Government." Chris took a bite of his grilled cheese, served on a Styrofoam plate with a cup of tomato soup, canned peaches, and red Jell-O with Cool Whip.

"Oh, here comes trouble!" Linda looked up at two male teachers approaching them with a female teacher, and Chris recognized the woman from his research because she was a drop-dead-gorgeous brunette, her great body shown to advantage in a trim black dress with black suede boots. Her name was Courtney Wheeler and she taught French, coached Cheer Club, and was married to a mortgage banker named Doug.

"Abe, Rick, Courtney, come here!" Sue motioned them over.

Chris shifted his attention to one of the male teachers, who was Abe Yomes, nicknamed Mr. Y. Abe was a tall, reedy African-American who taught Language Arts in eleventh grade, which was why Chris had researched him. Abe had on a trim checked shirt, pressed khakis, and polished loafers. He was gay and lived in town with his partner, Jamie Renette, who owned Renette Realty.

"I'm Abe Yomes, the famous Mr. Y, and you must be the new kid." Abe grinned as he set his tray on the table.

"Pleased to meet you, Abe. Chris Brennan." Chris reached across the table, and Abe shook his hand, with a smile.

"Welcome to Stepford. My partner Jamie's a Realtor, in case you decide to buy." Abe's dark eyes twinkled with amusement behind his hip rimless glasses. "I see you're drinking the Kool-Aid—I mean, eating the grilled cheese. These people, they're a cult. I tell them, the grilled cheese sucks out loud. The fact that it's a double-decker only makes it twice as gummy. I speak truth to power, and by power I mean the cafeteria ladies."

"Good to know." Chris chuckled, genuinely.

"Chris, meet Rick Pannerman, our resident hippie. He was born to teach Art. Actually he was born to be Picasso, but somebody else got the job." Abe gestured to the other male teacher, who was bald and chubby, with bright blue eyes and a smile buried in his long grayish beard. He dressed in a worn flannel shirt and jeans.

"Chris, good to see ya," Rick said, extending a meaty hand. "Welcome to the Island of Misfit Toys."

"Ha!" Chris smiled, and so did Abe.

"That's what he calls our table. Now you're one of us freaks. Gooble-gobble." Abe pulled out a chair as Courtney came walking over with her tray. "Last but not least, this lovely creature is Courtney Wheeler. She's married to Doug The Lug, the world's most boring white guy, and that's saying something."

"Abe, hush." Courtney sat down, smiling.

Abe pushed her chair in with a flourish. "Courtney is my bestie, and Prince Harry is my spirit animal. Don't you think we look alike, he and I?"

Courtney answered slyly, "Well, you both breathe oxygen."

"Not true. Oxygen breathes *him*." Abe sat down, focusing again on Chris. "So welcome, Central Valley virgin. What do you teach again?"

"Government and Criminal Justice," Chris answered, finishing the first half of his sandwich.

"I teach Language Arts, playing to type. I'm sensitive, yet curiously strong, the Altoids of teachers. Where're you from?"

"Wyoming."

"Wait. Whaaaat? Wyoming?" Abe's eyes flew open behind his rimless glasses. "Are you kidding me right now?"

Courtney burst into laughter. "Oh my God!"

Rick grinned in a goofy way. "Ha! What are the chances?"

Chris didn't like the way they said it. "Why? Have you been there?"

"*Been* there?" Abe repeated, his lips still parting in delight. "I *grew* up there! It was my childhood home! We left when I was nine but my parents moved back there, they liked it so much!"

"Really?" Chris arranged his face into a delighted mask. "What a coincidence."

"I know, right?" Abe bubbled with enthusiasm. "I'm adopted, hello. My dad was a real outdoorsman. Wyoming born and bred. He was on the Game and Fish Commission—fun fact, Wyoming is one of the few states that have a Game and Fish Commission, as opposed to a Fish and Game Commission. Anyway, my dad taught me to hunt and fish. We ate fresh elk burgers for dinner! You know how many elk are up there, and mule deer, bison, grizzlies . . ."

"Don't I know it," Chris said, though he didn't.

"Whereabouts in Wyoming are you from?" Abe leaned over, ignoring his lunch.

"Well, I'm not really *from* Wyoming—"

"I thought you said you were."

Courtney blinked. "Meanwhile Abe is being rude as usual, asking a million questions and not letting you eat."

Abe recoiled. "I'm not being rude. I never met anybody else from Wyoming out here. It's amazing!" He returned his attention to Chris. "I didn't mean to be rude, I just got excited. I'm an excitable boy. You get that, right?"

"I understand, no apology's necessary."

"I didn't think so." Abe glanced at Courtney triumphantly. "See, henny? Boyfriend and I speak the same language, though he doesn't have an accent." Abe turned back to Chris. "You don't have an accent. You must've lost it."

"I guess I did—"

"Right, you lose it. I lost mine. Can you imagine looking like me and sounding like a ranch hand? We're talking *major* cognitive dissonance."

Courtney rolled her lovely eyes. "Abe, you had the double-shot again, didn't you?"

Rick turned to Chris with an apologetic look. "We got a Starbucks in town, and Abe lives there. Buckle up."

Abe ignored them, turning back to Chris. "Anyway so are you from Wyoming or not?"

"No, I'm from the Midwest but I went to Northwest College in—"

"Powell! Of course! My dad's alma mater! In the Bighorn basin!"

"You know Northwest College, too?" Chris was kicking himself. This was a problem.

Courtney interjected, "Abe loves Wyoming. He even dragged us all out there to see it. Pretty, but really? Boring."

Rick shrugged. "I didn't think it was boring. Sachi wants us to retire there. All that natural beauty."

"Hold on a sec, I got snaps!" Abe slid his iPhone from his back pocket and started touching the screen.

Chris turned to Courtney to change the subject. "So Courtney, what do you teach?" he asked, though he already knew.

"French." Courtney smiled. "I started here five years ago, after I got married."

"Look!" Abe interrupted, holding up his phone across the table, showing a photo of a rock formation around a body of water. "This must bring back memories, doesn't it?"

Chris plastered on a startled smile of recognition. "Man, that's great!"

Abe turned the picture around. "It looks like a lake, but it's not. I had my first kiss there—with a woman *and* a man! Tell 'em what it is, Chris! Everybody went there to make out, didn't they? That's what my dad said."

"Not me, I was a good boy. I studied hard so I could grow up, become a teacher, and eat double-decker grilled cheese." Chris took a bite of his sandwich, then acted as if he'd gotten food stuck in his throat. Suddenly he pushed away from the table, fake-choking, letting his expression reflect mild alarm, between hairball and Heimlich.

Rick's blue eyes went wide. "Chris, are you *choking*?"

"Oh no, drink something!" Courtney jumped up with a water bottle and hurried to his side.

"Chris!" Abe rushed around the table and whacked Chris on the back as Rick, Sue, and Linda came rushing over.

Chris doubled over, fake-choking as heads began to turn. Each teacher's face registered concern, then fear. He kept it up while Abe, Sue, and Linda clustered around him, calling "Oh no!" "He's choking!" "Do the Heimlich maneuver!" "Call 911!"

"It's okay, I guess it went down the wrong pipe." Chris

acted as if he'd swallowed his sandwich, fake-gasping. The last thing he wanted was someone to call 911, bringing the police. They could start asking questions, which could ruin everything.

"My God!" Abe frowned with regret. "So sorry, I should have let you eat!"

"Not your fault, Abe. It was the sandwich."

"Let's sue the district," Abe shot back. Rick and Courtney laughed, and the other teachers broke into relieved smiles, then went back to their tables.

Chris smiled, but he knew that the Wyoming questions wouldn't go away forever. Abe would want to reminisce and compare notes.

Which presented a problem that he needed to solve.

Chapter Five

Heather Larkin stood by the entrance to the Lafayette Room, scanning the tables in her station, four eights in the left corner. The luncheon was for the Auxiliary Committee of Blakemore Medical Center, and fifty-two well-dressed women had been served their appetizer, mixed-greens salad with goat cheese crumbles, beet shavings, and walnuts.

Everything was going smoothly, and the room looked perfect. It was storming outside, but indirect light poured from Palladian windows and the occasional clap of thunder didn't disturb the chatter and laughter. The lights were low, emanating from tasteful brass sconces on the ivory damask walls, which matched the ivory tablecloths and slipcovered chairs. White tulips filled the centerpieces on each table, and the air smelled like costly perfume and raspberry vinaigrette dressing.

Heather kept an eye on her tables, since it was a club rule that members shouldn't have to wait for service. She wondered if they knew how many eyes were on them, waiting on them so they didn't have to wait. Waiters. Waitresses. It was even in the job name.

Heather's makeup was light, and she'd pulled her straight, brown hair back into a low ponytail. She had on her uniform, a mint-green dirndl with a drawstring bodice intended to show her cleavage to golfers on their third Long Island Iced Tea. She hated the uniform and the required shoes, which were white with a stacked heel. But she picked her battles, and her uniform wasn't one of them.

She had waitressed at the Central Valley Country Club for fifteen years and was excellent at her job. But lately she'd been wondering if she'd gotten too good at waiting. Patience was a virtue, but there were limits. She wondered if a decade of waiting on people had trained her to wait for things to happen, rather than making them happen, or to meet other people's needs instead of her own, like an expert codependent.

Still Heather was lucky to have the job, especially as a single mother. There were cost-of-living increases, pooled tips at Christmas, plus full benefits that she and her son Jordan were eligible for. Jordan was a junior in high school, hopefully heading for college on a baseball scholarship. But what was *she* heading for? She only had two years of college because she quit when she'd gotten pregnant. Still, she never thought of her son as a mistake. Marrying his father was the mistake. Divorcing him corrected the mistake.

Heather scanned the tables. The women looked so nice with their highlights freshly done, and they had on pastel pantsuits with cute cropped jackets, undoubtedly bought at the mall. Club members didn't shop at the outlets, so they didn't have to hide the Sharpie mark on an irregular or the pulled thread of a defective garment. Heather had stopped wanting to be them, but would have settled for being somebody who wore her own clothes to work. She wanted a desk and chair, so she could sit down. She wanted a job that went somewhere, with a brass name-plate with her full name, instead of a name tag, HEATHER.

"Heather," said a voice behind her, and Heather came out of her reverie, turning. It was Emily, the new Food & Beverage Manager. Emily was still in her twenties, but her heavy makeup made her look hard and her short brown hair was stiff with product. She had on a mint-green polo shirt with khakis, the uniform upgrade for management employees.

"Yes?"

"I need you to stay until six tonight. The luncheon is going to run late because they're going to do the silent auction and raffles after the speeches."

"Sorry, I can't. Like I said, I'd like to be home for Jordan." Heather picked her battles, and this was the one she'd picked. Her regular shift was breakfast and lunch, from 6:00 A.M. to 3:00 P.M. That would get her home so she could make dinner and they could have a meal together. It had never been a problem with her old boss Mike, and Heather had assumed that a female boss would be even more understanding. But nobody could knife a woman like another woman.

"I need you to stay." Emily pursed her lips, shiny with pink lip gloss.

"Can't Suzanne?"

"I'm not asking Suzanne. I'm asking you."

"Can't you ask her? She doesn't have kids." Heather reflexively scanned the tables but nobody needed anything.

"Your *kid* is in high school." Emily's blue eyes glittered.

"So?" Heather didn't explain that in one year, Jordan would be gone, off to college. Everything felt like the last time. "You said you'd accommodate—"

"I said I'd accommodate you *if I can*."

"But you're not trying to accommodate me. You didn't ask Suzanne—"

"Heather, if you value your job, you will do what I ask, when I ask it." Emily glanced around the dining room.

"What's that mean? You fire me if I say no?"

"Yes." Emily met her eyes directly. "When I took over, I was given carte blanche to do what needed to be done. You can take the job or leave it. Your choice."

Heather felt the blood drain from her face. She had heard the rumors that new management had been hired to cut catering costs. If Emily was looking for reason to fire her, Heather couldn't give her one. "Okay, I'll stay until six," she said quickly. Suddenly she noticed one of the women lifting an empty glass to signal a refill. "I'd better go."

"Hurry," Emily snapped. "You should've seen that earlier. Don't you know who that is? That's Mindy Kostis. She's sponsoring the luncheon."

"Okay, on it." Heather recognized the name because Jordan was on the baseball team with Evan Kostis, Mindy's son.

"Whatever. Go, go, go."

Heather made a beeline for Mindy. The Kostis family was in the Winner's Circle, the top tier of contributors to the Building Fund. Heather hadn't met or served Mindy and felt suddenly relieved that her name tag didn't have her last name. Even so, she doubted that Mindy would recognize the name, since Jordan had just made varsity.

Heather reached the table, extended a hand for the empty glass, and smiled pleasantly. "May I get you a refill, Ms. Kostis?" she asked, since it was club rules to address members by name.

"Yes, please. Tanqueray and tonic." Mindy smiled back, pleasantly enough. She had curly blonde hair, round blue eyes, and a sweet smile. She was dressed in a pink-tweed suit with a patch that read Chanel, and Heather tried not to let her eyes bug out of her head. She had never seen a real Chanel jacket.

"My pleasure," Heather answered, a scripted reply, also per club rules.

"Do I know you? You look so familiar." Mindy squinted at Heather's name tag.

Heather's mouth went dry. She didn't know how Mindy knew her. Heather didn't go to the games because she worked. She was about to answer, *My son is on the baseball team with your son,* but she stopped herself. "No, I don't believe so," she answered, her tone polite.

"Oh, okay, sorry." Mindy smiled, blinking.

"My pleasure," Heather said again, like a CVCC fembot. The other women at the table kept chattering away, paying no attention to the conversation, which, to them, was Mindy talking to The Waitress. She turned to them. "Anyone else need a refill?"

"Uh, no," said one, without looking up, and the others didn't reply.

"Thank you." Heather left, flustered. She didn't know why she hadn't told Mindy who she was. Mindy hadn't demeaned Heather at all, so why had Heather demeaned herself? She didn't consider herself less than Mindy, so why had she acted that way? Mindy was Winner's Circle, but what was Heather? Loser's Circle?

She practically fled the Lafayette Room, heading back toward the bar, and it struck her that the luncheon had just started, but Mindy was the only woman on her second cocktail.

Chapter Six

It was pouring outside, and Susan Sematov stood at her office window, her cell phone to her ear, dismayed to hear her call go to voicemail. Her older son Ryan hadn't come home last night, and she was worried. He was nineteen, an adult, but that didn't mean she didn't worry about him anymore, especially after last year. Her husband, Neil, had passed away after a brutal battle with pancreatic cancer, and Susan, Ryan, and their younger son, Raz, were still reeling. Neil had gone from diagnosis to death in only two months, and Ryan had dropped out of Boston University, where he'd just finished his freshman year.

Susan ended the call and pressed REDIAL to call Ryan again, keeping her face to the window, so it looked as if she was surveying ValleyCo One from her window. Susan was Marketing Manager of ValleyCo, the biggest developer of outlet malls in Central Valley. The ValleyCo One outlet mall also held their corporate headquarters, a three-story brick box designed to coordinate with the brick outlet stores that lay outside her window in a massive concrete square.

Susan's call to Ryan rang and rang, and she sent up a prayer, asking God to please let him pick up. Her older son had taken his father's death so hard and felt lost at home. His friends were still at BU and their other colleges, and he was spending all day sleeping on the couch, and at night, going out drinking with God-knows-who.

Susan's call went to voicemail again, and she hung up, scanning the outlet mall. At the top of the square, its north side, were the Vanity Fair outlets—Maidenform, Olga, Warner's, Best Form, and Lillyette—which everybody in the office nicknamed BoobTown. To her right on the east side was Lee, Wrangler, Reef, Nautica, and JanSport—naturally nicknamed BallTown. To her left was Pottery Barn, Crate & Barrel, Lenox, and Corningware—or HousePorn. Behind her, out of her view, was Land of Shoes; Easy Spirit, Famous Footwear, Reebok, Bass Factory Outlet, and Gold Toe Factory. Susan had been hired straight out of Penn State as an administrative assistant in the Marketing Department and had worked her way up to running the department by the time ValleyCo Five was in blueprints.

Susan glanced at the clock—1:35. She didn't want to call the police because she knew Ryan would throw a fit. She didn't know where Ryan had gone because he'd left the house while she was on a conference call with the West Coast. Presumably he had told his younger brother Raz where he was going, but one work call had led to another, and before Susan knew it, Raz had gone up to bed without telling her where Ryan had gone.

Susan thought it over. The two brothers were thick as thieves, or at least they used to be before Neil had died, but her sons were each reacting to their father's passing in different ways; Ryan, her mild child, had grown more inward, keeping his grief inside, but Raz, her wild child, had gotten more out of control. Raz had idolized his father, and they were both baseball fanatics.

Susan let her thoughts travel backwards in time, to those memories. Raz and Neil would hit balls in the backyard for hours, and Neil went to every one of Raz's games, proud to see his son pitch for the Musketeers. Neil's illness had derailed Raz emotionally, and she had gotten recommendations for therapists, but neither boy would go. She'd started therapy, and the plan was to try to convince them to come with her, but that had yet to come to fruition.

Susan scrolled to the text function, found her last text to Raz, and texted him: **Honey, please call when you can. It's important.** Students were allowed to keep their cell phones with them, only with the sound off, and they weren't permitted to look at them during class. It was a rule more honored in the breach, and Raz and rules were never on good terms.

She slipped the phone back in her blazer pocket and went to her desk, which she kept uncluttered except for her nameplate, a digital clock, a jar of pencils and pens, and family photographs of Neil and the kids. She sat down and scanned the photos, wishing that she were in at least a few of the photographs with Neil, so she could see them over time. They'd met in college, fallen in love, gotten married upon graduation, and been happily married almost every day since then. Susan couldn't have asked for more. Except now, all she asked for was more.

Her gaze found her favorite photo, the one of Neil hugging Ryan and Raz at Ryan's graduation from CVHS. They had been so happy then, and even she didn't believe that they had had such a successful marriage, given their upbringing. She wasn't perfect, nor was he, but they were imperfect in the same way, a union of two doers who loved nothing so much as checking off boxes on a Things To Do List.

Susan shooed the thoughts away, then checked her phone, but Raz hadn't texted her back. She texted him again. **Honey, please call. Worried about Ryan.** She set the phone down, trying not to *catastrophize,* as her therapist Marcia said. Marcia had taught her to cope by occupying her mind, so Susan tapped the mousepad on her laptop. The screen filled with the red ValleyCo logo, a stylized mall nestled in the V of Valley, a branding decision made before Susan's time.

She opened an email and a PDF of a BoobTown ad for her approval. The top banner read THIS MOTHER'S DAY CELEBRATE MOM AND YOURSELF! Underneath was a photo of a pretty mom with a little boy, a stock image aimed at their target market. Susan had been that woman, the shopper who was ValleyCo's sweet spot, the kind of mom who put the date of a sale on her calendar the first time she heard it. That was why Susan made sure that in every ad, the sale date was the largest thing on the page, and in their email blasts, the sale date connected automatically to My ValleyCo Calendar, an app that she had commissioned herself.

My ValleyCo Calendar enabled the customer to schedule the sales at any ValleyCo outlet mall and send herself alerts at one- and two-week intervals. Susan's bosses, all male, had been skeptical, wondering why any woman would agree to be harassed, but the app took off. Susan hadn't been surprised. Its success was due to the innate belief that doing everything right would lead to happiness, a credo that she had ascribed to until Neil died.

Susan approved the ad. It was good enough. She was losing her edge now that Neil had died. He'd been her biggest supporter, and only after he was gone did she realize that she had been performing for him all along.

Susan picked up her phone. It read 1:45 P.M., which

meant that Raz was in seventh period, but he hadn't called or texted. She swiped to her Favorites and pressed three—Neil would be forever number one, and Ryan was number two. The phone rang but it went to voicemail.

"Damn!" Susan said aloud, glancing behind her, but her secretary wasn't looking. Everyone had been so wonderful to her after Neil had passed, but lately her office felt like a fishbowl. Every time they looked at her, she saw herself the way they saw her: a new widow, trying desperately to keep herself and her family from coming apart at the seams, like a factory second. The Sematovs were Irregulars now.

Susan pressed REDIAL, the phone rang twice, and finally, Raz picked up. "Raz—"

"Mom, *what*?" Raz asked, his tone irritated. "Why are you calling me? I'm at school."

"This is your free period, isn't it? I'm worried about Ryan. He didn't come home last night."

"So?"

Susan sensed he was with friends. "So he doesn't do that. He's been out all night."

"Mom." Raz snorted. "Is this what you think is important? He's a big boy. He's *out*."

"Did he tell you where he was going last night?"

"I don't know!" Raz raised his voice.

"Where did he say he was going?"

"'I don't know' means I don't know! I don't *remember*."

"Raz, please think," Susan said, softening her tone. "Something could've happened to him."

"He probably got laid!"

"Raz!" Susan glanced over her shoulder and caught her secretary looking at her. "I'm worried about him."

"There's nothing to worry about! He's fine. I have to go!"

"Raz, you don't know that he's fine. Think about what he told you. Did he say where he was going or who he was with—" Susan stopped when she realized Raz had gone unusually quiet on the other end of the call.

She looked at the phone, and Raz had hung up.

Chapter Seven

Chris headed to baseball practice, more tired than he'd expected. He had no idea how teachers did it, day after day. He'd had to teach the same lesson twice, saying the same exact things to two classes of AP Government and two classes of the non-AP level, since the class size at CVHS was restricted to thirty students. Plus he had to teach his elective, Criminal Justice. He'd identified two more boys in his non-AP course and one in Criminal Justice, but neither as promising as Jordan or Raz.

Chris threaded his way down a packed hallway, having changed into his coach's gear, a blue polo shirt that read ASSISTANT COACH MUSKETEERS BASEBALL, royal-blue nylon sweatpants, and sneakers. Framed group photos of past CVHS classes were mounted on the white walls, and inspirational posters hung at regular intervals: MUSKETEERS MAKE EMPATHY A HABIT. BE THE CHANGE—NOTICE, CHOOSE, ACT. VALIDATE OTHERS. He passed a window overlooking a courtyard filled with flowerbeds. It was raining out, so practice had been moved inside to the gym.

Chris was looking forward to seeing Jordan and Raz, so he could make a final decision. He had tentatively eliminated Evan because of the boy's alpha behavior with the snacks and choice of the Bill of Rights team. Raz had also chosen the Bill of Rights team, so he was now on the bubble. Jordan was the frontrunner since he had chosen the Constitution team, suggesting that he was a boy comfortable with structure and authority, perfect for Chris. He needed a boy he could use and manipulate. Tuesday was coming up fast.

Suddenly Chris noticed that two of his players had turned onto the hallway, Trevor Kiefermann and Dylan McPhee. Chris hadn't met them yet, but he had researched them, and the two boys couldn't have been more different. Trevor was a tall, blocky redhead with a freckled face and an obsession with kettlebells and weight lifting, according to his social media. Dylan was the tallest kid on the team, at six-five, but reed-thin and wiry with wispy blond hair, fine features, and heavy wire-rimmed glasses that slid down his nose. Dylan's social media consisted of photos from NASA, the Astronomy Photo of the Day, and photographs of outer space, sent by whatever astronaut was currently orbiting the earth.

Chris flashed them a smile. "Hey guys, I'm Coach Brennan, the new assistant coach."

"Hey Coach, Trevor Kiefermann, nice to meet you. I play third base." Trevor shook his hand, squeezing it firmly.

"Coach, I'm Dylan McPhee, center field." Dylan shook Chris's hand, too, but his hand was slender, though his grip equally strong.

"Good to meet you both." Chris fell into step with them down the hallway, and Trevor seemed eager to talk, the more outgoing of the two.

"They say you're a cowboy. Moved here from Montana, right?"

"Wyoming, but news travels fast here." Chris allowed his features to reflect mild surprise.

"Raz told us. Where'd you coach before?"

"I didn't. I almost played minor-league ball but I tore my ACL the week before tryouts." Chris knew his alias couldn't be found online on any minor-league roster, should they look him up. Interestingly, the Internet made lying easier and harder, both at once.

"Sucks." Trevor shook his head. "Where'd you play?"

"Class A, Midwest League. If I tell you which team, you're gonna laugh. The Fort Wayne Tincaps of Fort Wayne, Indiana."

"What a name!" Trevor chuckled.

Dylan smiled. "Is that real?"

"Yes, totally." Chris smiled back, feeling the humor break the ice, as usual. "Still, it coulda been worse. Would you believe the Cedar Rapids Kernels."

"Ha!" Trevor laughed, and so did Dylan.

"So how's the season?" Chris asked, though he already knew. The Musketeers were on a losing streak.

"Not so good." Trevor's expression clouded. "The season started April 1, and we're zero and five. Coach Hardwick might replace Raz with Jordan for tomorrow's game. We play Upper Grove, and they're undefeated."

"Is Jordan the better pitcher?"

"I think so. He just made varsity and he doesn't throw as hard as Raz, but his accuracy and control is unreal. He just stays calm, no matter what."

Dylan interjected again, "Jordan's a contact pitcher. The batter might get a piece of the ball, but they won't get a base hit. The ball will be a grounder or fly out, easy to catch."

Chris mulled it over. "So they're competing for starting pitcher and they're friends? That can't be easy, can it?"

"They're buds, but hey, it happens on a team. Only one can be the ace."

Chris was settling on Jordan, but he would need to separate him from Raz to exert the maximum influence on him. The competition for starting pitcher might be the wedge, and all Chris had to do was hammer it hard.

The hallway ended at the entrance to the boys' locker room, and the door was propped open. Trevor gestured inside. "I'll show you where the coaches' office is. Coach Natale should be there, the JV Coach."

"Lead the way, boys."

Chapter Eight

Chris followed the boys down a ramp to a lower level and they entered a large locker room with benches and blue lockers, which was emptying. Trevor and Dylan dropped him off, and Chris walked the short hallway to the coaches' office, spotting Coach Natale through the window. Chris knew from his research that Natale taught Health, his wife Felicia was a reading specialist at the high school, and their twin girls were in fifth grade at CVMS. They owned a white poodle but Chris didn't remember the dog's name. Then it came to him—Snowflake. Confirming, *no imagination.*

"I'm Chris Brennan, the new assistant," Chris said, when he reached the entrance to the office, and Victor crossed the room with an eager grin, his meaty hand extended.

"I'm Victor Natale, welcome!" Victor pumped Chris's hand with vigor. Natale was short and chubby, with an affable Italian-guy vibe. He had large brown eyes, a big nose, and thick lips, his fleshy face framed by thick black hair. "I coach the JV team with my assistant Dan Bankoske. He's already in the gym. So I hear you're from Utah?"

"Wyoming. Everybody knows everything here, am I right?"

"Bingo!" Victor laughed. "My wife told me. She's on the Instructional Support team. She heard it from Anne in the office." He spread his arms broadly. "Well, this is our palace. The empty desk is yours."

"Thanks." Chris crossed to the empty desk and set his backpack on the black desk chair. The windowless room held four black desks facing the wall, and the other three desks were cluttered with forms, three-ring notebooks, and *Inside Pitch, Coach & Athletic Director,* and *Covering All Bases* magazines. Black file cabinets lined the opposite wall next to a dorm-size refrigerator, old microwave, and a Keurig coffeemaker.

"So, Chris, what's your deal? You single or married?"

"Single."

"Girlfriend?"

"No."

"Looking to meet somebody new? My sister-in-law's about to free up. You can take her off my hands. I can't get her out of my house."

"Not yet, thanks." Chris thought Victor was likable but he didn't need a friend.

"Lemme know. Did you get the free iPad? It's from the Boosters, God bless them."

"Yes." Chris unzipped his backpack and took out his new iPad.

"You downloaded the software, right? It's like that app, MLB Dugout."

"Right." Chris had downloaded the coaching software as per Hardwick's emailed instructions, but he had also created secret player files. "Any pointers for working with Coach Hardwick?"

"Ha!" Victor's dark eyes glittered. "The kids call him Hardass behind his back. Also Hardhead, Hardwood, Hard On, and Hard Dick."

Chris chuckled, happy to be taken into confidence so quickly. "He's not exactly Santa Claus."

"Understatement of the year."

"Are you friendly with him?"

"Is anybody? That's why Kwame left. Couldn't take it another minute. Hardwick goes through assistants like Kleenexes." Victor chuckled. "You know the secret to getting along with him? Follow the Bible."

"Really? I didn't know he was a man of faith." Chris hadn't seen anything in his research about Coach Hardwick's being religious or he would've worn a crucifix.

"No, not that Bible. Hardwick's Bible. He emailed it to you. He calls it the Bible."

"Oh, *that* Bible." Chris remembered the packet of information that Coach Hardwick had emailed him. He had it with him in his backpack.

"The Bible is the Gospel According to Hardwick. If you follow the Bible, you'll get along fine with him. The Bible is his program, his rules, rain or shine, off-season to postseason. To be fair, you can't argue with results. He wins." Victor yakked away. "I follow the Bible because it's good for JV and varsity to be consistent. But I use more emotional intelligence than he does. I like to get close to my players, get to know them personally. Hardwick's not like that. He's old-school."

"I think it's okay to get close to the players. You can still retain your authority." Chris processed the information. If Hardwick didn't get close to the players, it gave him an opening with the boys.

"I agree." Victor smiled, his approval plain. "But keep it to yourself. Follow the Bible. Stay in your lane. The kids, too. They know what's expected. If the kids follow the Bible, Hardwick doesn't sweat anything. Like hair, for example. Take Raz. Mike Sematov."

"I have him in class."

"Good luck. What a wackadoodle. He pitched last season. Throws hard. A great fastball but major control problems on and off the field." Victor snorted. "If you have him in class, you know what he's like. Hair down to his shoulders like Lincecum. Wears a man bun. Hardwick doesn't care. He even told Raz that his hair had superpowers like Samson. Now the kid'll *never* cut it."

Chris smiled. "So Raz is the starting pitcher? What about Jordan Larkin? I heard Coach Hardwick might start him instead."

"Larkin? Love that kid." Victor's coarse features lit up. "He played for me on JV last season. He's a great kid. A quiet kid, shy, but great."

"Really." Chris was targeting Larkin, more and more.

"Then over the summer, he grew. That's the kind of thing that happens in high-school ball, I see it all the time. The kids grow, put on muscle. Or they sharpen their skills, improve their mechanics, go to a camp. Larkin came into his own. He's got the stuff. He's *bringin'* it. The team's losing with Raz pitching. I think Hardwick will start Jordan."

"How did Larkin improve so much?"

"God knows. He didn't go to camp, he can't afford it."

"Do you think Raz taught him?" Chris was fishing. "Or maybe he learned from his father?"

"I don't know if Raz taught him. If he did, he regrets it." Victor frowned. "FYI, neither Larkin or Raz have a dad. Raz's dad died last summer, helluva guy. Neil, came to all the games. Larkin's dad skipped out when the kid was little. He's got a mom, a waitress. He's an only child."

"Too bad." Chris had thought as much. There had been no mention of a father in Larkin's social media.

"Yeah, it's a tough break. Larkin's praying for a scholarship."

"Guess we better get going, huh?" Chris gestured at the clock, getting a plan. They left the office and went down the hallway. The air felt hotter, and the heat intensified a weirdly strong odor.

"The stench is Axe body spray. Good luck getting it out of your clothes. My wife can smell it in my hair." Victor fell in step beside him, and they continued down a long corridor to the gym entrance, double-wide with the doors propped open. "Wait'll you see how big the gym is. Batting nets, weight room, the whole nine. Again, the Boosters buy it all."

They reached the gym entrance, and they went inside. Boys were rolling nets, dragging blue mats, and lugging mesh bags full of equipment this way and that. The noise echoed throughout the gym, ricocheting off the hard surfaces. Chris scanned for Jordan, who was with Raz, talking with Coach Hardwick.

"See what I mean? Awesome." Victor gestured with a flourish.

"It's amazing." Chris couldn't have cared less, though the gym was immense, with a high-peaked ceiling of corrugated material, bright strips of fluorescent lighting, and blue-and-white championship banners hanging from the rafters. The walls were white cinder block, and the bleachers, also royal blue, had been folded against the sidewalls, revealing a glistening hardwood floor.

"Today varsity and junior varsity are practicing. I run my guys, you run yours. They're setting up the equipment." Victor pointed to the four corners of the gym.

"I see." Chris kept his eye on Coach Hardwick, who was talking to Raz more than Jordan. The discussion seemed to be heating up, with Coach Hardwick gesturing and Raz shaking his head, no. "Victor, I'd better go check in."

"Good luck." Victor flashed him a warm smile.

Chris took off, beelining for Coach Hardwick. He plastered on a smile, but Hardwick only frowned back, and the harsh lighting of the gym showed the furrows on his forehead and the lines from his bulbous nose to his weak chin. It struck Chris that Coach Hardwick resembled the Central Valley Musketeer, the angry colonist whose painted likeness scowled from the center of the gym floor.

"You're late." Hardwick glared. Up close, his glasses looked dirty, and their bifocal windows magnified his brown irises.

"Sorry, I'm Chris Brennan. Good to see you again—"

"You were talking to Victor. Don't. He talks too much, he's Italian. Stay away from him. It'll take years off your life."

Chris let it go. "I read your email and I know what we're practicing today. I'm good to go."

Hardwick's frown eased. "Call the kids over here. Holler. We don't use whistles. They're not dogs."

"Will do." Chris turned away, cupped his hands, and shouted, "Varsity, come on over!"

Heads turned, and the boys came running almost immediately. Raz jogged over ahead of Jordan and Evan.

"Come on over and take a knee, please!" Chris clapped his hands together. The boys settled down, looking up at him with eager faces, probably twenty-five of all different shapes, sizes, and races, all of them in their blue Musketeer Varsity baseball T-shirts and shorts.

Coach Hardwick put his hands on his hips. "Boys, I'm going to make this short and sweet. Today we're going to practice hard. The Musketeer standard is excellence, on the field and in the gym. Nothing less wins."

Chris kept his game face on, noticing the boys' rapt attention. They showed every emotion on their young features, and they so wanted approval. Chris would exploit that very emotion, starting today. Jordan, Evan, Dylan, and Trevor were paying attention, but Raz's shaggy head was down, and he was picking his cuticles.

"Boys, let me tell you a story before we get started. It's from the legendary Coach John Scolinos, who coached at California Polytechnic. Coach Scolinos used to say that in high-school baseball, in college baseball, in the minor leagues, and in the major leagues, home plate is seventeen inches wide."

Chris watched as the boys listened, especially Jordan. Only Raz kept picking his cuticles.

Hardwick continued, "Baseball is a game about seventeen inches. If you don't reach those seventeen inches, the plate does not get bigger or wider to help you. It's a standard. The standard on this team is excellence. *You* reach the *standard*. The *standard* does not reach *you*."

Chris nodded, as Hardwick kept speaking.

"How do you reach that standard? How do you reach excellence? You must hold yourself accountable at all times." Coach Hardwick gestured to Chris. "Boys, meet our new assistant coach, Coach Brennan."

"Oh, hi." Chris smiled as all the heads turned to him.

Coach Hardwick continued, "Coach Brennan was late to practice today by two minutes. Coach Brennan might be thinking, two minutes doesn't matter. It's *only* two minutes. Coach Brennan might be thinking, two minutes isn't as late as five minutes. Or ten. Or *seventeen*."

Chris felt himself flush. This would not further his plans. He needed to be an authority figure to Jordan to gain his trust. He could see their smiles fade when it dawned on them that Coach Hardwick was about to make an example of him.

"Boys, if Coach Brennan is thinking any of those things, he is sorely mistaken. Coach Brennan may have been hired by the school district, but he will not stay on this team. If any of you are thinking the way Coach Brennan thinks, you will not stay on this team, either."

Chris kept his head high. Evan started to smirk, out of nervousness or derision. Trevor and Dylan frowned. Jordan averted his eyes, and Raz kept looking down.

"Boys, the standard is arriving at practice on time. The standard never changes. Why? Because the standard is excellence, and excellence is the *only* thing that wins. The way to achieve excellence is through accountability. If you do not account to yourself, then you will fail. If Coach Brennan does not account to himself, he will fail."

Chris realized he'd been thinking about this the wrong way. After all, the boys were identifying with him, seeing him as relatable, which was exactly what he needed. So Chris played it up, lowering his gaze as if utterly ashamed of himself.

"Tomorrow we play Upper Grove. We are ready. We have been accountable. And we will win." Coach Hardwick stood taller, hitching up his pants. "Now, boys, line up at your regular practice stations. If you read the Bible, you know the drill."

The boys scrambled to their feet, then jogged off quickly.

Chris turned to Coach Hardwick. "Coach, it won't happen again."

"Damn right it won't."

Chris took it on the chin. "I saw you talking with Jordan and Raz. Anything I should know?"

"Raz wants to stay as starting pitcher."

"Over Jordan?"

"No, over Cy Young."

Chris smiled at the bad joke. "From what I hear, Jordan doesn't have the stuff to start."

"What?" Hardwick's eyes narrowed behind his glasses. "Did Victor tell you that? What does *he* know? He coaches JV for a reason. He hasn't seen Jordan throw since last season. You don't believe me, go see for yourself."

"You mean have a catch with Jordan?" Chris asked, which was exactly what he wanted.

"Yes. Let him show you what he's got. I know talent when I see it. Hmph."

"Okay, Coach. Will do." Chris jogged off after the team, smiling inwardly. He was looking forward to his catch with Jordan. Just the two of them, alone. Like father and son.

Or so Chris imagined.

Chapter Nine

Chris approached Jordan, who was standing in line for batting practice. “Got a minute?” he said, tossing the boy a glove. “Coach wants us to have a catch, so I can see what you got.”

“Okay.” Jordan came out of line, and a few of the boys glanced over, including Evan and Raz.

“Let’s go on the other side of the curtain, for safety’s sake.” Chris started walking along a blue plastic drape that hung from the ceiling, sectioning off a portion of the gym. Chris had already moved the portable pitcher’s mound and other equipment to the other side.

Jordan said nothing, trailing him. The gym was filled with the activity and noise of fifty boys running, drilling, and catching.

“I hear a lot of nice things about you from Coach Natale.” Chris kept his tone light, to get some good vibes going. “He told me he really enjoyed coaching you.”

“Oh.” Jordan half-smiled, head down.

“He also said you’ve really improved.”

Jordan didn't say anything, walking in his characteristic stooped fashion along the plastic curtain.

"It's hard to improve, I find. But you did it. You made varsity."

Jordan nodded, with a slight smile.

"You might even start tomorrow."

Jordan nodded again.

"How did you do it?"

"I don't know." Jordan shrugged.

"Somebody teach you?"

"Not really."

"You wanna know who taught me to play baseball? My mom." Chris rolled his eyes, self-deprecating, as they reached the opening in the curtain and entered the isolated part of the gym, which was empty.

"Huh." Jordan half-smiled, and Chris decided to carry the conversational ball, hoping to lay a foundation for Jordan to open up.

"My mom is awesome, *was* awesome. I was close to her. Unfortunately, my dad was a real jerk. A drunk, actually." Chris heard the ring of truth in his words, since one of his foster fathers had lived inside the bottle. "My mother tried to be the mom and a dad, both. She was tall and bowled in a league. She's the one who bought me my first glove, even helped me oil it. She took me to the park and taught me how to throw."

"Huh." Jordan met Chris's eyes for the first time. "I learned from YouTube."

"Really?" Chris couldn't remember when YouTube had started.

"Sure, I watched a lot of YouTube videos. I still do. There are professional ones like MLB Network. They have Pedro Martinez talking about Colon. I like them but I like the amateur ones, like, from college and high-school coaches. They take it slower and explain. I think that's how I got better. I worked on my mechanics. That's what recruiters look for. Good mechanics."

"It's true, you can't get to the next level without good mechanics." Chris realized that Jordan warmed up when the subject was baseball. "I like videos, but some aren't worth it. Is there one you recommend? A favorite?"

"Yeah, it's from Texas. It's mad technical but the coach explains it in a way you can understand."

"Can you send me the link? My email's on my teacher page."

"Sure."

"Thanks." Chris had just opened up a line of communication to the boy. "I also heard you picked up some new pitches."

"Yeah. I had a fastball, two-seam, and a change-up. My curve was okay. I added a four-seam, a slider, and a sinker."

"Wow, terrific." Chris imagined Jordan training himself with only videos for guidance. Overall, Chris was hearing solitude, even loneliness, which he would exploit to his advantage.

"Plus I worked on my legs. They were too skinny. I was all arms before, when I pitched."

"Legs matter."

"The power comes from the legs and hips."

"Exactly. Good for you." Chris decided to plant another seed. "Hey, listen, before we get started, I'm sorry about what happened at the beginning of practice, with me and Coach Hardwick. That was kind of, uh, embarrassing."

"I know, right?" Jordan's eyes flared. "On your birthday, even."

"Right." Chris had totally forgotten that it was his fake

birthday, but Jordan hadn't, an excellent sign. "I was late because I was talking to Coach Natale, but I don't want you to think I disrespected the team."

"No, Coach, I wouldn't think that. I don't think that."

"I care about the team as much as I care about my class. Coaching and teaching, they're two sides of the same coin." Chris looked down as if he were feeling shame anew, then screwed the baseball into his glove. "Did you enjoy class today, by the way? It was fun, right?"

"Sure, yeah." Jordan smiled.

"Okay, let's have a catch. You need to warm up, and I need to blow off steam."

"Okay." Jordan smiled, warmly.

"Then we'll move into your new pitches. I heard so many good things that I wanted to see it for myself." Chris backed up, and Jordan walked in the other direction. Chris rotated his arm to loosen it up, ignoring the ache from his batting-cage workouts, then threw to Jordan. The boy threw it back effortlessly, the ball making a smooth arc that was a product of innate athletic talent and muscle memory.

Chris caught it and tossed it back harder to establish some credibility, and the ball made a solid *thump* when it reached Jordan's glove. Jordan threw it back harder, too, and as they went back and forth, Chris could discern an overall relaxation of the boy's body, his movements becoming more fluid, throwing and catching as if at play. Jordan even laughed when Chris's throws went wide or high, and each time he did, Chris made sure to say "attaboy" or "well done."

Chris realized that playing catch was a bonding thing, better than conversation, especially with a boy who was more comfortable with action than words. He thought of that old movie *Field of Dreams,* about the son who wanted to have a catch with his father. Oddly, Chris found himself wondering why so many fathers were missing, including his own. He only rarely thought about his father anymore, a man he'd never met. It was past.

Chris tossed the ball to Jordan for the last time. "You good to go?"

Jordan nodded.

Chris got the face mask, put it on, and positioned himself about the right distance, then dropped into a catcher's crouch. "Okay, don't kill me!"

Jordan stepped up onto the pitcher's mound, of white rubber. "Don't worry, if you got good insurance!"

"Ha!" Chris put down one finger, an old-school signal for a fastball.

Jordan wound up, lifting his front leg and rearing back, then pitched perfectly, releasing at the right moment and following through, back leg raised. The ball zoomed toward the strike zone.

"Nice!" Chris caught the ball, impressed. The ball speed had to be at least eighty or eighty-five miles an hour. He threw it back.

"I can do that better!" Jordan called out, catching the ball.

"That was terrific!" Chris crouched again, put down four fingers, and wiggled them, signaling for a change-up.

Jordan wound up, reared back, and pitched the ball again, following through. The ball zoomed toward the strike zone, where it changed speeds at the last instant, dipping down the way God intended.

"Very nice!" Chris tossed the ball back and then put Jordan through his three-seam fastball, a sinker, a slider, and only one curveball because there was no point adding to the wear and tear on his arm. When they were finished, Chris rose, took off the face mask, and walked forward. "That'll do!"

"Okay!" Jordan jogged off the mound, reaching him with a happy, relaxed smile.

"Okay, Coach?"

"More than okay! Awesome!" Chris clapped him on the shoulder.

"Thanks." Jordan grinned.

"Really, your hard work paid off. You're throwin' heat." Chris sensed a new closeness between them, so his mission had been accomplished—or at least part of it had. He wanted to get closer to Jordan, but he also wanted to separate Jordan from Raz. Chris couldn't get as close to Jordan as he needed to be if Jordan had a best friend, and the crack in the relationship between the boys was already there. All Chris had to do was stick a chisel in the fissure and hammer it into pieces.

Chris motioned beyond the curtain. "Now, run and go get Raz."

"Raz?" Jordan hesitated. "Why?"

"You'll see. Hurry, go. We don't have much time."

"Sure okay. Be right back." Jordan took off, tucking the glove under his arm. He ran through the opening in the curtain and arrived only a few minutes later with Raz jogging behind him, his dark eyes flashing with eagerness and his glove already on.

"Raz, hi. I need you." Chris motioned to him.

"Sure, Coach." Raz tucked a strand of hair into his man bun.

Chris turned away pointedly from Raz and faced Jordan. "Jordan, I was thinking it would be a great idea to videotape you. Between us, I have a buddy who knows a scout. I can send him the video through back channels, if you know what I mean."

"Really?" Jordan's eyes rounded with delight. "What school?"

"I can't say." Chris was improvising. Of course there was no scout, no school, and no back channel. "Just leave it to me."

"That'd be great! I appreciate that, Coach."

"Good, and keep it on the QT." Chris turned back to Raz. "Raz, you catch while I film Jordan."

Raz blinked. "Then are you gonna film me, too?"

"No, just Jordan."

Raz cleared his throat. "But Coach Brennan, I pitched last season. I'm the pitcher."

"So?" Chris faked confusion. "Raz, are you telling me you can't catch Jordan?"

"No, I can catch him, of course I can catch him, but *I'm* the pitcher. Not Jordan."

Jordan recoiled. "Raz, I pitched last season."

"On JV." Raz waved his glove at him dismissively.

"I'm on varsity now."

"Because you're a tryhard, Jordan."

"No, I'm not!" Jordan shot back, pained.

"Whoa, boys," Chris broke in, acting surprised, as if he hadn't instigated the conflict. He didn't need it to go too far. He only needed to turn one boy against the other. He frowned at Raz. "Can't say I like your attitude, Raz. This is a team. We function as teammates. And don't give me attitude."

"Sorry, Coach Brennan." Raz swallowed hard. "But yo, can I pitch after Jordan? Like, can you film Jordan, then film me? And you could send the video of me to your friend and—"

"Not today. It's late." Chris motioned Raz backwards. "Get in position now. Catch."

Raz stalked away, simmering.

Chris took Jordan by the arm and walked him toward the pitcher's mound. "Jordan, I didn't know he'd react that way. I'm trying to do a nice thing for you. Where did that come from?"

"I know." Jordan walked with his head down. "He wants to stay as the starter. He just brought it up with Coach Hardwick."

"Coach Hardwick will make that decision, not Raz."

"That's what Coach says."

"I'm surprised Raz would take that to Coach Hardwick. I thought you and he were friends." Chris paused, letting the silence do its work. The implication was that Raz wasn't acting like a friend. "Well. You're not doing anything wrong. You understand that, right?"

Jordan nodded, walking.

"You worked hard and you improved. You put in the time, built up your legs, studied the videos. You earned this shot. A good friend would be happy for you."

Jordan pursed his lips as they reached the other side of the gym, where Chris motioned to the pitcher's mound.

"Okay. Put Raz out of your mind. Get up there. Give it everything you've got, you hear me?"

Jordan nodded, averting his eyes, then headed toward the mound. He threw a practice pitch, then started pitching in earnest, but the fight with Raz had gotten to him. His pitching had none of its earlier brilliance, and one of his fastballs went wild. Chris hadn't been sure that would be the result, but even if it hadn't been, it worked for his purposes. Now Jordan would be mad at Raz for causing him to blow his big chance. Chris filmed the debacle and patted Jordan on the back afterwards, telling him they'd do it again, another time. Jordan and Raz didn't say another word to each other for the rest of practice and they left the gym separately.

It couldn't have gone worse for Jordan and Raz.

And it couldn't have gone better for Chris.

Chapter Ten

After practice, Chris sat in his Jeep, pretending he was talking on the phone. The dashboard clock read 6:15, and the sky was darkening. Lights in the parking lot cast halos on the empty spaces. He kept an eye on his rearview mirror, watching the players walk toward the student parking lot. It was too dark to see their faces, but he recognized Jordan's lurching gait and Evan at the center of the group. Raz lagged behind, alone.

Chris left the faculty lot and turned into the student lot, slowing and rolling down his window when he reached the boys, who were clustered around a brand-new BMW M 235i convertible coupe, gleaming darkly under the light. The engine thrummed like six cylinders of German precision engineering.

"What's up, guys?" Chris shouted to them, though he knew.

"Coach Brennan!" "Yo!" "Hi, Coach!"

"Coach, you like my ride?" Evan grinned, sitting next to Jordan in the passenger seat. Raz was trying to shove himself into the backseat, which was nonexistent.

"Love it! Is it really yours?"

Raz interjected, "He got it from Daddy!"

"Wow!" Chris acted surprised, though he had seen Evan's posts about the car on Instagram. "Hey listen, I was about to email the team. I'm having a get-together at my house tomorrow night, to introduce myself to the team. Why don't you guys come over? Have some pizza?"

Evan answered, "Okay!"

"Sure, okay, yes!" the others called back.

"For your birthday?" Jordan asked from the passenger seat.

"Coach, it's your birthday?" "Whaaaa!" "Happy Birthday!"

Meanwhile, Chris palmed his smartphone, thumbed to Settings, then to WIRELESS. His screen filled with the wireless networks, including **Evan4EvaEva,** which had to be Evan's car. Chris pressed the screen to connect. Most people didn't think about cyber-security in their cars, but the software that operated most cars, especially new ones, had plenty of vulnerabilities, and any wireless signal could be hacked—even a car's braking system.

"Coach, what time you want us over?" Jordan called out.

"How about eight?" Chris kept his grin on.

"Woohoo, party!" Evan shouted, and Jordan and the other boys laughed, turning up the music again.

"Drive safe, gentlemen! See you tomorrow!" Chris waved good-bye, fed the car gas, and drove through the lot. **Evan4EvaEva** evaporated, and he took a right turn onto Central Valley Road, passing development after development. In no time he reached the entrance of Valley Oaks, where balloons lay deflated on the fresh sod, tethered to the MODEL HOME AVAILABLE sign.

He turned into the driveway, and the development was dark, with only the newly built sections lit up. There was a segment of new homes still under construction, their wood frames wrapped in Tyvek HomeWrap, and he drove to Building 12, parked in the pocket lot behind, then entered the building and let himself into his apartment on the second floor. He walked through the living room to the kitchen, a small rectangle with white cabinets, no-name appliances, and beige counters. He opened the refrigerator, which was packed with groceries for his party, grabbed a bottle of beer, and uncapped it, returning to the living room.

Chris surveyed the apartment, a two-bedroom with a rectangular living room furnished with a rented sectional couch, a teak coffee table, and end tables with glazed pottery lamps—but otherwise, the place was designed to make a teenage boy feel like it was a cool place to hang. An entertainment center with a large-screen TV and an Xbox system occupied one side of the room. The bottom shelf held Halo, Call of Duty, and Grand Theft Auto, and Chris had bought the games used, so it looked like he played, which he didn't. He knew what real violence was like, and gaming had none of the thrill.

On the opposite wall was his locked gun case with a thick glass front, which held several hunting rifles, two long guns, an AR-15 assault weapon, and two handguns, a Beretta and a Colt .45 revolver. Chris had the appropriate licensing for each one, and they were unloaded and under lock and key. The case was intended to invite the admiring eyes of teenage boys, and he bet that most of his team had gone hunting, with brothers or dads. Chris was an excellent shot, though nobody but him would know that.

He wanted to make sure everything was set for tomorrow night, so he set down the beer bottle and crossed to the digital clock, turned it upside down, and checked the connection, which was fine. Though the clock looked normal, it was a hidden camera with audio. He double-checked the camera in the artificial plant in the corner and in the electrical outlet on the wall.

Chris scanned the ceiling fixture, which was a hidden camera, like the smoke detector. In the kitchen, there was a hidden camera on top of the refrigerator and behind the coffeepot. He couldn't be everywhere tomorrow night, but the cameras could pick up all sorts of stray information. He needed to know as much about these boys as soon as possible, for step one and beyond.

Chris picked up his backpack and went to his office, which was small with two windows, bare white walls, and a massive computer workstation with two large monitors aglow, stacked with files. He had a lot of information to absorb, so it was going to be a long night.

A teacher's work was never done.

Chapter Eleven

Heather Larkin wished she had time to make a decent dinner, but tonight it was scrambled eggs. She loved Ina Garten and wanted to be a home cook, but there was a difference between imagination and reality, beginning with her kitchen—too small to be a galley kitchen, she called it an "alley" kitchen—with refaced brown-wood cabinetry, Formica-knockoff countertops, and ancient appliances from a scratch-and-dent store. Their apartment was two bedrooms in a low-rise complex between a do-it-yourself car wash and a Friendly's. Their view was the lighted Friendly's sign, and at night, if she drew the curtains, the apartment took on a radioactive red glow.

Heather turned off the eggs, scooped them onto the plate, and brought them to Jordan, who was studying at the table. "Sorry, honey. I wanted to make chicken, but the witch kept me late again."

"No problem, Mom," Jordan said without looking up, and Heather knew he meant no disrespect. He was supposed to have read *The Great Gatsby,* but he hadn't gotten it done. His schedule was as busy as hers, with school, homework, baseball practice, and games. He grabbed the upside-down bottle of ketchup from the table, popped the top, and squeezed it onto his eggs.

"How about I make chicken tomorrow night?"

"Sure, fine." Jordan picked up a fork and plowed into the eggs, then turned the page of his book, tucking it underneath the rim to keep it open.

"Let me get your toast." Heather went back to the kitchen, plucked the pieces from the toaster, put them on a plate, and brought them back to the table with her new Kerrygold butter. She had overheard the members at the club talking about Kerrygold like it was magical, but Whole Foods was the only store that carried it. Heather didn't shop there because it was expensive, but she'd made an exception to get the Kerrygold. She didn't realize until the checkout line that she was the only customer in a uniform—with a *name tag,* for God's sake. Self-conscious, she'd zippered her coat up.

"Thanks," Jordan said through a mouthful, opening his lips to let the heat from the eggs escape his mouth.

"Want coffee, honey?"

"If it's made already."

"It is." Heather cheered up as she went back into the kitchen, feeling a wave of gratitude for her son. He kept his room clean, took their garbage to the incinerator chute, did his own laundry in the machines in the crummy basement. He'd set up her email, showed her how to G-chat, and fixed Netflix so they could use her sister's account. Jordan never gave her a moment's trouble. She didn't know how she'd gotten so lucky, in him.

"How was practice?" Heather asked from the kitchen, sliding the pot of coffee from Mr. Coffeemaker and pouring him a mug, then herself. They both drank it black, which made her feel good, for some reason. They were no-frills, a tough little half a family.

"Fine." Jordan turned the page, then tucked the paperback under his plate.

"How was school?" Heather brought the mugs back and placed Jordan's coffee in front of him.

"Fine."

"Good." Heather pulled out the chair and sat opposite him. She wasn't hungry because she had eaten at the club, scarfing down so many leftover pigs-in-blankets that she felt like one.

"Got a new assistant coach."

"Oh? What's his name?"

"Brennan. I have him for AP Government, too."

"Is he nice?"

"Yes. I got a game tomorrow. I might start." Jordan glanced up with a quick smile.

"You mean you might be the starting pitcher?" Heather asked, surprised. "Not Raz?"

"Yep." Jordan nodded, returning to his book.

"Good for you, honey!" Heather felt happy for him, though she knew he would have mixed feelings, competing with Raz. She could have asked him about it, but she'd learned not to bug him. She wished she could go to his games, to cheer for him, to be there for him, but she had to work, which was just another way she fell short.

Heather sipped her coffee, keeping him company, or maybe he was keeping her company. Either way, silence fell between them. Jordan didn't talk much, but on the plus side, he never complained. She used to worry that he *internalized* his emotions, like it said in the magazines, but he was a boy, after all, and so much like her father.

Heather laced her fingers around her mug, and her gaze traveled to the window. She hadn't closed the curtains yet, and it was already dark outside. The Friendly's sign glowed blood-red—TRY OUR HUNKA CHUNKA PB FUDGE—and the lights were on in the Sunoco gas station.

Traffic was congested on Central Valley Road, and car exhaust made chalky plumes in the night air. Jordan had been spooked by exhaust when he was little.

Mommy, are those ghosts coming from inside the cars?

No, honey. They're farts.

Heather smiled to herself, wondering if she had been a better mother then or if it had just been easier. Her mother always said, *big kids, big problems,* and Heather worried constantly about college for Jordan, where he would get in, how they would pay for it. Heather lowered her gaze, watching him. She loved watching her son eat, even though she watched people eat all day, but that was different.

Suddenly a text alert sounded on Jordan's phone, which was on the table, and Heather glanced over to see a skinny banner pop onto the screen:

From Evan K: bro

Heather blinked, surprised. Evan K had to be Evan Kostis, Mindy's Kostis's son. It was funny, since she'd seen Mindy just today at the luncheon.

Do I know you? You look familiar.

Heather felt a tingle of excitement at the thought that Jordan could become friends with Evan. Jordan didn't have any close friends besides Raz, but Raz was such a wacko. A popular kid like Evan could bring Jordan out of his shell. And Evan was the captain of the baseball team and in the local newspaper, whether for National Honor Society or some other thing. Evan was Winner's Circle, like his parents. Maybe the Larkins could get out of the Loser's Circle, or at least Jordan could.

The banner flashed a second time, but Jordan kept reading and Heather watched the phone screen go black. Her father always said, *it's not what you know, it's who you know,* and she saw proof of that every day, watching the club members exchanging business cards, taking each other's stock tips and vacation-spot recommendations, hiring each other's lawyers, doctors, babysitters, whatever.

"Jordan, you got a text." Heather rose, reaching for his plate to clear the table, but he grabbed the other side of the plate, stopping her.

"You don't have to clear, Ma. I will."

"If I clear, you can text Evan back."

"I'm not like you, Ma. I don't get excited every time I get a text. I'm not an *olds*." Jordan stood up with a crooked smile, picking up the dirty plates, silverware, and crumpled napkin, stacking them the way he learned to at the club, where he bused tables in summer.

"I just think if Evan texted you, you should text him back."

"I don't."

"Why not? Don't you want to see what he wants?"

"I know what he wants." Jordan walked into the kitchen with the plates and silverware, then opened the dishwasher only wide enough to slide the plates in the bottom rack and drop the fork and the knife in the silverware bin.

"What does he want?" Heather could see Jordan getting testy, but she had him in her clutches and wasn't about to let go.

"He wants to go to the movies Saturday night."

"That sounds like fun," Heather said, too quickly. "Are you going to go with him?

"I can't."

"Why not?"

"I'm doing something with Raz."

"Did you already make plans with Raz?"

"I always do things with Raz on the weekend. You know that."

"But it's not like you have plans."

"I'm *not* gonna ditch Raz." Jordan frowned.

"You're not ditching him if you don't have plans."

"Mom, I have homework to do." Jordan went to the table, palmed his phone, and grabbed his paperback.

"I'm just saying. Maybe you can go out with Raz on Friday night and Evan on Saturday night." Heather followed him into the living room, knowing she had already said too much. She always said to herself, *with boys, say as few words as is humanly possible.* The hardest part about being a mother was shutting up.

"Don't want to." Jordan walked through the living room, where he'd left his backpack, and Heather dogged his heels.

"Or why not go with Evan, but see if Raz can come, too?"

"No." Jordan swung his backpack over his shoulder, its black straps flying.

"Why not? Why can't you take Raz?" Heather went after him, talking to his back.

"Evan doesn't like Raz." Jordan disappeared down the hallway.

"Wonder why," Heather said, but by then, she was talking to herself.

Chapter Twelve

Mindy Kostis took a sip of her G & T, on her laptop at the kitchen island. She knew the alcohol wasn't helping her diet, but no matter what she did, she couldn't lose weight anyway. She worked out with a personal trainer and had just started yoga, but she knew it wouldn't work. Her goal weight was 125, and Mindy was pretty sure she would be 125 years old before she reached it, then she would be dead. Her epitaph would read SHE REACHED HER GOAL WEIGHT, THEN DIED OF SHOCK.

Mindy scrolled down on the Photos page, scanning their vacation pictures. They'd spent spring break in the Cayman Islands, and she wanted to pick the best photos for a Facebook album, **The Kostis Family in the Caymans!** The vacation was a true getaway for her, her husband Paul, and their son Evan. She'd scheduled parasailing, paddleboard, and scuba lessons, and Evan had left his phone behind, which was a miracle. Mindy had even gotten Paul's attention, a rarity of late.

She eyed a photo of Paul gazing out at the water. He was a hematology oncologist at Blakemore Medical Center, and his cases often weighed on his mind. But this was different. She knew him better than that. They'd met in the cafeteria line at Blakemore, where she was a nurse and he was a resident. They had been married twenty-two years, happy until he'd had an affair with a nurse fifteen years younger and thirty pounds skinnier. Mindy didn't know which hurt more.

Mindy glanced at the clock on her laptop, surprised to see that it was 10:16. It was strange that Paul still wasn't home. He'd said he'd be home by ten. She prayed he wasn't having another affair, but she couldn't bring herself to ask him. Last time he'd denied it, and she'd believed him. But that time, she had proof. This time, she had nothing but an underlying worry that drove her to read his texts while he was in the shower, go through his pockets before she dropped his clothes off, and try to get into his email, though it was password-protected.

"Mom?" Evan scuffed into the kitchen in his sweats and slides, holding his phone. "I need a check for our jackets tomorrow."

"Jackets?" Mindy couldn't focus, wondering where Paul was. She glanced at her phone. There were no calls or texts from him.

"Yes, for the team. You know. Tomorrow's the last day to bring in the money."

"Oh, right, of course." Mindy shifted mental gears. She herself had organized the bulk purchase. She went into the side drawer and found the checkbook they used for household expenses. She dug around for a pen, wrote the check, then tore it off and handed it to him. "Here we go."

"Thanks." Evan turned to leave, starting to text.

"Did you finish your homework?"

"Yes." Evan walked away, and Mindy felt a pang. On vacation, they'd had nice, long walks on the beach, and Evan had told her about girls he was dating, Ashley

Somebody, a freshman at CVHS, and Brittany Somebody Else at Rocky Springs. Mindy was pretty sure he'd had sex already. In fact, he was probably having more sex than she was. But maybe not more than his father.

"Honey, hold on," Mindy called after Evan, on impulse.

"What?" Evan turned, texting. She couldn't see his face, and the lights were recessed spots on a dimmer, and the granite countertops, black with orange flecks, glistened darkly around him. The kitchen was state-of-the-art and top-of-the-line, but sometimes it struck her as a stage set, since they never ate at the same times.

"Did you get dinner?" Mindy hadn't gotten home in time to feed him.

"Sure."

"What'd you have?"

"A sandwich. The leftover tuna."

"How was school?"

"Okay," Evan answered without looking up, texting.

"How's Ashley and Brittany?"

"Fine."

"Is that who you're texting?"

"Mom . . ." Evan didn't have to finish the sentence. Mindy had already agreed it was rude to ask him who he was texting.

"Okay, so how's the car?"

"Awesome!" Evan looked up with a smile. "The sound system is incredible."

"Good!" Mindy felt cheered. It had been Paul's idea to get Evan the BMW for his birthday, and she'd gone along with it because she'd rather have him in something with state-of-the-art safety. The best use of their money was taking care of their only son, and their standard of living was the trade-off for Paul's long hours, after all.

"Can I go now, Mom?"

"Sure, honey. Don't spend too long on the phone. Love you."

"Love you too."

"Good night now." Mindy blew him a kiss, but Evan didn't look up, shuffling from the kitchen. She swiveled back to the laptop, where the vacation picture was still on. She found herself getting back on the Internet, going to Gmail, and logging in as Paul.

She took another stab at guessing his password.

Chapter Thirteen

Susan Sematov clutched her cell phone like a security blanket. It was 10:30 P.M., and Ryan still wasn't home, nor had he called or texted. She stood in the family room and looked out the picture window, which ghosted her reflection against the Dutch colonials, clipped hedges, and green recycling bins. Her makeup had worn off, emphasizing the bags under her eyes and the shine on her upturned nose. Her eyes were tired, and her mouth made a tight line. Her brown hair hung limply to her shoulders, and she still had on her navy suit from J.Crew Outlet and brown pumps from DFW. ValleyCo employees were required to shop its outlets, which had been Susan's idea.

The scene outside the picture window was dark and quiet. They lived on a cul-de-sac, and their neighbors were home, so if any headlights appeared, they would belong to Ryan. Susan had spent the entire day worrying about Ryan. She'd called the local hospitals, the police, and two of Ryan's high-school friends, but neither of them had heard from Ryan in months. Still she couldn't just stare out the window.

Susan went to the bottom of the stairwell, calling upstairs. "Raz, I'm going out to look for Ryan!"

There was no reply. Raz was probably G-chatting and texting while he did his homework. She worried that he was rewiring his brain circuitry, being on electronic devices all the time.

"Raz? Raz!"

No reply.

Susan considered going upstairs to talk to him, but she didn't want to have a fight. He hadn't apologized for hanging up on her today, and his angry outbursts were becoming common. She'd been walking on eggshells around him and she told her therapist that Raz was turning into a bully. She texted him, **I'm going out to see if I can find Ryan.**

Raz texted back, **wtf mom.**

Susan didn't like profanity. She texted, **See you in an hour. Let me know if he comes home in the meantime.**

Susan crossed to the console table and got her car keys out of the basket, her gaze falling momentarily on Neil's. Her first thought was, *Oh no, Neil left his keys,* then her mouth went dry. She wondered when that would stop happening, if ever. She took her keys, turning around and half expecting to see him. He wasn't there, but everything reminded her of him. The family room had a pseudo-country look made real by the greenish-blue end tables that he had painted. She loved old furniture, which Neil would refinish and paint whatever color she wanted, back when they were young and all about each other, before the kids. It made her feel like a bad mother to admit it, but she had felt more special then.

Susan's reverie was interrupted by a noise upstairs, and the next moment she turned to see Raz coming downstairs, his expression predictably cross.

"Mom, what are you doing?" Raz reached the bottom of the stairs with a thud, his tread heavy. He was a good-looking boy, even when he was angry, his thick, dark eyebrows knitted together, dramatic against his long dark hair. He had his father's big brown eyes, and his nose had a bump, also like Neil's, but it fit his face. His mouth was big, in more ways than one.

"I'm just going out to look for Ryan."

"Where? You don't even know where to look."

"I'm just going to look around at some of the places in town."

"Where?"

"Houlihan's. TGI Fridays. He could be at any of those."

"He doesn't go places like that." Raz strode toward her, and Susan edged backwards, unaccountably.

"Where does he go then? Enlighten me."

"I don't know, that sketchy bar on Stable Road."

"What's the name of it?" Susan didn't know.

"Oh God." Raz rolled his eyes. "This is so dumb, Mom. He's fine."

"What's the name of it? Where is it?"

"I told you. It's on Stable Road. You don't have to go out looking for him like he's a dog."

"I want to," Susan replied, modulating her tone. "I can't sleep anyway. I'll just take a nice drive and see if I can see him."

"He's not gonna be at Houlihan's."

"Okay, I know, you said that. Then I'll go to Stable Road and look for the bar there."

"You won't find it."

"If you remember the name, I'll find it. I'll look it up."

"It's easier just to show you." Raz stalked past, heading for the door.

"You don't have to do that. It's late." Susan didn't want

him to go with her. She didn't want to fight with him in the car. She would have preferred a peaceful drive through town, alone. She was officially the worst mother in the world, avoiding her own son.

"Let's go already!" Raz stepped outside, letting the screen door bang behind him.

"Okay." Susan left the house, locking the front door and following him to her car, a white Lexus sedan. She backed out of the driveway and left the cul-de-sac, with Raz texting. They traveled north, heading into town. Silence fell between them, making her tense. She hadn't had a chance to talk to Raz since she'd been on the phone for the dinner hour. They'd had pizza delivered, again.

"How's school?" Susan asked, after a time.

"Fine," Raz answered, his head down, texting.

"How's the season going?"

"We're losing."

"Oh, sorry about that." Susan tread lightly. "How's your arm? Feeling good?"

"Fine."

"I looked at the schedule and your next home game is tomorrow, right? I was thinking that I could leave work early and come see you." Susan turned right. Large homes lined the street, their warm yellow lights on, the families within safe and sound. The Sematovs used to be one of those families.

"You mean, watch the game?"

"Yes, of course." Susan kept her tone light. Neil was the one who went to the games, not her.

"You don't have to."

"I want to." Susan couldn't see his expression. His hair fell in his face, lit from below by the bluish light of his phone, where the text bubbles were floating by.

"You have work."

"I can get out early. I'd love to come."

"No you wouldn't. If you did, you would have come before."

Susan's mouth went dry. "I'd like to go," she said anyway. "I know Dad used to go, but I'd like to go. I'd like to see you pitch."

"I might not be pitching."

"Why not?" Susan took a right turn, heading into Central Valley proper.

"I don't know. I just might not pitch. It's not, like, a given."

"Who would pitch, if not you?"

"Jordan."

"But he's JV, isn't he?" Susan knew Jordan Larkin, a great kid. Jordan and Raz were good friends. Jordan had even cried at Neil's funeral, and Susan had been touched. Raz had cried, too, but not Ryan. Ryan kept it all inside. Now both of her sons were losing their way.

"Jordan made varsity. He's gotten better."

"Oh." Susan knew it was bad news for Raz. "Well, even if you don't pitch in the beginning, you'll get in the game. You'll play even if you don't start, right?"

"Does it matter?"

"What do you mean?"

Raz didn't reply.

"It doesn't matter to me if you don't start," Susan answered anyway. "Does it matter to you?"

"Not at all. I'm stoked. I can't wait to sit on the bench with my dick in my hands."

"Raz, really?" Susan didn't like that language. "If starting pitcher is what you want, maybe you can get the position back."

"How would I do that?"

Susan was about to answer, then stopped. Neil was the answer. Neil had taught Raz to pitch. Neil would've taken Raz in the backyard, and the two of them would have drilled forever. "Okay, well, I'm sure there's a way. Maybe there's someone I can hire, like a tutor. A coach. A pitching coach."

"I don't want to work with a pitching coach. You're not gonna hire me a pitching coach. It's stupid."

"No, it's not. There's nothing wrong with helping yourself. If you were nearsighted, you'd wear glasses."

"I knew you would say that. You always say that."

Susan spared him the lecture on goal-directed behavior. She wasn't certain of it herself lately. Her goals had scaled down to: Last the entire day without blubbering like a baby. Save the kids. Keep the wheels on your life.

"Mom. I don't want a pitching coach. How many times do I have to say it? No pitching coach!"

"Okay, fine." Susan felt her temper flare, but reminded herself again to stay patient. Raz wanted only one pitching coach, his dad.

"What if I don't play? What if I don't even get in?"

"You'll get in. They need more than one pitcher a game." Susan was pretty sure that was true. "In any event, I'm going to the game."

"Whatever," Raz answered, leaving Susan to her thoughts. She had to face the fact that the kids had been closer to Neil than her. She didn't know if she could ever bridge that gap. Worse, she couldn't shake the sensation that they thought the wrong parent had died. She even agreed.

Suddenly her phone rang. They both looked over, and the screen read **Ryan calling.**

"Thank God." Susan grabbed the phone and swiped to answer. "Ryan, are you okay? Where are you?"

"I'm at the police station in Rocky Springs. Can you come?"

Chapter Fourteen

The morning sun shone through the classroom windows, and Chris stood as the students went to their seats, dug in their backpacks, and opened spiral notebooks. Evan slipped his phone away, but Jordan was already writing in his notebook. Raz was late, and Chris hoped he showed up. He had to make the final choice between Jordan and Raz today. There was too much to do before Tuesday. He wanted to pull the trigger after class, and he had one more trick up his sleeve.

"Good morning, everyone!" Chris began. "We're going to start with an exercise about the Bill of Rights."

Suddenly Raz hurried into the classroom and sat down heavily in his seat, dropping his backpack loudly on the floor. "Sorry I'm late," he mumbled, but Chris kept his attention on the class.

"Okay, gang, your homework was to write an essay about which Amendment is the most important. But our forefathers didn't write the Bill of Rights by submitting a paper. They hammered it out together. So that's what we're going to do today, have a real debate." Chris returned his attention to Raz, slumped in his chair. "Raz, which Amendment did you decide was the most important?"

"Um, the Second?"

"Okay, come on up here." Chris gestured to the front of the classroom, and Raz rose uncertainly. Chris looked back at the class. "Now, let's get an adversary." Chris turned to Jordan, apparently spontaneously. "Jordan, which Amendment did you think was the most important?"

"The Fourth."

"Then come on up."

"Okay." Jordan rose and lumbered to the front of the room, barely glancing over at Raz.

Chris stood between the two boys like a boxing referee. "Raz and Jordan, you will each state your case. If anybody has a question, they can ask and you have to answer, then keep going. The class will decide who wins, and that will be the end of the first round. We'll keep going until we see which Amendment is left."

Raz raked back his hair, and up close, he looked unusually pale, even drawn. "Well, uh, I said the Second Amendment was the most important because everybody should have a right to protect themselves, like, against whatever. Like bad guys. You're not safe if you can't protect yourself and that should be your right as a citizen—"

"Raz, what's the Second Amendment?" one of the boys shouted. "It's called a *definition*. We learned it in middle school."

The class laughed, and Raz looked shaken. "The Second Amendment is the right to bear arms. It says that a citizen has a right to bear arms and the government can't take that away from them."

Sarah raised her hand. "My dad says the militia is allowed to have the arms, not the people. It says it right there, 'a militia,' doesn't it?"

"My mom says that's from lobbying—" shouted another boy, but Chris shot him a warning glance, not wanting a gun-control debate. He knew more about guns than these kids ever would, and that wasn't the point of the exercise.

"Raz," Chris interjected, "what do you think is the reason the Second Amendment is the most important?"

"Well, um, see," Raz fumbled. "Because you gotta *live*. You can talk about the pursuit of happiness, or free speech, but none of it makes any difference if you're *dead*. Once you're dead, you're *dead* and *gone* . . . and it doesn't matter what your rights were or whatever happiness you were pursuing because, let's face it, you're . . . like, dead."

The class burst into laughter.

Sarah's hand rose. "Raz, is your argument that if you're dead, you don't have any rights? Is that really the best argument you can come up with? That dead people don't have rights?"

"It's not that." Raz licked his dry lips, his dark eyes filming. "You have to be able to protect yourself! You have to be able to live! Do you want to die? Do you really want to *die*?"

"What?" Sarah and the class laughed, but Chris waved them into silence, realizing that Raz was probably talking about his late father.

"Okay Raz, time's up. Thank you." Chris gestured to Jordan. "Jordan, state your case."

Jordan faced the class, surprisingly poised. "I wrote that the Fourth Amendment was the most important. It says that citizens should be safe in their houses, and that the government is not allowed to have unreasonable searches and seizures."

"Good *definition*!" the boy in the back said pointedly, and the class chuckled.

Jordan paused. "Most of the Amendments are about making sure you're able to do something, like the right to speak freely or to practice whatever religion you want, but the Fourth Amendment says you don't have to do *anything*."

"It's the chillest Amendment!" another boy called out, and everybody laughed.

Jordan smiled shyly. "In a way, it is. It says you have the right to be free and happy in your own home. The right *to be left alone*. Justice Brandeis of the Supreme Court said that, and that's what makes the Fourth Amendment the most important. Thank you."

The class erupted into applause, which Chris silenced by motioning to them. "Okay, class, now that you have heard both arguments, it's time to vote. Clap if you think Raz is the winner of the debate."

Only two students clapped, and the others giggled. Raz sagged, embarrassed.

Chris gestured to Jordan. "Now clap if you think Jordan won the debate."

Everybody else clapped, and Jordan stood taller. Raz looked away.

Chris made his decision. He was going with Jordan. The boy had risen to the occasion, overcoming his natural reserve to defend himself and his position, performing under pressure and thinking on his feet. The classroom exercise paled in comparison to what lay ahead, and Chris couldn't rely on a boy who might fall apart when things got tough.

And lethal.

Chapter Fifteen

Chris chewed his sandwich, eating at his desk. He'd brought lunch from home to avoid the other teachers. He didn't need an instant replay of yesterday and he could choke credibly only so many times. He had his laptop open as if he were working in his classroom, but he sat scanning his files on Jordan, confirming the correctness of his choice.

"Chris, you're working through lunch?" someone called out, and Chris looked up to see Abe, Rick, and Courtney standing in the threshold, holding trays of cafeteria food. Abe looked stylish, Rick looked organic, and Courtney looked tempting, but they were the last thing Chris needed right now.

"Guys, I have to look over a lesson plan." Chris hit a key so that the local newspaper, the *Central Valley Patch,* would come on the screen.

"Listen to you—'lesson plan'! I like when you talk dirty." Abe pulled up three desks around Chris's desk. "I came to talk about Powell with my new best friend!"

"Ha!" Chris hid his dismay. He had gone online last

night and learned as much as possible about Powell, Northwest College, and the Bighorn basin, but he didn't know how long he could keep this up.

Rick hesitated. "We don't mean to bother you, Chris."

Courtney shot Abe a sideways glance. "Abe, I told you this was a bad idea. Chris has to work."

"Oh, sit down, everybody." Abe set down the tray with sodas, a slice of pizza on a styrofoam plate, and a garden salad. "Chris, don't be such a goody-goody. We're the mean girls of Central Valley. On Wednesdays we wear pink."

"We're not the mean girls, they are." Courtney sat down. "They hate us because they ain't us."

Rick smiled in his goofy way, as he took a seat. "We won't stay long, Chris. We didn't want you to feel left out."

Courtney's phone started ringing in her purse, and she slipped it out and looked at the screen. "I swear, Doug has radar for when I get a minute to breathe."

Abe smiled. "Courtney, he knows your schedule. B Lunch is 11:15 to 11:45."

"Excuse me." Courtney rose with the phone, answering the call on the way out of the classroom.

"'Hi Courtney, this is Lug,'" Abe said, mimicking a caveman voice. "He's one *big* beefsteak patty, but she loves the guy, what can I say? And she's loyal. She's stuck with me through thick and thin. I was so sick a few years ago, and she was there, every step of the way."

"What was the matter, Abe?" Chris asked, to keep him talking about anything but Wyoming.

Rick fell suddenly silent, eating his pizza, which turned the beard hairs around his mouth reddish.

"I had anorexia. I was manorexic!" Abe fluttered his eyes behind his hip glasses. "My whole life, off and on, I just couldn't beat it. For me it was about depression, anyway, blah blah, that's my tale of woe." He leaned forward. "So Chris, we're sons of Wyoming! Tell me you had your first kiss at the reservoir, too."

"I swear, I didn't." Chris had determined that the body of water in Abe's photo was a reservoir. "I had my first kiss at fourteen in the hayloft at my granny's farm."

"Well, quite the junior achiever! Where was the farm?"

"Little town on the west side of the state, Evanston."

"You ever get up to Jackson? Can you believe the changes in Jackson?"

"Tell me about it," Chris said offhand. *No, really, tell me about it.*

"The place is so chichi now! The celebrities, ski-in developments, and the shopping. It even has its own *Hermès*! Courtney taught me how to pronounce it so I sound cool."

"And you do," Chris said, tense. Sooner or later, Abe would figure him out, and he couldn't deny it was a problem.

"I took Jamie there on vacation and he said the only way he'd go back to Wyoming is if we went to Jackson. But I told him, Jackson is *not* Wyoming."

"Damn straight."

Rick finished his pizza. "Sachi and I were just talking about that trip last night. She loved it."

"Right?" Abe flashed Rick a happy smile, then returned his attention to Chris. "Where did your dad go to high school, Chris?"

Chris had an answer, as of last night. "Sheridan."

"Whoa, small."

"Right. I didn't get that far out."

"Nobody does, except cattle." Chris had hoped as much, which was why he'd picked it online. He was trying to contain the damage.

"So what's it like?"

"Mountains, mountains, and more mountains."

"I heard your parents died in a crash. Sorry about that."

Rick interjected, "Yes, condolences."

"Thank you." Chris wondered if Abe could check his fake backstory with anyone he knew back in Wyoming.

"And you have no brothers or sisters?" Abe asked, resuming the conversation.

"None," Chris answered, with growing tension. So Abe had heard that, too.

"Unusual for out there. My parents adopted six kids. Three of us are black, and three are white. My dad said we were his retirement package and he was hedging his bets." Abe chuckled. "My dad knows everybody. I emailed him about you but he hasn't emailed back. He only checks his email when he remembers to."

"Uh, I forget." Chris didn't like the way this was going. He picked up his water bottle, and his gaze fell on his laptop, his attention drawn by a familiar name under the headline, LOCAL YOUTH ARRESTED:

> Central Valley resident Ryan Sematov, 19, was arrested last night by Rocky Springs Police Department for attempted burglary of the Samsonite factory store at the ValleyCo Outlet 11. Police were called to the scene when the burglar alarm sounded and nearby residents dialed 911. Sematov was charged with attempted burglary, vandalism, and malicious mischief, and was released on his own recognizance pending a preliminary hearing.

"Oh no, look at this!" Chris said, seizing the excuse to change the subject. He realized that the arrest must've been one of the reasons that Raz was late this morning. "This is terrible news. I have his brother Raz in my class."

"What?" Abe came around the desk and read the screen.

"Oh no, that *is* terrible. I had Ryan in my class last year. He was a terrific student. I have Raz now, he's nutty. I feel bad for the family. The father died over the summer."

Rick joined them, looking at the laptop. "That's too bad. I liked Ryan, and Raz is okay. He's a free spirit, that's all."

Courtney entered the classroom with her cell phone. "What's the matter?"

Abe answered, "Ryan Sematov was arrested for burglary."

"Are you serious?" Courtney grimaced. "I never had him, but that's so sad about that family. The father died over the summer."

"I know." Abe shook his head. "Ryan tried to break into a store at a ValleyCo mall. I seem to remember his mother is a higher-up at ValleyCo, in the corporate office."

Courtney came around the desk. "That can't be good for her. What a shame."

"That's tough." Chris sounded troubled, but not about Ryan or Raz.

About Abe.

Chapter Sixteen

Mindy couldn't get into her husband's Gmail, so she was upstairs in his home office going through their credit-card receipts, since they had a joint Amex and Visa. Last night, he'd come home at eleven o'clock, and when she'd asked why he was late, he'd said only that he'd gotten held up at the hospital. But he wouldn't meet her eye and bit his cuticle, which he never did. As a surgeon, he was meticulous about his hands and nails, even getting manicures to keep them neat.

A wife always knows, her mother had told her.

But that was completely untrue. Mindy had scrutinized Paul for clues about whether he was having another affair, but she had no idea what to look for. The last time, she'd had no idea that he was having an affair. She'd thought they were both happy, communicating well, and having sex as often as most married couples. She'd been fooled by an excellent liar, her own husband.

Mindy's cell phone rang, and she checked the screen. She only had until one thirty, when she had to leave for the game, bringing party trays, bottled water, and soda.

Alcohol wasn't allowed at the games, but nobody would know her reusable water bottle held a G & T.

Her phone screen showed that one of the Boosters was calling, so Mindy answered the call. "Ellen, what's up? I'm in the middle of something."

"Did you hear about Ryan Sematov?"

"Is that Raz's older brother?" Mindy asked, regretting having taken the call. She had more important things to do than gossip. Like play Nancy Drew.

"Yes, he was arrested for burglary last night."

"Oh no." Mindy felt a pang. She had adored Neil Sematov, who was one of the saner parents. She tuned Ellen out and eyed the credit-card receipt.

". . . and he broke into a ValleyCo outlet. You know the mother works for ValleyCo . . ."

Mindy scanned the list of their credit-card charges, noting the name of the restaurants. They were all places she or Evan had been, so far. The only thing that had surprised her was that Evan was eating out so much at lunchtime. She didn't know why he couldn't buy in the cafeteria like everybody else. Or God forbid, bring a lunch from home. Maybe he really was becoming entitled, getting *affluenza*.

". . . I mean, I feel bad for her, truly I do, but let's be real . . ."

Mindy kept scanning, then froze. There was a charge from Central Valley Jewelers for $327.82, processed two weeks ago. She felt her gut twist. Paul had bought that nurse a bracelet from the same store, the last time around. And he had charged it on their joint credit card, which made no sense unless he were trying to get caught, a theory they'd discussed in approximately 172 therapy sessions.

". . . if your kids are having psychological problems, you can't pretend it's not happening, especially not these days . . ."

Mindy felt her heart start to pound. She wanted to know if he was having an affair—and she didn't, both at once. Was it really true? The charge was undeniable, its machine-printed numbers staring her right in the face. Did Paul buy this for another woman? Would he really do this to her again? At the same store? Did he really want her to divorce him? Or did he just want to hurt her?

". . . you can't stick your head in the sand these days, as a mother . . ."

Mindy flashed-forward to Ellen on the phone, calling everybody to gossip about her. *Did you hear? Paul is running around on Mindy again. You can't stick your head in the sand, as a wife today.*

". . . but you know what they say, everything happens for a reason. So maybe now she'll . . ."

Mindy felt stricken. The dark obverse of everything-happens-for-a-reason was that the reason should have been identified, and prevented. If Paul cheated on her again, there had to be a reason, and it was her fault. Her weight, for starters. Mindy had *let herself go.* She could almost hear her mother saying it, right now. *You blew up, dumplin'. What did you expect?*

Mindy had thought she was over it, but she wasn't, not if it was happening again. She had forgiven Paul, or at least she hadn't asked for a divorce, because she loved their family. And she loved Evan, who loved them both. But she couldn't go through it again. Everybody deserves a second chance, but nobody deserves a third.

Mindy felt her thoughts racing, rolling into a giant bolus of anxiety, anguish, and confusion. And still, part of her reflexively wondered if she was jumping to conclusions. Maybe Evan had bought a gift for one of the girls he was dating. He was supposed to ask first, but he had done that before. Or maybe the charge was fraud or a clerical error. That had happened before, too; once somebody charged $150 worth of athletic equipment at a Foot Locker in Minneapolis, using their credit card.

"Mindy? Did I lose you? Mindy!"

"Oh sorry, I think it cut out." Mindy came out of her reverie. "The reception is bad upstairs."

"You have cold spots in your house? I have a wireless guy. I'll text you his contact info."

"Great," Mindy said, wondering about the cold spots in her house. Lately her entire house was a cold spot. She set the statement aside. "I should really go, okay?"

Chapter Seventeen

Heather heard her text alert coming from her uniform pocket, but it was probably nothing. The only texts she got were from creditors, written in a deceptively friendly way; *Oops, life happens! Reminder, your bill is ready.* Blue Cross texted her, too; *You have a private message waiting. Tap link to view.* It sounded tantalizing, but it was the same message. *You're late with your payment.*

Heather hustled to the kitchen. She was working yet another luncheon, this time for the Women's Service League of Central Valley. She entered the warm kitchen and grabbed three plated entrees, avoiding the new chef, a drama queen. She pushed through the swinging door for outgoing, expertly balancing the plates on her forearms. She crossed the hallway, entered the Lafayette Room, and beelined for the table. Coincidentally, it was the one in the corner, where she had served Mindy Kostis yesterday.

You look familiar to me.

Heather dismissed the thought, sidestepping fancy handbags and managing not to elbow anyone in the head, though she might have wanted to, since the Women's Service League had decided at the last minute to hold its speeches and raffles before the meal, backing up the entire schedule, so that Heather had no hope of getting out on time again. She reached the table with a professional smile, served as unobtrusively as possible, and headed back to the kitchen, hearing another text alert sound, which gave her pause. It could be Jordan. Something could've gone wrong at school.

Heather stopped by the wall near the restrooms, sliding her phone from her uniform pocket. The banner on the screen showed the text was from Jordan, and it had the first three words, **whoa mom u,** which she didn't understand, so she swiped to read the whole text.

whoa mom u wont believe it im starting

Heather read the text in astonishment, because something good had happened. Jordan had taken the top spot. Her heart filled with happiness and another emotion—hope. She felt unaccountably as if her son had lifted up their entire family in just one stroke. She texted back: **you're STARTING!?**

yes ☺

Heather felt wetness come to her eyes. It was the emoticon that got to her, a generic representation of a smile that was too damn long in coming. On impulse, she scrolled to her phone function and called him.

"Ma, hold on," Jordan answered, his voice low. Heather assumed he was going where he could talk to his mother without fear of embarrassment.

"Jordan, is this really true? You're starting pitcher for *varsity*?"

"Mom, do you believe it?" Jordan asked, his voice filled with happiness.

"No, no I don't!" Heather felt tears come to her eyes, but she blinked them away. "I'm so proud of you! You deserve it! You worked so hard, you practiced so hard!"

"Mom, it's unreal! Coach Hardwick just told me, like, in front of everyone. I felt bad for Raz, though."

"He'll be okay. What did Coach Hardwick say?" Heather wanted to know every detail.

"He said, 'starting roster for today' and read off the names, and when he got to the pitcher, he said my name. Awesome, right, Mom?"

"*So* awesome! So what did you say when he said that?"

"There was nothing to say. I got my glove." Jordan laughed, a carefree giggle that Heather remembered from when he was younger.

"Where are you now?"

"In the locker room, in a *stall*." Jordan laughed again, and Heather realized that he had no one to share his happiness with except her. Raz was his closest friend, so there was nobody else left. She wished she could be there to watch him pitch, and wetness returned to her eyes. She cleared her throat.

"Well, you have a wonderful game, sweetheart. Knock them dead!"

"I will. Love you, Mom."

"Love you, too, honey," Heather said, hoarsely. She had no idea why she was getting so choked up. The emoticon. That giggle. Her son, who had worked so hard for so long, had finally caught a break.

"Bye." Jordan ended the call.

Heather wiped her eyes with her fingers, then looked up to see her manager, Emily, striding toward her.

"Heather, what are you doing on the phone?" Emily asked, glaring.

"Sorry." Heather looked Emily directly in the eye. She wasn't about to deny it. She would take her lumps.

"Was it a personal call?"

"Yes. My son."

"Was it an emergency?"

"No."

"Doesn't your son know not to call you at work?"

"He didn't call me, I called him."

"For what reason?"

"None of your business." Heather felt anger flicker in her chest, underneath her name tag.

"Did you have an emergency?"

"No."

Emily's blue eyes hardened like ice. "You know you're not allowed to make personal calls at work. We're in the middle of a luncheon. We're trying to get everybody served."

"My station is completely served."

"How do you know they don't need anything? They could need something while you're outside in the hall, making personal calls."

"The call lasted three minutes, maximum. I was just in the dining room and I can go back in right now."

"Not the point. You broke the rules and you should know better. This is a warning, and if you do it again, you're fired. And you were on more than three minutes. You were on four."

"Are you *serious*?" Heather felt the anger burn brighter. "You timed my phone call?"

Emily didn't bat an eye. "Yes, that's my job."

"No, your job is to make sure the luncheon is going well and the club members are happy, which they are, at my station. You're just trying to catch me in a mistake because you have it out for me, from day one."

"And you made a mistake. Because you're not committed to this job."

"Of course I am! I've been doing it for seventeen years. If you look up 'committed' in the dictionary, you'll see a picture of me in this stupid dirndl."

Emily crossed her arms. "I don't like your attitude."

"I do. I *love* my attitude, and you know what, you don't need to fire me. I quit."

Emily's eyes flared. "You better think about what you're saying."

"I have," Heather said, though she hadn't. She was tired, finally of waiting. For nothing. For everything. For her life to start. She found herself untying the back of the white apron that went over the dirndl, which wasn't easy considering that she still had her cell phone in her hand.

"What are you doing?"

"What do you think I'm doing? I'm stripping in the freaking hallway." Heather balled up the apron and threw it on the rug. "And if I could, I'd take off this effing dress, too."

"Are you serious right now?" Emily asked, surprised.

"Abso-effing-lutely." Heather didn't know why she was using profanity. She never talked that way. Meanwhile, one of the new waitresses walked by, averting her eyes, and Heather thought that if this were a movie, people would clap, like at the end of *Bridget Jones*. But in the real world, people looked away. They didn't want to see somebody jump off a bridge. "Take this job and shove it" was a song, not a career move.

"Fine then." Emily snorted. "We'll send your last check to your house."

"Thank you." Heather turned away, heading for the locker room, her eyes suddenly dry and her thoughts newly clear. She would get her purse and change into her clothes. She was going to a baseball game to watch her son pitch for varsity.

One of the Larkins was in the Winner's Circle.

Chapter Eighteen

Susan slipped on her sunglasses and hurried through the parking lot to the baseball game. Thank God it was a sunny afternoon because she didn't want anyone to see her puffy eyes. Everyone would know about Ryan's arrest by now. She'd considered not going to the game, but she couldn't sacrifice Raz for Ryan.

Susan prayed Raz was pitching today. He derived so much self-worth from being the pitcher, believing that his athletic skill was the only thing he had over his more academic older brother. Susan saw so much in Raz that he didn't see in himself—his open heart, his carefree way of looking at life, his absolute joy in meeting people—all of it so much like Neil. But because those things came naturally to Raz, he didn't value them, and nothing she could do would convince him.

You're as smart as your brother, honey, Susan remembered saying to him when he brought home another borderline report card. *You can get better grades, if you try.*

Raz had laughed it off. *I'm fine being a dumb jock, Mom. And I'm so much hotter than Ryan.*

Susan squared her shoulders, putting the memories from her mind. She felt exhausted after the endless night at the police station. She'd called a lawyer who had negotiated a plea agreement. Ryan would be charged with a misdemeanor and sentenced to probation, a fine, and restitution. The lawyer had said *this will go away,* but Susan felt absolute mortification. She'd called her boss to apologize, Community Relations to make a general statement, and her assistant to let her know that she was taking a personal day. By noon, Ryan's mug shot was on TV news. Her reliable son, who never gave her a moment's worry until his face was above the red banner, **ValleyCo Vandal.**

She passed the high school, a massive redbrick complex with two new wings, their construction supported by developers like ValleyCo. Susan herself had arranged for the top ValleyCo brass to be at the ground-breaking, posing with shiny shovels. She used to feel proud she worked for ValleyCo, but now she felt guilty. She had to scale back. Something had to give.

She approached the crowd of parents clustered to the left of the dugout, watching the game. It seemed like a big crowd, maybe fifty people standing, sitting in blue-cloth sling chairs, or eating the food that covered a long picnic table against the dugout wall. Susan reached the fringe of the crowd, still not able to see the pitcher's mound. She didn't know any of the other parents, so she didn't try to talk to them.

Joyful cheering came from the students hanging onto the cyclone fence, and Susan walked around the back of the crowd to home plate, behind the super-tall cyclone fence, angled down at the top. A player from the other team was at bat, and though Susan didn't remember who they were, they had on bright red uniforms, so she could tell the difference. That meant the Musketeers were pitching.

Susan kept walking and got a view of the pitcher's mound. Raz wasn't pitching, and Jordan was, in his place. She felt terrible for Raz. The change to the lineup would've been another blow, when he was least able to deal with it. This morning before he'd left for school, he'd looked as exhausted, raw, and ragged as she had been. He'd skipped breakfast and left with his long hair dripping wet from the shower, making a soggy collar of his Musketeers baseball T-shirt, which he practically lived in.

Susan looked over at the dugout, and at this angle, she could see Raz silently watching the game from a folding chair behind the Musketeers cheering at the fence.

"Susan?" said a voice beside her.

Susan turned, but didn't recognize the woman approaching her, a pretty, heavyset mom with a halo of blonde curls, bright blue eyes, and a sweet, if concerned, smile. She had on a Musketeers sweatshirt and jeans, which was obviously the right thing to wear at the game, because the other parents had on team logowear. Susan was wearing the black cable sweater and khakis she wore on casual Friday at work.

"I'm Mindy Kostis. Good to see you again."

"Oh, Mindy, right. Hi." Susan raced to remember what Neil had told her about Mindy. Nice lady, doctor husband, popular son. Evan was the catcher. Raz talked about Evan, too, though Susan got the impression that Evan was too popular a kid to be friendly with Raz.

"I just wanted to tell you, I'm so sorry." Mindy's face flushed with genuine emotion.

"Thanks." Susan swallowed hard, unsure what she meant. Ryan? Neil? *Pick a calamity, any calamity.*

"Neil was such a terrific guy. He used to help me so much at the games. We're all missing him today. I know you must be, most of all."

"Thank you." Susan's throat thickened. Meanwhile, if

Mindy knew about Ryan, it didn't show. Maybe this was the best way to handle the situation, just pretend it hadn't happened.

"The Boosters would like to make an impromptu memorial to Neil at the end of the game, if that's okay with you. I didn't know you were coming today, so I took the liberty of asking Raz and he was fine with it."

"Of course, thanks." Susan felt gratitude, and dread, both at once.

"Would you like to say a few words at the ceremony?"

"No, no, thank you." Susan couldn't, not today, not ever. She had been a mess at the funeral. She realized she was still a mess.

"Then I will, don't worry about it. I know what to say." Mindy patted her arm, frowning in a sympathetic way. "How have you been?"

Susan didn't know how to answer. Mindy seemed to want an honest answer, but it wasn't the time or the place to open up. Susan didn't know if she needed to make a friend among the moms, or even how to start. It always seemed like a clique she wasn't a part of, though Neil had been, ironically. Besides, she doubted they had anything in common. Mindy was the Queen Bee of the Boosters with a perfect life, as compared with the Sematov Shit Show.

"Fine, thanks," Susan answered, turning away.

Chapter Nineteen

Chris thought the scene at the baseball game looked typically suburban. The sun shone high in a cloudless sky, and cheering spectators clustered around a perfect baseball diamond and a lush green outfield. He understood why baseball was America's pastime, but it just wasn't his. Sports bored him. He preferred higher stakes.

Chris stood at the edge of the dugout watching, and Jordan had been striking out one batter after the next, until the third inning, when one of the Upper Grove batters connected and the ball hopped into the infield. Jordan had fielded it on the fly and thrown it to first base in the nick of time, and the crowd went crazy. The Musketeers players cheered for him almost constantly, yelling at the top of their lungs, shouting "Jordan, Jordan!" "Number 12!" "Get it!" and "Bring it!"

"Strike three!" barked the umpire, ending the inning.

Jordan and the rest of the team jogged toward the dugout, and Chris fist-bumped each player as they passed by him. Raz, who'd subbed in the outfield, was up next in the batting order, and the team cheered for him, shaking the cyclone fence in front of the dugout. One of the Musketeers played Raz's walk-up music on the boombox, and the team went crazy, rapping at the top of their lungs.

The Upper Grove pitcher threw a fastball, and Raz swung quickly, missing.

"Strike one!" barked the umpire.

Jordan and the Musketeers cheered louder. "You can do it!" "Shake it off!" "You got this, you got this!"

The Upper Grove pitcher threw another fastball, and Raz swung again, missing.

"Strike two!" yelled the umpire.

The Musketeers hollered, "Cool down, Raz!" "Wait for your pitch!"

Chris noticed two moms cheering for Raz behind the fence and he recognized them from his research—Evan's mother Mindy and Raz's mother Susan. He'd been hoping to meet Jordan's mom Heather, but she wasn't here, and he assumed she was at work.

The next pitch flew across the plate, and Raz swung wildly, missing yet again.

"Strike three, you're out!" the umpire yelled.

Suddenly Raz whipped the bat into the air and threw it into the fence behind home plate. Raz's mother and Evan's mother jumped back, shocked.

"Son, you're out of here!" the umpire shouted, then Coach Hardwick scurried to home plate.

Chris used the delay to jog from his coaching spot at third base to the dugout to speak with Jordan, patting him on the back. "Don't let this get to you. You're doing awesome. Keep it up."

Jordan nodded, tense, and the team watched as Coach Hardwick marched Raz to the dugout, where everybody parted for him, stunned and nervous. Raz stalked inside and kicked the folding chair.

"Raz, enough!" Coach Hardwick bellowed, then pointed to Evan, who was next in the lineup.

The Musketeers burst into cheers for Evan, and as the game went on, they dominated inning after inning, scoring three more runs, and Jordan hit as well as he pitched. Chris spotted Jordan's mother Heather arriving late, an attractive woman with dark blonde hair in a white sweater and jeans, and he kept his eye on her throughout the game, waiting to make his move. He needed to get as close as possible to Jordan, and winning over his mom would help the cause.

The final score was five to nothing, the Musketeers' first win, and the team rushed Jordan on the mound, piling onto him and each other. They shook hands with Upper Grove, then streamed to the grassy area behind the visiting dugout, where snack food and drinks had been put out by the Boosters. Coach Hardwick said a few words, parents started talking to him and each other, and Chris made his way to Jordan's mom, standing at the periphery. He approached her with a grin, sticking out his hand.

"Hi, I'm Chris Brennan, the new assistant coach. Are you Jordan's mom? I saw you cheering for him."

"Oh, nice to meet you. Yes, I'm Heather Larkin." She extended her hand, and Chris clasped it warmly.

"Great to meet you. I also have him in AP Government and I'm so impressed with him. He's able, responsible, and hard-working. You guys raised a great son." Chris knew there were no "guys," only Heather, but he couldn't let on he knew.

"That's true, he really is." Heather beamed, and Chris noted she didn't correct him.

"I was thrilled to see that he started today, and you must be very proud of him."

"Oh, I am, I really am!" Heather's hazel eyes shone. "I'm so glad I came. It's my first game! I can't believe how great he played!"

"He really came into his own, and it's wonderful that you were there to share it with him."

"That's just how I feel!" Heather bubbled over with happiness. "I'm so happy I quit my job!"

"What?" Chris didn't know if he'd heard her correctly.

"I quit my job and I feel so great!" Heather burst into laughter. "I hated it, only I didn't *realize* I hated it! The new bosses are terrible! I'll find another job and I feel so happy to be free! And I got to be here!"

"There you go! Some things are meant to be, aren't they?" Chris grinned, though inside, he was shaking his head. She was a sweet person, but somebody should tell all the sweet people in the world, *Don't volunteer so much to complete strangers. Don't tell them the most personal things. Don't post every detail about your private life. You have no idea who is out there, preying on you, using that information to their advantage. Like me.*

"It really is meant to be! Thank you so much for coaching him!"

"I've only coached him for a day, but I'll take the credit." Chris laughed, and Heather joined him.

"Why not? That's the spirit!"

"Right!" Chris said, but just then, a stray sniffle came from one of the moms nearby, evidently about Raz's father.

Heather's pretty face fell. "What a shame. Neil was a great guy. He used to drive Raz and Jordan everywhere until they got their licenses." She leaned over, lowering her voice. "I think Jordan feels bad about starting instead of Raz."

"I can tell." Chris matched her subdued tone, liking the way this was going. The more compliments he paid

Jordan, the happier she got, like any good mother. "He doesn't relish beating his friend. He's got a good heart."

"He wouldn't let it show though. He's not like that."

"I know he's not, he reminds me of someone—basically me." Chris was ad-libbing, but Heather smiled again, so he kept going. "I'll tell you what I told Jordan about the situation with Raz. I told him, 'You have every right to this position because you earned it. You are a combination of God-given talent and hard work, and that's what this is all about. Baseball, life, everything. You can't let anything hold you back. You're stepping into your destiny.'"

"You told him that?" Heather's eyes went wide, and Chris worried he was laying it on too thick, but she was lapping it up. She was eager to hear him, and he could tell she was lonely. She was cute in a natural way, with a great body, but he shooed his horniness away. His goal wasn't to take her to bed, but to manipulate her, so he kept talking.

"I love coaching baseball, but the thing you have to know, is that baseball is about these kids and their maturity, and helping them grow into who they were really meant to be. That's how I think of it. That's why I got into teaching in the first place."

"Really." Heather beamed.

"In fact, just FYI, I'm having a get-together tonight at my apartment for the team to introduce myself. Now it will be a victory celebration, thanks to Jordan."

"Oh." Heather blinked. "He didn't mention that to me, but he doesn't always tell me what he's doing."

"Of course, he wouldn't." Chris could see her falter, so he rushed to reassure her. "I didn't keep my mother posted on everything I did, either. No boy does."

"Right." Heather's smile returned.

"I just wanted you to know that I'm going to take very

good care of him. And if you ever need to reach me, my number and email's on the website."

"Thank you so much." Heather nodded.

"I better go. Congratulations."

"You should say that to Jordan!" Heather shot back, with a final smile. "I'm just the mom."

"I meant congratulations for quitting your job."

"Oh, right!" Heather rolled her eyes, adorably. "God knows what happens next."

"We'll see!" Chris knew *exactly* what happened next, but that was for only him to know.

Chapter Twenty

Chris scanned the party under way at his apartment. Coach Hardwick had declined to come, but the players filled the living room, wolfing down pizza and talking among themselves. Everyone had arrived except Jordan, Evan, and Raz, and Chris was concerned. He hoped it didn't suggest a reconciliation between Jordan and Raz. He was looking for an opportunity to solidify his relationship to Jordan and finish Raz.

"I wonder where Jordan is." Chris stepped onto the balcony, which overlooked the pocket parking lot. A few of the players were freestyling, which gave Chris a headache, but Trevor and Dylan stood talking against the rail, so he went over to them. "Hey guys, great game! Way to go!"

"Hey, Coach!" Trevor shook his fist in the air. "Awesome! Larkin's the man!"

"Trevor, I give credit to you guys, too. It's a team victory."

"Thanks, Coach." Trevor beamed.

"It's the truth. You hit two doubles today. And you,

Dylan." Chris turned to the boy. "Dylan, that home run! I think that ball went four hundred feet."

"Not *that* far," Dylan corrected him, pushing up his glasses with a tight smile.

Suddenly their attention was drawn by noisy rap music coming from below, and they all turned to see Evan's BMW pulling into the parking lot with its convertible top down, blasting hip-hop. Evan was driving, Jordan was in the passenger seat, and Raz was wedged in the nonexistent backseat, his knees tucked under his chin. Evan parked and cut the engine, abruptly ending the music.

"Musketeers!" Trevor called to them, but Dylan looked over at Chris, worriedly.

"Are your neighbors going to be pissed at the noise?"

"Don't worry about it." Chris waved him off.

"Musketeers, pizza's hot!" Trevor hollered.

"Zaaaaaa!" Evan hollered back, looking up with a grin as he opened the car door and got out of the BMW.

Trevor pointed down at Raz, laughing. "Raz, you look like a dog! Did you put your head out the window? Did you get a treat?"

"Shut up, Trevor!" Raz called out, climbing out of the car, and just then, Chris thought he heard the telltale clink of a bottle from below. They must've been drinking, and he didn't approve. Alcohol was an X factor he didn't need right now.

Trevor called back, "Yeah, Raz, you're a good dog! What tricks can you do? Besides throwing your bat? That was smooth, dude!"

The boys on the balcony burst into laughter, and the players who were inside the apartment came out. "Yo!" they started calling out, "Raz! Evan!" Then they broke into a chant, "Jordan, Jordan, Jordan!"

Chris watched Jordan get out of the car and follow Evan and Raz to the back door, which he'd left open. "Excuse me, gentlemen," Chris said, making his way off the balcony and into the apartment, then opening the front door just as Evan and Jordan reached the top of the stairs with matching grins.

"Hey, Coach Brennan!" they both said in unison, then started shoving each other, Evan saying "Jinx," and Jordan saying, "What are you, in middle school?"

"Welcome, guys!" Chris clapped them both on the shoulder. "Come in and have something to eat. We're celebrating. Big home victory!"

"Totally, Coach!" Evan said, crossing into the apartment.

Chris shook Jordan's hand. "Jordan, you played incredible today. Congratulations."

"Thanks, Coach."

"Great to see your mom there, too."

"I know, right?" Jordan smiled, shyly. "She never came before."

"She brought you luck." Chris could see Raz coming up the stairs but didn't hurry to acknowledge him. "I introduced myself to her. We had a great talk about you. She was so proud of you."

Jordan shuddered. "She didn't say anything embarrassing, did she?"

"Of course she did. She told me what a good boy you were when you were a little baby."

"You're kidding, right?" Jordan's eyes flared in mock-alarm.

"I'm kidding. You did terrific today. You should be proud of yourself."

"Thanks, Coach." Jordan glanced over his shoulder at Raz, who lurched forward.

"Coach, your crib is sick!" Raz pushed past him.

"Hey, Raz." Chris caught a whiff of beer on Raz's breath, but not on the other boys. He closed the apartment door, watching as Jordan followed Evan toward the food table.

Raz stopped to look at the gun case. "Whoa, Coach! Are they loaded?"

"No," Chris answered, going over. "You like?"

"Awesome! Are you a good shot?"

"I'm not bad. How about you?"

"Never tried." Raz kept looking at the guns, and Chris couldn't tell if it was to avoid looking at him. Either way, it was time to twist the proverbial knife. There were many kinds of weapons in the world, and words could be the most lethal.

"Raz, I have to say, I was really disappointed when you threw the bat—"

"Sorry," Raz said, sullen. He raked back his hair, loose to his shoulders.

"I know you have a lot going on with your older brother, but—"

"I *don't* have a lot going on," Raz shot back, shifting his gaze back to the gun collection.

"Okay, then I stand corrected." Chris had brought it up because he wanted to see how Raz would react. "I'm talking to you, as your coach and as your friend. I'm looking out for you. You can't have a bad attitude. Between us, my buddy was there today. He saw what you did."

Raz's head snapped around, his dark eyes newly troubled. "You mean the guy you sent Jordan's video to?"

"Yes, but that's between you and me. I'm not even going to tell Jordan that. You've got to do better next time." Chris patted him on the shoulder, like *tough break*.

"What if there's not a next time, Coach?" Raz grimaced.

"I'm sure there will be," Chris answered, but his tone suggested exactly the opposite.

"But, there'll be other games. I'll get in as reliever, won't I?"

"That's up to Coach Hardwick, not me. You're going to have to dig yourself out of a hole."

"I got a single."

"True, but that's not the problem."

"What's the problem?"

"An attitude problem is the kiss of death for recruiters."

"'The kiss of *death*'?" Raz's frown deepened.

"That's what my friend told me. No school will touch a kid with an attitude problem. They don't need the aggravation on the field or in the dugout."

Just then, Evan and Jordan came over holding plates of food, and behind them was Trevor and Dylan. Evan laughed. "Raz, we were just saying, that might've been your best pitch ever. Except that you pitched your *bat*."

Trevor burst into laughter. "Raz, what do you call that pitch? Was that a fastball? Or fast *bat*?"

Dylan smiled. "Dude, I think it was more like a curve. Don't you think it was a curve *bat*? I thought I saw it curve right before the plate. Or the *fence*."

"Or my *mom*!" Evan joined in, his eyes comically wide. "Raz, you almost cracked my mom's skull wide open!"

Trevor added, "And his *own* mom! He almost clocked his own mother! He pitched a curve bat!"

"Trevor, shut the hell up, you meathead!" Raz shouted, shoving Trevor.

"You shut up! Get your hands off me!"

Chris delayed acting for a half second, and just then, Raz shoved Trevor harder, and Trevor shoved Raz back.

"You're crazy, Raz!" Trevor shouted. "You're outta your mind!"

"Boys, Raz, stop it!" Chris reached for Raz, but just then, Raz threw a punch, missing Trevor, upending Evan's plate of food, and connecting with Jordan's face.

"Arhh!" Jordan jumped backwards, his hand flying to his cheek.

Raz whirled around on Jordan. "Oops, did I hurt you, rock star? You going to get a mark on your face now?"

Jordan recoiled, shaken. Raz's punch had broken the skin, making a cut that started to bleed, dripping down Jordan's cheek.

Trevor yelled, "You *suck*, Raz! You can't take it! You never coulda pitched the way Jordan did today!"

"I could so!" Raz lunged for Trevor in anger, knocking Evan and Jordan to the side.

"Stop, Raz!" Chris decided this had gone as far as he needed it to go. He grabbed Raz by the shoulders from behind, forced him backwards, and pressed him into a sitting position on the cabinet in front of the gun case, looking the boy in the eye. "Raz, you've been drinking, haven't you?"

"So what!" Raz yelled in Chris's face, and the boys fell stone silent. Jordan wiped blood from his cut, leaving a pinkish smear on his cheek.

Chris turned to Evan. "Evan, were you drinking, too?"

"No."

"Are you okay to drive?"

"Yes."

Chris believed him, only because Raz didn't call Evan a liar. "I want you to take Raz home."

"Okay, Coach."

"Thank you." Chris took Raz by the arm and lifted him off the cabinet. "Raz, get it together. You're your own worst enemy."

"Leave me alone, *buddy*!"

"Good-bye." Chris walked Raz toward the door, with Evan behind. When he opened it, Raz wrenched his arm away, stalked out of the apartment, and hurried down the stairs. Chris put a hand on Evan's shoulder. "Take him right home, please. No monkey business, no drinking."

"Okay, Coach." Evan motioned to Jordan. "Jordan, you coming?"

Chris interjected, "Evan, I want Jordan to stay. I need to check out his cut and see if he needs to go to the hospital."

Jordan shook his head, and blood dripped like a red tear down his cheek. "Coach, I don't need to go to a hospital. It's nothing."

"That may be, but I'll take you home. I'm responsible for you. I met your mom today. You can't go home and tell her you got injured at my house without her hearing from me. That can't happen, Jordan."

"Okay," Jordan said reluctantly. "Later, Evan."

"Later." Evan waved them off, leaving the apartment and going down the stairs.

"Jordan, let's take a look at that cut." Chris closed the door, satisfied that he'd accomplished his mission—or Raz had, for him.

And he wouldn't mind seeing Jordan's mother again.

Chapter Twenty-one

Chris stood next to Jordan as the boy opened the apartment door, and Heather looked up from her laptop. She was sitting on the couch in a sweatshirt and jeans, with her hair in a ponytail. She had one of those *Housewives* shows on mute, and her expression morphed from sleepy to shocked when she saw Chris entering with Jordan, who had a fresh wound on his cheek.

"Hey, Mom." Jordan closed the door behind them. "I'm okay, don't freak."

"Oh no, what's that on your face?" Heather moved the laptop aside, jumped up, and went over to Jordan, peering at his cheek. It had swollen pink, but the bleeding had stopped. "What happened, honey? Chris, what's going on?"

"It's nothing, Mom. I'm fine."

"He really is," Chris added.

"Tell me what happened. Did you fall?" Heather squinted at the cut, gripping Jordan's arm as if he would otherwise run away. "I hope you don't need stitches."

"I don't think he does," Chris interjected, speaking

from experience, though it wasn't an experience he could share. "I looked at it carefully, cleaned it up, and left it uncovered so it could get air."

"I'm totally fine," Jordan said again. "It's really nothing,"

"So how did it happen?" Heather looked from Jordan to Chris. "Did it happen at your house? At the party?"

Jordan hesitated, and Chris realized they should've discussed this before now. The party had continued after Evan and Raz had gone, and Jordan had hung out, even helping Chris clean up afterwards. They'd talked about other things on the ride here, like the game and pitching mechanics, of course, always mechanics. Chris had been glad to get closer to Jordan at his most vulnerable, and Jordan's friendship with Raz had to be dead meat after tonight.

"Mom, it doesn't matter," Jordan answered, but Heather looked at him like he was crazy.

"It matters to me, Jordan." Heather wheeled her head back to Chris, her blue eyes so frank that it unsettled him. "What happened, Chris? You tell me, since my son won't."

"I'm sorry, but unfortunately, there was an altercation."

"An *altercation*?" Heather asked in disbelief. "With you?"

"No, with Raz," Chris rushed to explain. "I drove Jordan home to apologize to you, because it happened at my house."

"It wasn't really an *altercation,* Mom," Jordan said, edging away. "It's not a big deal."

Heather placed her hands on her hips, turning to Jordan as he backed toward the hallway. "Jordan, if it's not a big deal, don't make it one. What's the big mystery? Did somebody hit you? Tell me."

"Raz got in a bad mood, is all."

"Raz *hit* you? That's terrible!"

"He didn't mean to."

Chris didn't say anything. He knew that if he made Raz look bad, Jordan would only defend him.

Heather's eyes had gone wide. "Jordan, what do you mean? How do you unintentionally hit somebody in the face? Are you saying it was an accident? Was it an accident?"

"Mom, no, but it's not a big thing. It's fine."

"Then it was on purpose? He hit you under your eye. He could've ruined your vision. Why did he do that? Were you guys fighting?"

"No, not really." Jordan backed up toward the hallway.

"So then why did he hit you?"

"He had a bad day. You saw, at the game."

"Hmph! Yes, I did see. I saw him throw a bat. That's bad sportsmanship, and it's dangerous."

Jordan looked at Chris as he left the room. "Coach Brennan, thanks for everything. Good night. Good night, Mom."

Chris gave him a wave. "No worries, Jordan. I'll see you at practice tomorrow morning."

Jordan turned away and headed down the hallway.

"Jordan, we'll talk later," Heather called after him, then turned to Chris with an exasperated sigh. "Sheesh! Is he really okay?"

"Yes, I'm sure of it."

"It was nice of you to take him home."

"Not a problem."

"Would you like a cup of coffee? Or is it too late for you?"

"A glass of water would be great." Chris realized that he could get something accomplished here, if he stayed awhile. Plus she really was cute.

"I have some cookies, if you're a cookie guy." Heather led him to a small dining area that was part of the kitchen, then gestured him into a seat at the table.

"Of course I'm a cookie guy. Who isn't?" Chris sat down, taking in the kitchen and the dining room. It was modest, and a weird reddish glow came from the curtains, from the Friendly's sign next door.

"It's Chips Ahoy. Not gourmet or anything." Heather reached into a cabinet above the counter, and Chris could tell from her residual frown that her mind was on what had happened to Jordan.

"There's no such thing as gourmet chocolate chips."

"Yes, there is." Heather opened the bag of cookies, shaking a few onto a plate she took from the dish rack. "They cost twelve bucks a pound at Whole Foods."

"Not worth it."

"I agree. You really want water? I have milk." Heather brought the plate of cookies over to the table and set it down. "Milk and cookies is better than water and cookies."

"Water and cookies is fine. I just won't dunk."

"Ha!" Heather brightened, heading back to the kitchen. "Everybody in my family dunked, we're big dunkers. Toast got dunked in coffee. Doughnuts, too."

"I like to dunk toast in coffee," Chris said, realizing it was the first completely true sentence he'd said since he'd come to Central Valley.

"Me too." Heather turned on the tap and poured water into a glass, then went to the freezer and popped a few cubes into the water. "We dunk Italian bread in gravy and—"

"Gravy?"

"Gravy is tomato sauce, that's what we always called it. My mother was Italian, from Brooklyn. It's my ex who was from here."

"Oh." Chris caught the reference to her ex, so now he could officially know what he already knew.

"My mother even dunked her bread in salad dressing. Vinegar and oil."

"That would be extreme dunking."

"They were dunking professionals." Heather smiled.

"I'm a dunking *champion*." Chris found himself smiling back.

Heather laughed as she brought the glass of water over and set it down, then took the seat opposite him. The table was small, and the only fixture was an overhead light, which was unusually cozy—at least it was unusual to Chris, because coziness wasn't a feeling he'd had often. In fact, he couldn't remember the last time he felt cozy.

Chris got back on track. "Obviously, I think Raz is having a hard time being replaced as starting pitcher. You might want to discourage the friendship for the time being."

"Tell me about it, I've been trying. I thought they'd sort it out, but maybe not. This is ridiculous."

"It's not fair to Jordan."

"No, it's not!" Heather raised her voice. "I feel bad for Raz and I don't mean to be mean. Please don't think I'm a gossip, but I don't know if you heard, his older brother Ryan was arrested last night."

"Yes, I did hear that." Chris noted she didn't say it in a gossipy way, but her tone was sympathetic.

"Okay, so they're having trouble in the family. I saw Susan at the game, but I didn't get to talk to her. I feel terrible that Raz's father died, too. But still, none of that is Jordan's fault. Jordan earned the position, all by himself. Nobody helped him. Everything he does, it's on his shoulders. He was never given any advantages."

Chris heard the emotion behind her words and sensed she wasn't talking about Jordan anymore. He broke off a piece of cookie and popped it in his mouth.

"I probably should have mentioned this, but his father and I broke up when he was born. He's grown up without a father and he's 'risen above his raisin' as Dr. Phil says."

"I don't think you need to worry. As you said, Raz and Jordan will sort themselves out, and this too shall pass."

"Right, I know." Heather pressed a stray strand of hair from her eyes, with a new sigh. "It's been a long day, I guess. A long, weird day."

"The day you quit your job."

"Right, the day I quit my job." Heather rolled her eyes, with a self-conscious giggle. "It's settling in."

"What is?"

"Reality. I don't have a backup plan."

"I always have a backup plan," Chris said, another thing that was true.

"Is that supposed to make me feel better?" Heather lifted an eyebrow, and Chris realized he'd said the wrong thing, thrown off-balance by her.

"No, what I was about to say is that you don't need a backup plan. Just go to the next step."

"What's that?"

"Find a new job."

"Ha!" Heather laughed, but it had a hollow sound. "That's not as easy as it sounds. I was just online at monster.com and Craigslist. I applied to fifteen jobs already, but there's not a lot of places looking."

"Nothing's as easy as it sounds. You can't let that stop you."

"Now you're talking like a coach."

"Well, I am a coach," Chris said, without thinking.

"Okay, then, coach me. I'm open-minded." Heather leaned back, crossing her arms, and Chris tried to think of something a real coach would say.

"Be positive."

"Good start."

"I'm sure a lot of businesses would love to have someone like you."

"What makes you say that? You don't even know me." Heather looked at him like he was crazy, the same way she had looked at Jordan, which was very cute. Totally cute.

"I do, in a way," Chris answered, and he wasn't even talking about his research on her. "Through Jordan."

"What about him? You don't know him that well, either."

"I know enough to draw some reasonable conclusions. He turned out great, and you just told me that you raised him by yourself, on your own."

"Yes, so?" Heather blinked. "What are you saying, that I should get a job as a nanny?"

"No, not unless you wanted to. What I mean is, you need to view your skill set more broadly."

"Skill set?" Heather threw back her head and laughed. "I have a *skill set*? That's news to me."

"No, it isn't, it shouldn't be," Chris said, meaning it. His tone turned soft and he didn't even plan it that way. "It takes a lot of skills to be a single mother, raise a kid, and run a household by yourself. You have to pay the bills, repair what needs repairing, and make sure that Jordan gets to school and to the doctor and to practice, am I right?"

"Yes, when he was younger, I guess." Heather shrugged. "But I don't fix things, Jordan does. Or they don't get fixed."

"Then they didn't need fixing. And all the time you're working at a full-time job, so you have that to deal with. True or not?"

"True," Heather answered, with the trace of a smile.

"And I'm sure you were very good at your job, whatever you did, and you said you wanted to leave it, and you did that, too. So you have a broad skill set and you should move forward with absolute confidence."

Heather smiled, chuckling. "You're an excellent coach!

You're getting me to think positive. Gung ho! Clear eyes, full heart, can't lose, all that."

"So it worked?" Chris chuckled.

"It kind of did!" Heather threw up her hands. "Go, team, go!"

"Ha!" Chris burst into laughter, realizing that the weirdest thing had just happened. He had been playing the role of a coach and saying whatever a coach would say, but somewhere between him and her, the words had become true. And above all, they had helped her, which made him feel good. He felt not only like a coach, he even felt more . . . human.

Suddenly a cell phone started ringing in the living room, and Heather looked over. "Oh, excuse me, I have to get that, but I'll be only a minute. It's my cousin in Denver and she just had a baby—"

"No, that's okay, I should go," Chris said, standing quickly. He had to stop what was happening between them. Whatever it was, it wasn't according to plan, backup plan, step one, or step two. It was basically something that couldn't happen at all, especially not with Heather. He needed to use Jordan, and her. They could only be the means to an end, in a dangerous and deadly game.

"You don't have to go. Give me a second." Heather hustled for the phone. "I just want to see if she's okay."

"No, it's late. Good night now." Chris crossed to the door, pulled it open, and let himself out.

It was no time to grow a conscience.

Chapter Twenty-two

An hour later, Chris was driving through thick, dark woods to a meet. The night sky was starless, and clouds swept across the moon, carried by unseen winds. He tried to put Heather out of his mind and focus on what lay ahead, but it wasn't easy. He'd been with his share of women, but she was different. He didn't want to figure out how, because any relationship with her could end only one way. So it had to end now, before it started.

Chris turned into a dirt driveway, and his Jeep's headlights raced over a peeling white sign with faded letters, COMING SOON, CENTRE MALL & FOOD COURT. He parked and cut the engine, scanning the scene in the scant light. It was a construction site for a mall, but the project had evidently been abandoned after the pad had been installed, paving a footprint for the strip of stores. The concrete glowed darkly in the moonlight, surrounded by trees that had been cut to black stubs.

Chris got out of the Jeep, dismayed to see that the silhouette standing next to the car wasn't the one he'd expected. Neither was the car. It was a gleaming black Audi coupe, not the nondescript black Ford SUV he knew so well. The man standing next to the car had on a Phillies cap, and there was only one man Chris knew who wore a ball cap thinking he was a Master of Disguise. The cap's brim put his face almost completely in shadow, which was fine with Chris because Aleksandr Ivanov was ugly as sin.

Chris walked over. "Hey, Alek. Where's the Rabbi? He said he'd be here."

"He couldn't make it."

"Why?"

"What's the difference? You miss Daddy? Deal with me. What's going on?"

Chris bit his tongue. He wasn't looking for trouble. "Okay, I have a guy. I'm in."

Alek snorted. "By 'guy,' you mean a kid. A high-school junior. This is some next-level shit, Curt."

Chris thought his real name sounded strange to him, but didn't say so. He realized he was mentally betwixt and between, after the cookies with Heather. He had to get his head back in the game. Alek had a bad temper, and the stakes were too high to get distracted.

"Who's the kid?"

"Jordan Larkin." Chris felt a twinge offering up the name, like a betrayal. But he shooed the thoughts away.

"So what's the problem? You called the Rabbi and told him you had a problem."

"I said I might have a problem." Chris didn't want to talk it over with Alek, who was half as smart as the Rabbi.

"Gimme a break, Curt. I don't have time to jerk around." Alek checked his watch, a neat swivel of his head under the cap.

"Turns out one of the teachers is from Wyoming. He knows Northwest College."

"You said that wouldn't happen." Alek snorted again.

"The odds were slim to none. It's a fluke." Chris's chest tightened. Alek always reminded him of one of his foster fathers, the worst one. A bully to everyone around him, like a prison guard to his wife, his other foster son, even the cat. Milly was the cat's name, a calico. The night Chris had finally left, he'd let Milly out and she ran off. She would never look back. Neither would he.

"What's his name, this teacher?"

"Abe Yomes."

"So what are you telling me for? Handle it."

"The question is how."

"You're a big boy. Don't ask me. Handle it. I gotta go. What a waste of time." Alek turned away, got in the car, and started the engine.

Chris watched him go, wishing the Rabbi had come. Together they would have assessed the risk and figured out what to do about Abe.

But if Chris had to handle it on his own, he would.

"I don't know, but I bet that's the closet." Wavonne points to a pair of double doors on the other side of the bed. Her eyes are fixed straight ahead like a fox at the entrance to a hen house.

"I think I'd better call Christy, and see if she reached Raynell earlier." I pull out my phone as Wavonne creeps toward the closet. "You stay out of there," I say, but before I have a chance to make my call, Wavonne has already opened the doors to the Holy Land.

"This must be what heaven's like," I hear Wavonne say as she steps inside the closet.

Curiosity gets the best of me, and I can't help but follow behind her into the expansive space, which is literally bigger than my living room. More clothes than any one person should own hang from two sets of rods on both sides of us—one close to the ceiling and one about midway down the wall. In front of us is a complex shelving system adorned with a selection of shoes that could easily rival the footwear department at Macy's. There's even a ladder that runs along a track surrounding the entire room to reach the purses displayed on the highest shelves. In the middle of the room is a large dresser with cabinets and drawers on both sides.

"Leave it alone," I call to Wavonne as she looks at the dresser.

I watch as she slowly walks alongside the clothes, looking closely at certain pieces and trying to read the labels if there's enough space between garments to see them. I wonder if she's aware that her mouth is hanging open. I'm not a fashionista by any means, but even I'm awestruck by the sheer volume of meticulously organized high-priced clothing. I hate to admit it, but for a moment, I think we both forget that we were even looking for Raynell.

"I bet there's a few hundred thousand bucks worth of clothes and shoes in here." Wavonne approaches the dozens of shoes stored along the back wall. "Prada, Louboutin, Fendi, Valentino," she calls out as she peruses the designer footwear. "Oh my God, Halia! I saw these Manolos on the Neiman Marcus Web site for more than two thousand dollars!"

"Okay, Wavonne. I think we've had enough. I'm not sure where Raynell is, but we don't have any business poking around her closet. Come on."

I start to walk out of the closet, and Wavonne reluctantly follows. "So now what?"

"I guess we go. I'll give Christy a call on the way to Sweet Tea and set up a time to get the check, assuming they're still some funds in the reunion committee's account."

We're about to make our way out of the bedroom when Wavonne spies another door on the other side of the room. "You think that's Terrence's closet?" she asks as she steps toward the door.

"I don't know. It doesn't matter. No more closet snooping, Wavonne. Let's go," I say, but Wavonne, being Wavonne, grasps the doorknob anyway.

"Oh hail no!" I hear her shriek when she opens the door.

"What?" I scurry in her direction and look over her shoulder while she stands frozen in place. The door doesn't lead to Terrence's closet. It leads to the bathroom—there's a long deep tub, a pristine glass-enclosed shower, two gleaming white pedestal sinks presiding over a polished marble tile floor—a polished marble tile floor that would be lovely . . . just lovely, if it wasn't for the fact that Raynell is laying facedown on it with a pool of blood around her head.

CHAPTER 21

"Oh *hail* no!"

"You said that already," I retort, slightly dazed as my eyes take in the sight before us: Raynell, in nothing but a nightshirt, flat on the floor. A shallow puddle of red surrounds her head and, at some point, streamed into the grout lines between the marble tiles.

"And I'll say it again. Oh *HAIL* NO!!!"

I try to remain calm while I bypass Wavonne. I carefully step around the blood, and lower myself to pick up Raynell's hand. I feel her wrist. "There's no pulse. She's dead."

I gently lay her hand back on the floor and stand up.

"Not again." The words involuntarily come from my lips as I try to make sense of what lays before us. This is not the first dead body Wavonne and I have stumbled upon. Last year, when we came across the deceased body of one of my restaurant investors (a bit of a shady fellow) in the kitchen of Sweet Tea after closing, I made the big . . . HUGE mistake of not calling the police for fear of the effect such awful publicity would have on my restaurant. Wavonne and I dragged his body out of Sweet Tea in hopes of keeping my restaurant out of the news surrounding a murder investigation. The whole thing turned into a huge disaster with Wavonne almost going to jail. I'm *not* making that blunder again.

I grab my phone and dial 911. "I need the police. I've found a dead body."

The operator asks a few questions and connects me with the police. I provide the few details that I can, and the officer on the line advises us to stay put and not touch anything until the authorities arrive.

When I disconnect from the call, I maneuver myself around Raynell's body and cautiously step out of the bathroom. I stand next to Wavonne just outside the door. We both can't do anything but stare. As we take in the dastardly scene I oddly begin to notice the sound of birds chirping outside. It's already pretty hot even though it's still morning, but there is a light breeze coming through the open window in the bathroom, and the morning sunshine is cascading through a skylight in the ceiling. I can't help but notice how Raynell, lying lifeless on the floor, is such a sharp contrast to the beautiful day outside.

"Standing here staring at her is not going to bring her back to life." I lightly pull Wavonne by the shoulders a few steps back from the bathroom door.

"What do you think happened?" Wavonne asks.

"I don't know. Maybe she fell. She was really drunk when she left the reunion."

"Or maybe someone pushed her."

"Maybe."

"So what are we supposed to do now?"

"I don't know," I reply. "The officer on the phone said not to touch anything, so I guess we should just stay put."

Wavonne and I do just that for about five minutes. We are hovering next to the bathroom door when we hear a loud knock on the door downstairs.

"Prince George's County Police," I hear a male voice call up the steps.

"We're up here."

Wavonne and I hurry out of the bedroom and down the hall. We meet the officer at the top of the steps.

"She's in the master bedroom . . . the bathroom, actually."

"And you are?" the policeman asks.

"Halia. I'm Halia Watkins, and this is my cousin, Wavonne Hix. We came by to pick up a check from Raynell. When she didn't answer the door we became concerned."

"How did you get in?" he asks as the three of us quickly walk down the hall.

"The door was unlocked. We let ourselves in."

"You're friends of the deceased?"

"Yes . . . well, no . . . sort of. I went to high school with her. We planned our reunion together. It was last night. I catered the event, and Raynell was supposed to have a check for me this morning."

"Fine, fine," the officer says as we reach the bathroom.

He looks at Raynell and back at Wavonne and me. "Have you touched anything?"

"Aren't you going to confirm she's dead?"

"Don't need to. See how her feet are sort of a bluish brown color? That's blood pooling. She's dead." He says this like it's just another day at the office. I guess for him, maybe it is.

"Did you touch anything?" he asks again.

"No . . . well, the door handle to let ourselves in. Maybe the banister on the stairway."

"I opened the bathroom door," Wavonne says.

"And we opened the closet door over there when we were looking for Raynell . . . and I felt her wrist to check for a pulse. I think that's it."

"Have you seen anything suspicious or out of the ordinary since you arrived?"

I look at Raynell's dead body and then narrow my eyebrows at him.

"Other than the deceased, that is."

"No. Nothing that I can think of."

"You think she fell? Or did someone whack her?" Wavonne asks. "Girlfriend was not the most popular sista in PG County."

"I have no idea, but a crime scene team is on the way. For now, I think it's best if you ladies step outside until we get a formal statement from you."

He starts talking into his walkie-talkie, and Wavonne and I do as we are told and leave the bedroom. But before we make it out of the house, the homicide team arrives, and a small group of people walk past us on the stairs. They have their hands full with cameras and cases and plastic bags . . . and pay us zero attention.

"You!?" I hear from a male voice as Wavonne and I step outside the front door.

"Detective Hutchins. We meet again."

Detective Hutchins and I have a wee bit of a history. He was the homicide detective on the case that involved the first dead body Wavonne and I had the pleasure of stumbling upon. He mostly regarded me as a pest during that investigation . . . at least until I ultimately solved the case and identified the murderer.

"What are you doing here?"

"Wavonne and I found Raynell's body. We came by to collect payment for a catering job. When she didn't answer, we let ourselves in and found her in the bathroom. I—"

He cuts me off. "I'll have an officer collect a statement from you. Please wait out here."

With that he enters the house and leaves Wavonne and me to stand outside until someone sees fit to speak to us. I call Laura while we wait and, without giving any details, I tell her that Wavonne and I are delayed and ask if she can go into the restaurant and cover for me. She agrees even though I had promised her the morning off, which is fortunate considering nearly an hour and a half passes before the same officer who first came to the house comes outside and officially interviews us. By this time, Wavonne and I are misty from the heat, which has probably gone up ten degrees or so from when we first got here.

We go over our story again, give him details about last night including Raynell's condition when we last saw her alive at the hotel. I tell him that it's my understanding that her husband is at a church retreat in Williamsburg, so she was likely home alone last night. He asks a few more questions about the reunion and requests Christy's contact information as we told him that she drove Raynell home.

"Thank you for your cooperation. You're free to leave," he says when he's done questioning us.

I feel like saying, "What if I don't want to leave?" but I refrain. Instead I nod and motion for Wavonne to follow me as I walk toward the van.

"We're leaving?" she asks.

"Of course not," I say. "Has he gone back inside yet?"

Wavonne looks over her shoulder. "Uh-huh."

"Good." I stop walking. "We'll wait here until Detective Hutchins comes out."

"Can we wait in the van with the air conditioning on?" Wavonne wipes her brow with the top of her hand. "Much longer in this heat, and this wig's comin' off . . . and don't nobody need to see that."

"Fine." I hand her the keys. "Go wait in the van."

While Wavonne heads off to sit in the air conditioning, it occurs to me that perhaps I should call Terrence or maybe Alvetta, and she can break the news of Raynell's death to him.

I fumble for my phone in my pocket and tap the screen a few times. "Hey, Alvetta. It's Halia," I say after lifting the phone to my ear.

"Hi, Halia. How are you? Fun night last night. The food was just—"

"Alvetta," I interrupt her. "Sweetie, I have some bad news."

There's silence on the other end of the phone.

"It's about Raynell."

"What? What is it?"

"Gosh. Now I'm thinking I shouldn't have called you. I should deliver the news in person."

"News? What news? Just tell me."

"Alvetta." I take a deep breath. "Raynell . . . Raynell appears to have had a fall or something. It looks like she hit her head on the bathroom sink or the side of the tub . . . and . . . well . . . well, she didn't survive the fall."

"She's dead?"

I pause before responding. "Yes."

"Oh my God!"

"I'm so sorry."

I go into the whole story about why we came over, how we found her, and explain that the police are currently in the house, but I'm not sure she's really hearing any of it.

"Alvetta, are you at home?"

"Yes."

"I'll be leaving here shortly. Why don't you give me your address, and Wavonne and I will stop by and check on you. Do you want me to call Terrence, or would you rather do that? Or we could let the police make the call."

"No, no. He shouldn't hear it from the police. I will tell him."

Wishing I had just gone to see Alvetta in person to begin with, I try to wrap up the call as delicately as I can and remind her that we'll be over shortly.

I'm about to end the waiting game for Detective Hutchins and drive over to Alvetta's when he finally emerges from the house.

"What are you still doing here? Officer Taylor told me he asked you to leave."

"No. He said we were 'free to leave.' "

Detective Hutchins sighs.

"What did you find out? Do you think it was just an accident?"

"I'm sorry. I should be sharing details of a crime scene investigation with you *because?*"

"Because you know I won't leave until you do. Look, she was a friend," I lie. "And I'm the one who found her. Can't you just give me an idea of your initial thoughts?"

Another sigh. "It appears that she fell. You and your cousin both indicated that she was extremely inebriated last night. In fact," he says, opening a folder in his hand and looking at a piece of paper, "according to the statement by your cousin, and I quote, 'She was straight-up crunked out her mind when she left the party.' There are no signs of forced entry or that she struggled with an attacker. We'll need her husband to confirm nothing is missing, but we didn't find any indication of robbery, either. It's logical to deduce that she slipped in the bathroom and hit her head on the edge of the tub. If she did survive the fall, she probably was unable to get up or call for help. She likely either died from the impact or blood loss."

"Well, an autopsy certainly needs to be done to confirm the cause of death."

"*Really?* Thanks for the tip, Ms. Watkins. We never would have thought of that."

I roll my eyes.

"Of course there will be an autopsy, but it may be awhile. The OCME is backed up and cases way more suspicious than this will take precedence."

"OCME?"

"Have I stumped the all-knowing Detective Halia Watkins?" he asks with a snarky look on his face. "Office of the Chief Medical Examiner."

"Oh. Good to know," I say. "I assumed her husband has not been notified. I've asked a good friend of both Raynell and her husband to break the news to him."

"That's fine."

"Okay. Thank you, Detective Hutchins. I guess I'll be on my way."

I turn away from the house and join Wavonne in the car. The cool air emitting from the vents in the dashboard is a welcome relief from the heat. I'm about to put the van in drive when we catch sight of Raynell's body concealed in a gray plastic bag being wheeled out toward a white van.

"Guess that's the last we'll see of Raynell Rollins," Wavonne says.

"I guess so."

"Can't say I liked her much, but I will say this: the sista did have some good hair."

"Well, I'm glad you thought of something positive to say about her," I reply as I put the car in drive and head to Alvetta's home.

CHAPTER 22

"I can't believe she's dead," I say to Wavonne as we veer off the highway toward National Harbor, a haughty waterfront development on the Potomac River.

"I guess the phrase 'too mean to die' don't apply in her case."

"Detective Hutchins seems to think it was just an accident—that she fell over drunk."

"Detective Hutchins didn't know her, and how salty she was . . . and how many people hated her."

"The woman is dead, Wavonne. No need for name-calling."

"Just speakin' the truth, Halia."

"Maybe so . . . maybe so," I say. "Now, what's the building number again?" I ask as I maneuver the van down Waterfront Street and take in all the hotels, glitzy shops, and restaurants.

"Turn here. It's on American Way."

I make a left, and we head up a hill.

"There it is." Wavonne points to a swanky building about twelve stories tall. The awning over the main entrance reads "The Echelon."

Alvetta mentioned that we could park in the garage and get a visitors' pass from the front desk, but I see an open spot on the street and decide to grab it instead. I pay the meter and Wavonne and I walk toward the building. When we reach the entrance, I punch in a code that Alvetta gave us and hear a buzzing sound as the door unlocks.

"This looks more like a Ritz Carlton than an apartment building," I say to Wavonne as we step into the cool air and breathe in the scent of a mammoth display of fresh flowers on an elegant round table in front of the doorway. We step across the lightly hued bamboo floors and find that not only is there a front desk with a clerk clicking away on his computer, but, on the other side of the lobby, is a sharply dressed young lady sitting behind a wraparound counter with the word "Concierge" adorned across the front panel in gold letters.

"Classy." Wavonne takes note of the sleek furnishings and modern light fixtures on our way to the elevators.

"We in the wrong bidness, Halia. You should have opened a church instead of a restaurant."

I laugh. "It quite possibly would have been more profitable . . . and maybe less work."

We step into the elevator and Wavonne presses the PH button.

"I was thinkin' I needed to land me a pro football playa, but maybe what I really need is a minister."

I'm considering, once again, reminding her that she could actually try to earn her own money as we ride to the top floor of the building, but decide not to bother.

When the elevator doors open, Wavonne and I make our way to Alvetta's unit, and knock on the door.

"Hello," I say when she opens the door. "I'm so sorry."

"Thank you." She motions for us to come in.

For a moment the three of us just stand there in her softly lit foyer. I'm unsure of what else to say, and Alvetta doesn't seem to quite have it together. She's in a robe, and, while her eyes are looking at Wavonne and me, I can tell that her thoughts are elsewhere.

"I'm sorry," she eventually says. "Please. Let's go into the living room."

We follow her into an expansive living room decorated with contemporary furnishings, and Alvetta sits down on a long sofa.

"Talk about a 'deluxe apartment in the sky,'" Wavonne says under her breath as we lower ourselves into a pair of lounge chairs with polished stainless steel frames.

"That's a lovely view." I look past the sofa through the glass doors that lead to a terrace overlooking the Potomac River.

"It is. I was sitting out there having my coffee when you called . . . enjoying a rare Sunday morning at home with Michael out of town." Alvetta pauses for a moment. "It's really true? Raynell is really . . ."

"I'm afraid so. It looks like she slipped in the bathroom and hit her head."

"I just can't even wrap my head around it." Alvetta's looking at her lap. I can see her mouth begin to quiver as she tries to keep from crying. "She was just . . . last night . . . I just saw her last night. . . ."

Her attempt at holding back tears is unsuccessful.

"I know. I know. We are all shocked." I join her on the sofa and put my arm around her.

"I don't know what I'll do without her. We've been best friends for more than twenty years."

I keep a hold on her and just let her cry while Wavonne grabs a box of tissues from an end table and brings it to Alvetta.

"I wish I knew what to say, but . . ." I struggle to find words. "Have you reached Terrence?"

"Yes. Well . . . no . . . I talked to Michael, actually. He said he would break the news to Terrence. They should both be home shortly." She wipes her eyes with a tissue and tries to pull herself together. "Are the police sure it was an accident?"

"They seemed pretty sure. There was no sign of forced entry or struggle . . . or anything like that."

Alvetta wipes her eyes a second time and blows her nose. "I don't know . . . I wonder. I love . . . *loved* Raynell like a sister, but even I can admit that she had a mean streak. There's no shortage of people who might want her dead. Raynell probably had some sort of high school run-in with half the people at that reunion. Remember she was supposed to share a locker with Gina Holmes and threw her books all over the hallway. And how she thought it was funny to steal other girls' towels when they were in the shower so they had nothing to dry off with. And what she did to Kimberly Butler with the Nair. God bless Raynell, but she really could be horrible. And, back then, I guess I wasn't much better. I stood right along side her malicious reign. I think half the reason I stayed friends with her was because I feared the alternative."

"I don't dispute that she could be really awful. But do you really think anyone would still hold that much of a grudge? That they would kill her?"

"If you axe me," Wavonne says, "from what I've heard, she makes the chicks in that white teen movie about the 'mean girls' seem like Girl Scouts."

"She was rough in high school."

"She wasn't exactly Mary Freakin' Poppins as an adult, either."

"Wavonne, the woman is dead. Show some respect," I reprimand.

"She's right," Alvetta says. "Maybe she wasn't as mean as she was in high school, but girlfriend was still a little rough around the edges."

"A *little?*"

I give Wavonne a look.

"I'm just callin 'em like I see 'em, Halia. Like Alvetta said, there are probably people out there who wouldn't mind seein' her dead."

"It seems there're almost too many people to count," I say. "Gina Holmes, Kimberly Butler . . . every girl she ever stole a towel from."

"Even Gregory Simms might have a motive," Alvetta says.

"Gregory?" I ask. "What do you mean? Wasn't

he just working with Raynell to find a local property for his restaurant?"

"Yes, but him seeking out Raynell to work as his real estate agent always seemed odd to me . . . you know . . . given their history."

"What history?"

"Come to think of it, I guess few people knew, but Raynell and Gregory dated senior year."

"No way."

"Yes. Of course, in true Raynell-fashion, the whole thing was quite nefarious. Raynell was only using him."

"For what?"

"Haters can say what they want about Raynell, but she was a smart cookie with enough ambition for two people, which is why she was such a good real estate agent. She was very organized, detail oriented, and could market a house just shy of being condemned as 'a quaint fixer-upper with loads of potential.' But one thing she never could master was math . . . numbers, figures—she had absolutely no aptitude for them."

"And Gregory led the math team to a state championship," I say.

"Exactly. Raynell had the extracurriculars and the grades in everything but her math classes to get into the best colleges . . . and she could achieve a tidy score on the verbal portion of the SATs, but her math score was dismal. That's where Gregory came in."

"I don't remember them being a thing."

"No. You wouldn't. Raynell put the moves on him, and they started dating, but Raynell insisted they keep it on the down low. There was no way she was going to let the entire school know she was dating a math geek. At first she only got him to tutor her, but eventually she convinced him to let her cheat off him in calculus. And I don't know how, but somehow Raynell managed to engineer a swap when they took the SATs and Gregory completed her test, sacrificing his own score."

"Seriously?"

"Yep. Leave it to Raynell. Like I said, she was no dummy and could come up with schemes that would make a professional con artist jealous. She strung poor Gregory along for several months, but after he tutored her, let her cheat off him, and took the SATs for her, he was of no use to her anymore. By the spring, she'd gotten her college acceptance letters, and there was no way she was going to the high school social event of the year with a nerd. She dumped him a few weeks before prom, forbade him to tell anyone about their relationship, and managed to snag Trey Lotti as her prom date."

"I can't believe he never told me. Gregory and I were friends. We were on the debate team together. I never knew he had a thing going with Raynell. I actually ended up going to prom with him. I had no idea I was a rebound date."

"He was probably afraid to tell anyone," Alvetta says. "After the way Raynell treated him, it's odd that he reached out to her for help with his real estate aspirations. Although, maybe she reached out to him if she got word he was looking for space in the area and convinced him to come on board with her. Raynell is . . . *was* a master manipulator. She was able to cast a spell over him in high school. Maybe she did it again."

"Maybe," I say. "Who knows what Gregory's motives were, but I knew him pretty well in high school, and I just can't imagine he could kill someone—even Raynell."

"What about that Kimberly chick?" Wavonne asks. "We saw her eyes shootin' daggers at Raynell all night."

"Really?" Alvetta asks.

"Yes," I confirm. "She was visibly jarred when she caught sight of Raynell at the reunion. And rightfully so, given how terrible Raynell was to her. But I suspect Kimberly got her revenge by just showing up and looking fabulous."

Alvetta takes a breath. "All this speculation is probably silly. It sounds like it was an accident. We all saw how drunk she was when Christy drove her home."

At the mention of her name, I'm about to ask Alvetta if she is aware of any motive Christy would have for killing Raynell when we hear some clatter at the front door and see Michael walk into the apartment.

Alvetta gets up from the sofa to greet him, and he gives her a hug. "I'm so sorry," he says. "I still can't believe it."

"I know. I know," Alvetta responds. "How is Terrence doing?"

"I think he's mostly in shock. I was already on my way home when you called, so I had to tell him over the phone. It should have been done in person, but I wanted to tell him before the police did."

"Is he back in town? Should we go over and stay with him?"

"No. He drove on to Roanoke to tell Raynell's parents in person. He may stay there tonight or come back later this evening," Michael says, and just now seems to take note of Wavonne and me. "Hello."

"Hi, Michael," I say. "We just stopped by to check on Alvetta. We'll get going now that you're here."

"Thank you. I'm sorry you had to . . . to find her . . . well, you know."

"Yes. I'm sorry, too." I offer a polite smile. "Come on, Wavonne. Let's go and give them some privacy."

We hug both of them and then head toward the door.

"So sad," I say to Wavonne once we're out in the hall. "I'm glad Michael is there with her."

Wavonne pushes the button for the elevator. "So what do you think, Sherlock? You think Raynell buyin' the farm was an accident?"

"I don't know. It seems like it probably was, but if she were a nicer person, I'd be more confident that no foul play was involved. I know better than to not call the police immediately after finding a dead body, but I wish I had taken some time to look around the Rollinses' house before they got there, and see if anything seemed out of sorts. I had been to the house once before. I may have been able to tell if anything was out of place. Although I guess Terrence can do that when he gets home."

"Terrence? Terrence is a *man,* Halia. Men

don't notice anything unless it involves a football or a pair of titties."

I snicker. "That's not too far from the truth, Wavonne. Maybe we could swing by the house before going back to Sweet Tea. The cops may still be there. Maybe we can just say we stopped by to see if they needed any more information from us, and then I can try to poke around a bit." I look at my watch. "Actually, by the time we get back over there they will have probably gone. They were wheeling Raynell's body out of the house when we left earlier. I'm guessing they were probably about finished and locked the house. We won't be able to get in."

We step into the elevator.

"Promise you won't get mad?" Wavonne asks as the doors close.

"Mad about what?"

Wavonne raises her eyebrows at me.

"*What?* What did you do, *Wavonne?* Why do you look like a puppy that's just chewed up a pair of designer shoes?"

"If the cops are gone I might be able to help with the house being locked thing."

"How so?"

"You won't get mad?"

I take a deep breath. "No, Wavonne, I won't get mad."

"Well . . . I kinda helped myself to this on the way out." She reaches into the side pocket of her purse.

"Wavonne!" I say as she pulls out a gaudy Michael Kors keychain.

CHAPTER 23

"You took her keys?!"

"You said you wouldn't get mad."

I close my eyes for a second and take a deep breath. "Why . . . *why* did you take her keys, Wavonne?"

"I thought . . . I thought maybe I could go back at some point . . . I mean, she's got no use for all those fancy shoes and handbags."

"You were going to break into her house and steal her shoes and purses?!"

"I don't know if I would have actually done it, Halia. I guess I just wanted the option. And, we've had this discussion before. She's *dead.* It ain't stealin' if she's dead. She's got no use for any of that stuff."

"Unbelievable!"

"She just had such nice things, Halia. I'm so *over* cheap stuff—dresses that rip when I bend over. I'm tired of Gussini and Plato's Closet and

Ross Dress for Freakin' Less . . . and being the only black girl shoppin' at Latina Fashion."

"Then I suggest you save up some money so you can *buy*, rather than *steal*, some nice clothes."

"I wasn't goin to take any *clothes* . . . I couldn't fit all *this* into those outfits made for her short weeble-wobble body. But what's the harm in helping myself to a pair of Ferragamo shoes . . . or maybe a Michael Kors bag?"

"I *know* . . . let's just show up with a moving van and help ourselves to the whole lot . . . the shoes, the purses, the belts, her jewelry . . . hell, let's take the furniture . . . maybe the food from the kitchen, too. She's dead. What does she need with any of it?"

"All right, all right . . . pump your brakes, Halia. I was just talkin' about an item or two, and I probably wasn't goin' to do it anyway."

"Just give me those." I grab the keys from Wavonne.

"What are you goin' to do with them?"

"I don't know." I hesitate for a moment. "I guess we should take them back . . . put them back where you found them. And if we take a moment to look around while we're there, then so be it. Michael said Terrence wouldn't be back anytime soon, so if we're going to do it, we better do it now."

We step out of the elevator, and I call Laura at Sweet Tea to see how things are going and let her know that Wavonne and I will be further delayed. Laura assures me that she has things under control, so Wavonne and I return to my van and head back over to Raynell's.

"Here." I hand Wavonne the keychain and

continue to drive while digging through my purse with one hand for a Wet-Nap and a tissue. I eventually find both and hand them to Wavonne. "Hold them with the tissue and wipe them down to get any fingerprints off of them."

I'm hoping that, just maybe, the police are still there when we reach the house, so we can walk in without having to use the key, make up some excuse as to why we came back, and discreetly place the keys back on the console. Maybe we can just say we came back to tell them that we have seen Alvetta and Michael and wanted to let them know that Terrence was en route to inform Raynell's parents of her death.

Regrettably, we see no sign of the police when we arrive.

"What are you goin' to do?" Wavonne asks as we sit in the van in front of Raynell's house.

"I don't know. I thought the cops might still be here. I can't believe the place isn't even sealed off with police tape or something. Looking at the house, you wouldn't know anything out of the ordinary had just happened there."

"So we go home? Back to the restaurant?"

I grasp the steering wheel tightly while I think for a moment. "I'd really like to get in there for just a few minutes to look around. Detective Hutchins seemed to have all but determined that Raynell's death was an accident. If the police were convinced that there was nothing dubious about her death, they may not have conducted a thorough search."

"So we're goin' in?"

I take my hands off the wheel and clasp them

together tightly while I consider our options. Then I look around through the van windows and see if anyone is watching us. There is no one in sight. "Yes. I suppose we are."

"Fun!" Wavonne says.

I step on the gas pedal. "Let's park away from the house, so no one will see the van in case someone comes while we're still in there."

We drive a few blocks down from Raynell's house and park the van.

I've got a few boxes of latex gloves leftover from the catering job last night, so I grab one and pull out two pairs. "Put these on. We don't need to be leaving fingerprints."

We slip on the gloves, exit the van, and scurry up the sidewalk back to the Rollinses' home.

I take a last look around to make sure no one is watching. "Go ahead," I say to Wavonne. She slips a key into the dead bolt, and we hurriedly let ourselves in.

"Let's check upstairs first."

Wavonne shoves Raynell's keys in her pocket, and we climb the curved staircase to the second floor and walk down the hall to the master bedroom.

"You need to return those keys when we come back downstairs," I say as we reach the top of the steps. "Now, you stay out of that closet!"

"Yeah, yeah."

"It's all cleaned up," I say when we reach the doorway to the bathroom. "As if nothing ever happened."

"Sista-girl had no shortage of beauty supplies." Wavonne steps ahead of me into the bathroom and begins thumbing though Raynell's collection of creams and balms. "You'd think girlfriend would've looked a little less like a hedgehog with all these potions."

"Don't you stuff any of those cosmetics in your pocket!"

We continue to poke around the bathroom for a few minutes. Then we comb through the bedroom, looking through the dresser drawers and under the bed. We don't come across anything particularly suspicious, so we take a quick look in the guest bedrooms and bathrooms. I'm not sure what we are looking for, but whatever it is, we don't seem to be finding it upstairs.

"Let's check downstairs."

We descend the stairs and start our search of the lower level in a messy office off the foyer. The wraparound desk is piled high with mail and papers and various promotional materials for Raynell's real estate business. I'm about to start rifling through all the papers when we hear a knock at the front door.

"Shhh," I say to Wavonne. "Just stay here."

There's another knock and, when we still don't respond, whoever is at the door decides to let him- or herself in. We hear the doorknob turn, and then the sound of feet walking across the foyer and up the stairs.

"Let's get out of here while whoever just barged in is upstairs," I whisper to Wavonne.

I put a finger to my lips and tiptoe out of the office. Wavonne follows, and we both step lightly toward the front door. We're about halfway across the foyer when Wavonne stubs her toe on a chair along the wall. It makes a screeching sound as it scoots an inch or so across the floor. We immediately hear footsteps scurrying in the hall upstairs. Instinctively, I grab Wavonne's hand and lead her toward a side door. I quickly open it, and we dash into the garage.

"In here." I open the door of Raynell's SUV.

Wavonne follows my lead, and we climb into the Escalade and squat down out of sight.

"Who you think it is?"

"I don't know." I lift my head just enough to peer out through the side window. "But they're coming in here, whoever they are," I say as I see the knob on the door into the garage turn.

"What!?!" Wavonne says. "Suppose whoever it is killed Raynell?" She reaches up and pushes the garage opener, and then presses the ignition button.

Thanks to Raynell's key fob still being in Wavonne's pocket, the Escalade comes to life, and I watch as Wavonne uses the rearview cam to back the vehicle out of the driveway.

"What are you doing!?"

"Whoever it is pokin' around this house may have offed Raynell. They ain't killing us, too."

When we reach the end of the driveway and pull out onto the street, Wavonne sits upright in the seat and puts the car in drive. Just before she steps on the gas, I peek out through the window and see a woman hastily stick her head through the side door leading into the garage. It was very quick, but from the end of the driveway there's no mistaking who it is.

What is Kimberly Butler doing nosing around Raynell's house the very day Raynell was found dead? I think to myself as Wavonne stomps on the accelerator, and we hightail it out of Raynell's neighborhood toward the main road.

CHAPTER 24

"Have you lost your mind?!" I yell at Wavonne as she turns Raynell's Escalade onto the main road.

"Were we supposed to stay there and end up worm food like Raynell?"

I inhale deeply and try to collect myself. "I don't know" is the best response I can come up with.

I turn and look out the back window to make sure no one is following us. "It's bad enough we let ourselves into Raynell's house, but now we've taken her car. A judge may label such things 'breaking and entering' and 'grand theft auto.' "

"We had a key to the house, and we're only *borrowin'* the car. What choice did we have, Halia? God knows who was in the house and what weapon they had on them," Wavonne shoots back. "Who do you think it was?"

"I *know* who it was. I saw her stick her head out the door to get a peek at us."

"Who?"

"Kimberly Butler."

"Really? What do you think she was up to?"

"I don't know, but it's very suspicious."

"Sure is. Ain't no reason she should be snoopin' around a dead woman's house." Wavonne adjusts herself into a more comfortable position in the driver's seat. "Damn, this thing handles like a dream . . . rides so smooth. We need to ditch that raggedy-ass van of yours and get one of these babies, Halia."

"The car we need to ditch, Wavonne, is this one."

"Aw, let me drive it a bit longer. I ain't never driven a Cad-de-lac before. I feel like one of those hookers on the *Real Housewives of Atlanta.* I wish it was winter so I could try out these heated seats." Wavonne looks at all the buttons on the control panel. "Oh hell, let's turn them on anyway . . . heat up my bootie."

As soon as Wavonne flicks the seat warmer switch the Escalade starts to sputter.

"What did you do?!"

"Nothin'. I just turned the tushie warmer on. What's all that noise?"

The sputter turns into more of a clanking sound. Then there's a loud bang before the SUV loses power and abruptly cuts off.

Wavonne looks at the dashboard. "You got to be freakin kiddin' me! It's outta gas!"

Wavonne pulls the coasting vehicle over to the shoulder.

I lean over and see that the gas gauge is, in fact, on empty.

"Get out!" I holler. "Let's get out now before someone offers to help us."

"Where do you think we are?" Wavonne asks. "Freakin' Disneyland or somethin'? What makes you think any one of these fools whizzin' by is gonna stop and help us . . . unless I get out and show some cleavage."

"Just get out before someone sees us, and we're charged with stealing Raynell's car."

Wavonne and I hurriedly exit the Escalade and begin walking along the side of the road. I take a quick look back, and I'm glad to be reminded that the windows are heavily tinted, so while we saw Kimberly, she didn't see us.

"Hurry up," I say to Wavonne. "Let's go to that shopping center up ahead. We'll blend in with the customers there and call Momma to come get us."

"What are the two of you up to?" Momma asks as we get in her car.

"Nothing, Momma. We met up with Nicole to go shopping, and she had an emergency and had to leave. She didn't have time to take us back to the van."

"You, who hates to shop and has barely ever left the restaurant during the brunch rush, randomly decided to go shopping on a Sunday afternoon?" Momma looks up through the windshield at the signs on the façade of the "well past its prime" shopping center. "And at which one of these *destination* stores did you and Nicole specifically get together to go shopping? The Walgreens? The YMCA? The Afghan kebab place?"

Damn, I really should have thought through this whole shopping-with-Nicole thing a bit more.

"We were just makin' a pit stop, Aunt Celia," Wavonne calls from the backseat. "We were on our way to Pentagon City."

Momma turns and looks at Wavonne and then at me. She holds her gaze on me just long enough to let me know she doesn't believe that story, either. "I'll ask again. What are you girls up to?"

"Honestly, Momma, it's just better if you don't know," I say, hoping she will let it go.

"Make a left." I direct Momma out of the parking lot. "The van's in Raynell's . . . I mean Nicole's neighborhood. It's about a mile up the road."

"You girls have me worried. Now, tell me what's going on."

I really don't want to get into Raynell's death with Momma, and I certainly don't want to tell her that Wavonne and I had to abandon an Escalade we just stole out of her garage, so I do the one thing that I know will refocus her attention and distract her from wanting to know why Wavonne and I need a ride back to my van.

"Was that my phone?" I ask and pull it from my purse. "Another text from Gregory," I lie.

"Gregory?!" Momma turns toward me with excited eyes. "What did he say?"

"He's just wondering when's a good time for us to get together."

"Did you say 'about twenty years ago?' " Wavonne calls from the backseat.

Momma laughs.

"No. I need to look at the schedule at Sweet

Tea and confirm I can sneak away tomorrow night."

"Well, for Christ's sake, get back to him soon. You said he's only in town for a little while."

"Yes, Momma," I say. "Make a left up there."

Mom turns into Raynell's neighborhood, and I direct her to the van.

"Thanks, Momma."

Wavonne and I quickly step out of the car before she has a chance to ask anymore questions about our misadventures.

"Why don't you drive?" I say to Wavonne. "I want to look through the mail I grabbed from Raynell's office."

We hop in the van, and on the way to Sweet Tea I start sorting through the stack of envelopes.

"What do you think you're gonna find in there?" Wavonne asks.

"Who knows? Maybe a phone bill that notes some incriminating conversations or something like that."

"Like late-night phone calls between Raynell and Gregory?" Wavonne takes her eyes off the road for a moment and looks at me. "Are you tryin' to find a motive for Raynell's murder or just tryin' to figure out if Raynell had a thing goin' with your new man?"

"Gregory is hardly my new man."

I continue to riffle through Raynell's papers—there's an electric bill, a Bed Bath & Beyond coupon, some credit card promotions, another Bed Bath & Beyond coupon, some political advertisement, another Bed Bath & Beyond coupon, some grocery store circulars . . . junk mail, junk mail, junk mail. There doesn't appear to be anything in the pile that's going to yield any clues until I come across a plain white envelope. It's not sealed, so I open it easily and pull out a handwritten note.

"Get this." I start reading aloud. "'Hey, good-lookin'. Anxiously awaiting our next encounter when I get to wrap my arms around you and kiss your sweet lips.' It's signed *M.*"

"Ooh . . . Raynell's husband's name don't begin with no *M,*" Wavonne says. "That bougie ho was gettin' some bump and grind on the side."

"Sure seems like it."

"It's not signed *G.* So at least you know it ain't Gregory."

"I guess."

As we pull into the parking lot in front of Sweet Tea, I take a closer look at the note and read it again. "Something about it is familiar to me," I say to Wavonne as I continue to study it.

"The note? What?"

"I'm not sure . . . it's like I've seen it before."

"Where?"

I look at the ceiling and think for a moment. "You know, I'm not sure." I fold up the paper and put it back in the envelope. "But I intend to find out."

RECIPE FROM HALIA'S KITCHEN

Halia's Double-Crust Chicken Potpie

Crust Ingredients

1½ sticks salted butter (¾ cup)
⅓ stick butter flavored vegetable shortening (⅓ cup)
½ cup water
3 cups all-purpose flour
½ teaspoon salt
2 teaspoons sugar
Pinch of baking powder

Filling Ingredients

¾ cup sliced carrots
1 cup diced red potatoes (skin on)
⅓ cup butter
1 garlic clove, minced
⅓ cup finely chopped scallions
½ teaspoon salt
½ teaspoons pepper
⅛ teaspoon ground Cayenne/red pepper

⅓ cup flour
1¾ cups chicken stock
⅔ cup whole milk
3 cups torn, cooked chicken
¾ cup frozen peas

- Preheat oven to 375 degrees Fahrenheit.

- Place butter, shortening, and water in freezer for 20 minutes prior to use.

- Cut cold butter and shortening into 1/4-inch slices.

- In food processor, pulse together flour, salt, sugar, and baking powder. Add butter and shortening. Pulse until mixture clumps into size of small peas. While continuing to pulse, slowly add water until dough begins to form a ball. Remove dough from food processor and form into two balls. Insert balls in separate plastic bags, seal, and refrigerate for 30 minutes.

- On floured work surface, roll out one ball of dough into a circle (1/8-inch thickness/11 inches in diameter). If dough sticks to surface, work a small amount of flour (a tablespoon at time) into dough and re-roll.

- Lightly flour top side of crust prior to delicately folding it in half to transfer to 9-inch pie pan. Gently unfold in pan, pressing against edges. Trim excess crust and flatten evenly on rim of pie plate. Hold a fork at a slight angle and lightly press the tines into pastry to create a "fork edge" around the rim of the crust.

- Poke holes in bottom of crust with fork, line with parchment paper, and fill with pie weights. Bake for 20 minutes. Remove parchment paper and weights and bake for another five minutes or until golden brown. Remove crust from oven and cool.

- Boil carrots and potatoes in large saucepan for 8 to 10 minutes, until crisp tender. Drain.

- In large sauce pan, heat butter over medium-high heat. Add garlic and scallions. Stir constantly until garlic and scallions are fragrant (about 1 minute). Add salt, pepper, and red pepper. Slowly add flour. Continue to stir until sauce bubbles. Add chicken stock and milk, continuing to stir until sauce thickens. Stir in chicken, peas, carrots, and potatoes. Pour mixture into cooked pie crust.

- Roll out remaining dough and place over filling. Trim edges and create a "fork edge" around rim of top crust. Cut four slits/vents into top crust. Bake for 35 minutes or until top crust is golden brown.

Eight Servings

CHAPTER 25

This morning's antics took up so much time that by the time Wavonne and I finally get to Sweet Tea the brunch rush is long over. We have only a few customers when we walk through the front door.

I see Jack Spruce, a local police officer and Sweet Tea regular, having a late lunch at a table in the corner. He has one of our summer specials on his plate—fresh corn on the cob. I buy it by the truckload from June through August. We steam it and let customers decide if they want one, some, or all of the following on it: salt, pepper, Old Bay seasoning, butter, lemon, shredded cheese, and/or spicy mayonnaise. It's hugely popular with the customers despite the price, which I set at a premium—not because the corn is expensive, but because shucking hundreds of corn cobs a day cost me a mint in labor expenses.

Wavonne and I smile and wave hello to Jack on our way to the kitchen.

"Aren't you gonna go chat with your boyfriend?" Wavonne jokes. She's convinced Jack has a crush on me, and, I'll admit, she's probably right. I'm sure he really does love the food here, and we offer free soda and coffee to all the local police officers if they feel like stopping in when they're making their rounds. But Jack comes in the most of any of them and has asked me out a time or two. I've always declined as politely as I can. I do like him as a person. He's very nice, but I guess we all know "very nice" is the kiss of death when you're talking about someone with a romantic attraction to you. He's about my age with a dark brown complexion, closely cropped black hair, and a bit more of a belly than a police officer should probably be carrying—if he ever had to chase down a reasonably fit criminal, I'm afraid I'd have to bet on the criminal. But his being overweight isn't a problem for me. It's not like I'm not carrying around my share of extra pounds as well. There's just something a little *too* nice . . . or simple . . . or easy . . . or *something* about him. Much as I'd like to be attracted to him, I'm just not. I hate to admit it, but I need a man with a bit more of an edge.

"I'm so sorry you had to come in and deal with the Sunday-morning crowd after I left you here alone last night," I say to Laura after stepping inside the kitchen.

"No worries. We were busy and short a server with Wavonne being out, but we muddled through."

"Thank you, Laura. Why don't you take the rest of the day off? I'll be here until closing."

Laura gladly agrees to leave Sweet Tea to me,

and Wavonne and I go to the break room to drop off our purses. When we return to the dining room I see Tacy at a booth along the wall rolling silverware into linen napkins for the dinner service. Tacy's official title is prep cook, but he's sort of a jack-of-all-trades and just helps out with whatever requires some attention.

"Why don't you help Tacy with the silverware while it's slow?" I say to Wavonne.

Wavonne groans.

"What's with the groaning? Good Lord. I'm not asking you to mine coal in West Virginia. Come on. I'll help, too."

"What up, Tace-Man," Wavonne says when we reach the table.

"Nothing much. Trying to get the silverware done, so I can finish up the prep work in the kitchen for tonight's special."

"What's the special this evenin'?"

"Shrimp and grits."

"Ooooo, I'm gonna have me some of that," Wavonne says.

"It looked like we're almost ready with the special when I was in the kitchen with Laura a few minutes ago," I say to Tacy.

"There's still some chopping to do . . . parsley, scallions—"

"Bacon?" Wavonne asks. "I didn't hear you say nothin' about no bacon."

"The bacon has been chopped, Ms. Hix."

"Good. That's what makes it so delish."

Wavonne is at least partially right. We fry up the bacon first and then use the bacon fat to sauté the shrimp with some cream, lemon juice, fresh corn, parsley, scallions, garlic, just a touch of dry sherry, and, of course, chopped bacon. We serve the shrimp and sauce over two homemade triangle-shaped grit cakes. All the ingredients play a role in making the special so popular, but, like Wavonne said, the bacon, which I get from a local pig farmer just south of Frederick, is key—it gives the dish a different kind of richness than we would get from butter or olive oil.

"Tacy, why don't you go on back to the kitchen and finish your prep work, and Wavonne and I will take care of the flatware."

"Sure thing, Ms. Watkins."

"Why'd you send him away? Now we're gonna have to do all this ourselves." Wavonne gestures toward the basket of forks and knives on the table.

"It's not that much. And he's got work to do in the kitchen if we're going to have the shrimp and grits ready to go by dinner."

Wavonne grabs two forks and a knife and starts to wrap them in a napkin before shifting the conversation back to Raynell. "So, what do you think Kimberly was doin' at Raynell's house?"

"I wish I knew, but she must have been up to no good. Assuming Raynell was, in fact, murdered, the only reason I can come up with is that Kimberly killed her, and must have come back to try and cover her tracks."

"Too late for that considerin' the popo have already been there and canvassed the place."

"True, but she may not have known that Raynell's body had already been discovered until she got there. She could have thought she still had some time to go back and alter the crime scene.

Suppose she killed Raynell in a heated moment and fled last night. Once she regained her senses this morning, she might have decided to come back and try to get rid of her fingerprints in the house . . . or maybe she was going to try and hide Raynell's body to buy some time. Who knows. Whatever the reason, the police should really know she was snooping around."

"You ain't thinkin' of tellin' them?"

"No. Of course not. We can't tell the police about Kimberly breaking into Raynell's house without telling them about *us* breaking into Raynell's house. Maybe I'll just give Kimberly a call, and see what I can find out. I'll be right back."

I get up from the table and make a run to the break room to retrieve my purse.

"What do you need your purse for?" Wavonne asks when I return to the table and sit back down.

"Kimberly gave me her contact info last night. It should be in here somewhere."

My purse tends to be packed with stuff, and I really have to dig to find Kimberly's business card. While I'm looking around in my bag past makeup and tissues and ChapStick and notepads, I come across the church bulletin from Rebirth. I thoughtlessly stuffed it in my bag after I attended the service there last weekend. Putting my hand on it sparks a memory.

"You know what?" I pull the bulletin from my purse. "I think I remember where I've seen the handwriting on the note we found in Raynell's office."

"Where?"

I unfold the bulletin and hold it up for

Wavonne to see. "'The Word,' by Pastor Michael Marshall," I say, as I once again search through my black hole of a purse to find the note I took from Raynell's desk.

"Look." I lay the letter on the table next to the church bulletin featuring Michael's handwritten weekly column. "The handwriting is an exact match."

Wavonne walks over, sits next to me, and looks at the two papers. "Ba-bam!" she says. "That ho-bag was doin' the nasty with Michael. A *minister!*"

"Not to mention her best friend's husband."

"Damn, that Raynell was gettin' busy all over PG County."

"No kidding. If she was having an affair with Michael, that opens up a whole series of motives for killing her. The affair could have gone south, and Michael wanted her dead. Alvetta may have found out that her supposed best friend was sleeping with her husband and lost it. Or Terrence could have found out and flipped out as well. The possibilities are endless."

"Yeah, but, unlike Kimberly, none of them were slinkin' around Raynell's house today."

"Good point."

Wavonne's words remind me of why I was digging through my bag in the first place, and I continue my search for Kimberly's business card. Just as I'm pulling it out of my purse, Jack appears at the table.

"Hey, Jack. How are you today?" I ask. "Working on a Sunday?"

"Hello, ladies," he says to Wavonne and me. "Yes. I'm just finishing up lunch. Then I've got to get back out there and make my rounds. I thought I'd say hi and let you know that the fried pork chop I had for lunch was delicious as always. And that fresh corn on the cob hit the spot."

"Glad to hear it. I only use really thin chops so they fry up nice and quick and don't get too greasy."

"Is that why they come out perfect every time?"

I smile. "I guess so."

"Well, it was good to see you. I hope you have a good day."

"It can't get no worse," Wavonne says.

"Oh?"

"Let's just say it's been a long day already."

"Why?"

"One of Halia's old classmates croaked, and we were the sad suckers who found her body."

"Oh wow. I'm sorry to hear that," Jack says. "Wait. Your classmate wasn't that Rollins woman I heard some chatter about over the radio this morning, was she? The woman who was severely inebriated, slipped in the bathroom, and hit her head?"

"I'm afraid so. Although I'm not entirely sure she slipped. She had a lot of enemies, so her being *pushed* rather than *slipping* is not out of the realm of possibilities."

"Hmm," Jack says. "I know Detective Hutchins was at the scene. I'm sure he'll check out all the angles."

"I hope so."

"Well, I've got to run. Again, I'm sorry about your classmate, and what you had to go through this morning."

Jack's about to be on his way when he notices Kimberly's business card sitting on the table. "Who's that?" he asks.

"Another one of my high school classmates, Kimberly Butler."

"No kidding?" Jack picks up the card and looks at it closely. "I had an encounter with her late last night . . . early this morning really . . . about two a.m."

"Really?"

"Yes. I came across her sound asleep in her car at the Herald Shopping Center."

"The Herald Shopping Center? That's over by Raynell's neighborhood."

"I tapped on the window to see if she was okay and tell her the shopping center does not allow overnight parking or sleeping in your car on the property. It took a few hard taps to rouse her. She didn't look good. She said she wasn't feeling well and needed to pull over for a bit."

"Was she drunk?" Wavonne asks.

"No. She didn't appear well, but I wouldn't let her drive without a sobriety check. She passed a breathalyzer test and insisted that she was okay to drive home."

"That's very interesting," I say.

"How so?"

"Let's just say high school cruelties are not easily forgotten, and Raynell committed many of them against Kimberly. Isn't it a little suspicious that Kimberly was found asleep and out of sorts so close to Raynell's house the same night she died?"

"Hmmm . . . maybe."

"You'll pass this information on to Detective Hutchins?" I ask.

"Sure, sure. I'll tell him, but from what I heard coming across the radio today, all indications lead to an accidental fall that resulted in Ms. Rollins's death." Jack sets Kimberly's card back down on the table. "I really do have to run. I hope your evening is better than your morning."

"Thanks Jack."

"This is startin' to get interestin'," Wavonne says as Jack steps away from the table.

"It is." I grab my phone and start typing in Kimberly's number. "It certainly is."

CHAPTER 26

I try to sweep thoughts of Raynell from my brain as I walk into an Italian restaurant in Camp Springs. It's the day after Wavonne and I found Raynell's body, and I'm having a hard time letting go of her death and my feelings about whether it was an accident or the result of foul play.

I'm anxious to talk with Kimberly and find out what on earth she was doing prowling around at Raynell's house, so I invited her to come to Sweet Tea for lunch today, but she had already made plans. She did, however, agree to swing by the restaurant tomorrow. Until then, I'm in sort of a holding pattern with the whole thing. Given the events of late, I'm not really in the mood to go on a date, but I agreed to meet Gregory tonight nonetheless—he's in town for only a week or two, and some conversation with an old friend will do me good.

The smell of wood-fired pizza pleasantly wafts in the air as the door closes behind me. When I eat in restaurants other than my own I tend to favor ethnic establishments that offer food that's completely different from what I cook and serve all day. Now, don't get me wrong—I make some of the best food around, but sometimes a girl gets a hankering for something other than soul food. My tastes run the gamut—Italian, Greek, Chinese, Thai, Middle Eastern . . . I enjoy virtually any cuisine but Indian (not a fan of curry . . . the taste or the smell) or Ethiopian (never had it, but it looks disgusting).

The host is about to greet me when I see Gregory at a table behind him. I smile at the host and point to Gregory in an "I'm with him" fashion and make my way into the dining room.

"Hello." Gregory stands and greets me.

"Hi. Sorry I'm late. Trying to drive anywhere around D.C. this time of day is an exercise in frustration. Traffic is terrible."

"No worries. I was just answering e-mails on my phone."

"E-mails?" I inquire with a grin, eyeing his phone, which is currently lying on the table displaying an animated dragon and some colorful medieval scenery.

"Ah . . . you caught me." Gregory laughs. "Once a video game nerd. Always a video game nerd."

"Were you into video games in high school? I don't remember that."

"Into them? That's pretty much all I did outside of schoolwork. I didn't have much of a social life in those days. I spent many a Saturday night in front of Nintendo playing *The Legend of Zelda* and *Super Mario Bros.*"

"Really? I knew nothing about video games in high school . . . and I guess I know nothing about them now."

"I'll admit I still enjoy them. They help me relax."

"Hmm . . . maybe I should take up video games then. I could use some de-stressing here and there myself." I take a seat at the table, and Gregory does the same. "So, I'm guessing you've heard about Raynell?" I ask.

"I did. Word gets around fast these days. Such horrible news."

"It really is. I feel so bad for her husband and her family."

"It's just awful for her to die so young. I didn't really get the details, though. From what I know, someone found her at home . . . she'd had a bad fall or something."

"That's about all I know as well." I refrain from telling him that Wavonne and I were actually the ones who found Raynell's dead body. He doesn't appear to know, and I just don't feel like getting into all those details.

I find myself thankful when the waiter arrives at our table, giving us an excuse to cease conversation about Raynell.

"Hello. My name is Sam, and I'll be your server this evening. Can I start you off with a beverage?"

"Up for sharing a bottle of Chianti?" Gregory asks.

"Sure," I reply. "And some water as well, please," I say to the waiter.

"So, there must be something more pleasant to talk about than Raynell," Gregory says.

"Yes. There must be." Part of me would like to linger on the subject a bit longer, so I can ask him about his secret high school relationship with her and why he chose her, of all people, to help with his local real estate ambitions. But I can't begin to imagine that Gregory had anything to do with her death, so I don't really see any reason to bring it up and make him uncomfortable. Besides, Raynell has been on my mind for almost two days straight, and, quite honestly, I need a break. "So, tell me more about South Beach Burgers."

"Some people have spouses . . . children . . . pets. I have a restaurant chain. It's pretty much my entire world at the moment. It doesn't leave time for much else."

"I hear that. I only have one restaurant, and it's my world as well. But I'd be lying if I said I didn't enjoy it."

Gregory laughs. "Me too. Every day is different. I love the variety and the challenges . . . of which there are *many*."

"That's for sure. I could do without the irrational customers who want a free meal because a server messed up their drink order or brought them the wrong salad dressing . . . or the ones with substance abuse issues who pitch a fit when we cut them off at the bar . . . or the parents who think I'm supposed to magically make squash appear in my kitchen, so my already overloaded staff can stop everything to make custom zucchini fries for little Malik or Jayla instead of French fries."

"I'm sure we could trade all sorts of horror stories—the customers who use the bathroom for sexual trysts, employees showing up to work high as a kite reeking of marijuana—"

"Kitchen staff purposely messing up orders because they don't like the server who put the order in, employees with fake social security numbers, water leaks, broken equipment . . . we could go on for days."

"I'm sure we could, but overall it's a rewarding career, and it beats sitting in an office in front of a computer all day."

I agree with Gregory, and we spend the next hour trading stories over ravioli Florentina and pesto primavera. I had planned to stick with only one glass of Chianti, but I don't protest when Gregory refills my glass. I'm not much of a drinker, so two glasses of wine is enough to give me a little buzz.

By the time Sam sets down a large serving of tiramisu in the middle of us the conversation turns more personal.

"How is it you're still single?" Gregory asks as we both dip our forks into the dessert.

"I might ask you the same question."

"There have been a few relationships here and there. I had more time for that sort of thing before I opened South Beach Burgers. Now I mostly work and spend what little free time I have with good friends."

"No woman in your life? I find that hard to believe, Gregory. The girls in Florida must be all over you. Every woman at the reunion was practically tripping over each other to talk to you—like you were the last Cabbage Patch Kid at Toys 'R' Us on Christmas Eve."

Gregory laughs. "That's not true."

"Please. You had to have noticed all the attention."

"Maybe." Gregory takes another bite of the tiramisu. "But, you have to understand, Halia. All this attention from women—it's new to me. I haven't looked like this for that long. I'm sure you remember me in high school. I was definitely *not* a looker."

"Nonsense. I always thought you were handsome," I cajole, even though "handsome" isn't exactly the right word. In high school, I found Gregory "cute" in more of an endearing sort of way. He was gangly with big ears, but he was nice, and smart, and quite witty when he wasn't being shy.

"That's sweet of you to say, Halia, but we both know the truth. It wasn't until I started making some real money that I began to grow into myself. I think my success in business boosted my confidence, and women can sense that sort of thing. The financial rewards of my work also allowed for a personal trainer and a nutritionist . . . and better clothes . . ." Gregory lifts his hands behind his ears and pushes them forward. "And surgery to get these babies pinned back where they belong."

I chuckle as Gregory lets his ears fall back into place. "So you're just a different kind of handsome now."

"You sound like a politician, Halia. *You,*" Gregory says, putting his fork down on the table and leaving the last bit of the dessert for me, "on the other hand, were lovely in high school and have barely changed at all."

"Now who's the politician?" I ask even though I guess I don't think I've changed that much since high school. I was a thick girl back then, and I'm still one now. And if there is one advantage of being a full-figured sister, it's that it adds some plumpness to your face and keeps away the wrinkles.

"No. I mean it." Gregory smiles and gives me a long stare, and I'm not sure if it's the wine, or fatigue after a long day, or just the fine-looking man across the table from me giving me the eye, but I'm starting to feel light-headed.

When the check arrives I grab my purse and begin to pull out my credit card, but Gregory insists on paying. I thank him for dinner, and he walks with me to my van.

"I'm really glad we had this chance to reconnect," Gregory says as I reach for my keys and hover next to the car door.

"Me too."

Gregory lingers in front of me and, suddenly, we are like two awkward teenagers trying to navigate a good-night kiss. It's actually amusing to see traces of a clumsy adolescent emanating from such a polished man. "Sorry. I'm really bad at this," he says, and we both laugh. "So what now? A kiss, a hug . . . a handshake?"

"I think I'd feel a little slighted if all I got was a handshake," I joke, and a lumbering moment or two passes before Gregory leans in and kisses me. It's not an especially long kiss, but it is a nice one.

I feel myself getting light-headed again as our lips part, and I place my hand on the car to steady myself.

"I hope I can call you again before I head back to Florida."

"Sure."

"Great. I'll be in touch then. Drive safe."

"I will. See you soon."

I step inside my van and watch Gregory walk to his car. As I start the ignition I hear my phone chirp. I pull it from my purse and see a text from Wavonne.

aunt celia wants know how your date's going . . . thinks it must be going well since you're out so late . . .

I text back.

it was okay . . . we had dinner . . . mostly talked about the restaurant business . . .
on my way home now . . .

The evening definitely went better than "okay," but if Wavonne tells Momma that Gregory and I had a great evening topped off with a good-night kiss, Momma will have me in David's Bridal first thing in the morning trying on wedding dresses and talking baby names. *No,* I think to myself. *It's much better to play it cool and not let Momma get too excited.* But as I pull out of the restaurant parking lot it occurs to me that maybe it's not Momma who I'm worried about getting too excited after a promising first date with a handsome, single, gainfully employed man. Maybe it's *me* I'm worried about getting too excited. I haven't been on a good date in a long time, but I have been on some, and, needless to say, they have not led to anything significant.

What's it matter, I think to myself. *If nothing else it was a nice evening with an old friend over some good Italian food. If it doesn't lead to anything more, that's fine.* Yep, that's what I told myself . . . now if I could just believe it, too.

CHAPTER 27

I have got to stop letting it bother me, I think to myself as I look up from some invoices I'm reviewing at the bar and see yet another customer eating my food while looking at his phone. He's by himself, shoveling my chicken croquettes in his mouth with a fork via one hand and using his other hand to scroll and intermittently type. Occasionally he grins or even chuckles as if something on the screen is amusing him.

I see this behavior all the time, and I have to fight the urge to walk over and ask him why he doesn't just down a protein shake or stop into Wendy's for some rubber chicken on a bun if he's not going to pay any attention to what he's eating anyway. Yes, I know, I make money whether customers consciously eat my food or not, but my team and I put so much thought and work into every dish that comes out of the Sweet Tea kitchen that it just pains me to see people eating our food as if it were no better than a bowl of oatmeal.

I learned many of the recipes we use at Sweet Tea through years of helping my grandmother prepare Sunday dinners, and some of them were tweaked and refined over generations. Grandmommy developed the recipe for those chicken croquettes my customer is currently shoving in his mouth with no appreciation for the perfectly crisp coating that Grandmommy initially made with bread crumbs, but later crafted with corn flake crumbs to improve the taste and texture. I further updated the recipe with panko breadcrumbs (I *LOVE* panko breadcrumbs) to give them the ultimate crispness. I've tried using a full egg yolk and egg white wash as well as an egg white wash alone to see which one holds the coating better. The chicken stock we use in the recipe is made in house here at Sweet Tea. We chop fresh parsley and add a touch of lemon juice from freshly squeezed lemons to the chicken mix before we skillfully shape them into a traditional cone shape, affording not only a taste that's out of this world but visual appeal as well. Before bringing them to the table we top them with a piping-hot stewed potato gravy, fresh black pepper, and a sprinkle of paprika. All of this!—And, for the attention this young man is paying to them, I might as well have thrown a few Chicken McNuggets on a plate and slapped them down in front of him.

Truth be told, that's not the only one reason smartphones get under my skin. Of course, they've become a necessity of everyday life, and even I admit I can't imagine life without mine. But, let me tell you, they have been one of the worst things to hit the restaurant industry in decades. It has never been my desire to run a "turn and burn" establishment—I sincerely want my customers to have a relaxed outing where they enjoy my food and each other's company without feeling rushed, but smartphones have redefined what constitutes a "relaxed" evening. In the days before iPhones and Androids we would seat customers, they would order shortly after, enjoy some conversation and their courses . . . and then skedaddle, allowing us to seat new customers.

Now, after customers are seated, they might spend several minutes on their phone before even opening the menu, then take photos of themselves and their companions, and of course take photos of their food, which they then take the time to post to Facebook and Instagram. And when they're finished eating, these days, patrons tend to linger for inappropriate amounts of time just surfing on their phones, taking up valuable restaurant real estate, and costing me money. Over the years, we've learned to manage these customers and, if they linger for an extra lengthy spell following payment of their check, we'll generally approach the table and ask if there is anything else we can get for them. Fortunately, they typically take the polite hint and head on their way.

I remind myself once again to not let the man on his phone bother me. I'm about to return my attention to the invoices when I see Kimberly speaking with Saundra at the hostess stand. When we chatted on Sunday I asked if she would consider swinging by Sweet Tea to discuss commissioning some artwork for the restaurant. I only occasionally change up the artwork I have displayed in Sweet Tea as I'd never part with the family picnic mural I had painted along one wall when we first opened, and I've gotten attached to the old photos of church ladies preparing Sunday buffets we have hanging throughout the space. But I do switch out a piece or two here and there, and interest in her art was as good an excuse as any to meet with Kimberly and pump her for information.

I hop off the stool and walk over to greet her. "Kimberly. So good to see you again."

"Yes. You too. I'm glad to have a chance to finally check out your restaurant. I don't come back to the area very often, so I've never had the opportunity before."

I wait to see if she's going to mention anything about Raynell's death. When she doesn't, I decide not to broach the subject just yet. "Well, I hope Sweet Tea doesn't pale in comparison to those fabulous New York restaurants you must be used to."

Kimberly smiles. "I'm sure it won't. My parents are still close by . . . in the same house I grew up in, in Clinton. They dine here often and love it. I'm staying with them while I'm in town. If I go back there without some of your fried chicken, I'll have hell to pay."

"We can't let that happen. I'll wrap some for you to take," I offer. "So, why don't I show you around a bit and let you know what I'm thinking in terms of artwork for the restaurant, and then we'll have lunch?"

"Sure."

"I looked at your Web site—your paintings are

stunning. It's no wonder you've made such a name for yourself. I see you have a showing at a gallery in Greenwich Village next month." We step toward the back of the restaurant. "Over here"—I point to the wall behind the bar—"is my collection of antique photos and paintings. As you can see they're mostly of women preparing meals, family gatherings, church picnics . . ." I lead her farther toward the back of the restaurant. "And there's more along the back wall. That's my grandmother." I point to a large black-and-white photo of Grandmommy pouring waffle batter onto an iron. I had it enlarged when I opened the restaurant and made it the focal point of the rear wall. "Mrs. Mahalia Hix. I was named after her. People think Mahalia's Sweet Tea is named for me, but it's really in honor of her—such a special lady. I adore her smile in the picture. She loved preparing Sunday dinners, and her joy really shows in the photo."

"It really is charming," Kimberly says.

"I was wondering if you might be willing to create a painting from it." I had planned to ask her to create something original that we could add to the collection on the wall, but as I was looking at the painting of Grandmommy, the idea of a painting based on my favorite photograph of her came to mind. And it's something I might actually be interested in purchasing from Kimberly—maybe I didn't bring her here under false pretenses after all.

"Really? Hmm," Kimberly says. "That's not something I really do. I've never tried to create a painting from a photo before."

I'm about to respond that I understand, but she speaks again before I'm able to.

"But for you, a former classmate, and one of the nice ones, I'd give it a shot."

"That would be great. I can get you a copy of the photo to take back to New York. However long you need is fine."

"Yes, please send me a copy, but I'll just snap a photo of it with my phone for now," Kimberly says. "I have a few other projects I need to wrap up, but I could probably complete it in a few weeks."

"That would be great. So, what are you thinking in terms of price?"

Kimberly thinks for a moment, which makes me nervous. I saw on her Web site that some of her paintings have gone for tens of thousands of dollars.

"For you, I'll do it for a thousand dollars . . . oh, and that takeout fried chicken you promised for my parents."

"I think you've got yourself a deal." This is way more than I'd generally pay for artwork, but I'm genuinely excited about the idea of a custom painting of Grandmommy. "Why don't you have a seat?" I gesture toward the table next to us. "I'll get you a glass of the lemon blueberry iced tea we're serving today, and you can look over the menu and decide what you'd like for lunch. We have some chicken croquettes on special today."

A few minutes later I return with two glasses, a pitcher of iced tea dotted with blueberries and lemon slices, and a menu.

I offer the menu to Kimberly and fill the glasses.

"You know, I don't think I need to look at the menu. I haven't had chicken croquettes since I was a girl. I'll go with those."

"Good choice." I wave for Wavonne to come over to the table, and we watch her leisurely approach. "Sorry. Wavonne has three speeds: slow, slow, and slow. Unless there's only one pair of discount heels left on the shelf at DSW—then all of a sudden, she's Flo-Jo."

Kimberly laughs. "Aren't we all Flo-Jo when a discount pair of heels is at stake?"

"What are you two ol' hens cluckin' about?" Wavonne asks.

"Nothing. Just discussing shoes."

"Shoes? My favorite topic."

"It's good to see you again, Wavonne," Kimberly says.

"Yeah. You too," Wavonne replies, and turns toward me. "She tell you why Jack found her all loopy doopy in a parking lot by Raynell's house Saturday night?"

"Wavonne!" I say.

"Yeah. I figured you hadn't gotten to that point yet." Wavonne plops herself down next to Kimberly. "I personally wouldn't blame you if you did the bitch in. She had it comin'. Sista mess with *my* tresses and leave *me* bald, I'd take her down, too."

"What is she talking about?" Kimberly asks me.

"What she's talking about in her complete lack-of-tact way"—I glare at Wavonne before turning my attention back to Kimberly—"is that a local police officer happened to stop in for lunch yesterday when I had your business card out on the table. He recognized your photo and said he had an incident with you at the Herald Shopping Center in Fort Washington. He said he found you in your car in a peculiar state very late Saturday night . . . Sunday morning, really. I guess Wavonne and I just thought it was . . . well . . ." I'm trying to find a less offensive word than "suspicious" to use here. "*Curious* that you were found sleeping in your car so close to Raynell's house the night she died."

Kimberly's mouth drops. "Are you guys accusing me of something?" she asks. "Did you really ask me here to discuss a painting or to talk about Raynell's death?"

"Maybe a little of both, Kimberly." I reach for the pitcher on the table. "More tea?" I ask—a little gesture of goodwill before I begin pummeling her with questions.

CHAPTER 28

Kimberly quickly goes on the defense. "For your information, the Herald Shopping Center is on the way from the hotel to my parents' house. I didn't think I had drunk *that* much at the reunion, but once I got on Indian Head Highway, I really started to feel the liquor from earlier in the evening affect me. I didn't feel drunk as much as I just got a really bad . . . *terrible* headache. I didn't think I should be driving, so I pulled off the road to let it pass."

"I'm sorry, Kimberly. I didn't mean to upset you."

"Well, I hope I've explained myself. I only stopped at the shopping center because I was in no condition to drive. I've never gotten a headache like that from alcohol before—it was really intense." She starts to get up from the table. "I think I will pass on lunch. I don't have much of an appetite anymore."

"So, you explained why you were asleep in your car late Saturday night," Wavonne says just before Kimberly walks off. "Care to explain what you were doin' traipsin' around Raynell's house Sunday afternoon?"

Kimberly's eyes dart from Wavonne to me and then back to Wavonne.

"Yeah. We know *all* the good stuff," Wavonne says.

"How do you know that? That I was at Raynell's?"

"Does it really matter?" I ask before Wavonne has a chance to speak. "And come to think of it, when you came in, you said you were staying at your parents' house in Clinton. The reunion was in Greenbelt, Kimberly. Fort Washington is in no way on the way from Greenbelt to Clinton."

Kimberly gives me a long stare. "Okay. So I was at Raynell's yesterday . . . and, fine, Saturday night, too. But I swear I have no idea how Raynell died. I had nothing to do with whatever caused her death. All I wanted was a little payback."

"What do you mean?"

"You know what a wicked demon she was to me in high school. I was bald for most of junior year thanks to her. I still have post-traumatic stress from the *Nair incident*—I've spent thousands on therapy to get over my days of being bullied, and that hussy was so callous she didn't even remember what she did to me when we reconnected at the reunion. And on top of it, she wanted a favor from me. A *favor?* Are you freakin' kidding me?!" Kimberly takes a moment to collect herself and sits back down at the table. "I'm not sure I'd throw her a life raft if she was drowning, and she had the nerve to ask me to appraise a painting for her—so ridiculous! But at least her request gave me an excuse to show up at her house."

"Which you did? On Saturday night?"

Kimberly nods. "I wasn't crazy drunk by the time I left the reunion, but I had had a few drinks, or at least enough to get up enough gumption to even the score with Raynell. With a nice buzz from the liquor, I left the hotel, stopped by an all-night drugstore, and picked up a bottle of Nair. I had planned to go to Raynell's under the pretense of evaluating her painting, sneak into her bathroom, and put the hair removal cream in her shampoo bottle just like she had done to me."

"Ooh," Wavonne says. "I should be writin' this down, so I can sell it to BET."

"You were going to show up at Raynell's in the middle of the night to look at a painting? That wouldn't seem a little odd?"

"Yes, it would seem a little . . . *very* odd for me to come to her house at midnight to appraise some artwork, but I was tipsy and just seeing that awful woman got me going. I wasn't thinking straight. I figured I could tell her I had a change of plans and was leaving town early the next day. If she wanted me to look at the portrait, it would have to be then. I was afraid I'd lose my nerve if I waited any longer. When I got there, she didn't answer the door, but it was unlocked, so I snuck in and found her passed out on her bed. I simply tiptoed past her to the master bath, switched out the contents of her shampoo bottle, and left. I swear!

"I thought I was starting to sober up by the time I got to Raynell's, but on the way back to my parents' house, the drinking really caught up with me. My head hurt, and I felt more woozy and light-headed than liquor has ever made me feel before. But, somehow, I had the sense to get off the road and sleep off the booze before going back to my parents'. I still had a terrible headache when the police officer found me, but I blew a clean breathalyzer, so he let me drive home. Honestly, I still have a lingering headache, and it's been two days. I don't know what they put in the drinks at the reunion, but it was strong."

"So, why did you go back on Sunday?"

"Because, once my head cleared, I felt silly and juvenile about the whole thing, and, honestly, I was a little afraid of what Raynell would do when she likely figured out it was me who switched out her shampoo. It's been more than two decades since high school, but I got the sense that Raynell was as nasty as ever, and who knows what she would have done when she connected me to her bald head. I didn't even know she was dead when I went back. I was just going to knock on the door, feign interest in her painting, and make an excuse to use her master bath. I had planned to just drop the shampoo bottle in my purse and be on my way before she had a chance to use it. Most sisters only wash our hair once or twice a week, so I figure there was a good chance she hadn't used it."

"So, when you went back to her house on Sunday, you didn't know she was dead?"

"No. I heard about it yesterday evening when the news starting showing up on Facebook. Nothing seemed out of order when I was there until I heard someone downstairs . . ." Kimberly pauses for a moment. "Wait. It was you . . . it was the two of you who were downstairs when I was there . . . and the two of you who drove off in Raynell's Escalade."

"Don't be silly." I try to feign innocence, but I can feel the guilt showing in my face, and the quick looks Wavonne and I exchange erase any doubt that we were the culprits.

"How else would you have known I was there?"

"Fine," I admit. "I'm not convinced Raynell's death was an accident, and we were there Sunday looking for clues as to who might have killed her."

"Do you really think she was killed? So far everything I've heard indicates she fell."

"I don't know what to think. Believe me, you are not the only one who wanted revenge on Raynell. The woman racked up enemies faster than frequent-flier miles."

"Well, I assure you I had nothing to do with her death." Kimberly looks up and off to the right as if something just occurred to her. "But you know who might?"

"Who?"

"Gregory. Gregory Simms. Saturday night, just after I got back in my car, after switching out Raynell's shampoo with Nair, I saw a car pull up in front of her house."

"Gregory?" I'm hoping I misheard. Not only do I hate the idea of him possibly having something to do with Raynell's death, but I don't want to stomach him having a late-night rendezvous with her after he spent the evening flirting with me.

"Yep. It was dark, but I recognized him. Brother is looking fine these days."

"You got that right," Wavonne says.

Kimberly's demeanor has softened now that she's explained her actions to us. Her tone is friendlier and much less defensive. "Before I drove off, I saw him get out of the car and walk toward the front door. I figure if he and Raynell had a thing going, it was none of my business. But maybe his intentions were more sinister than an affair with a married woman. Not sure what his motive to kill her would have been, though."

"I guess he had as much motive as you did," I say. "Raynell did him dirty in high school just like you. And, oddly, he recently connected with her to help him find potential Maryland locations for his restaurant, which doesn't really make much sense. There must be a few thousand real estate agents he could have sought help from. Why did he decide to partner with the one who used and abused him so many years ago?"

"What did she do to him?" Kimberly asks.

"It's a long story," I say as Darius walks by with a tray holding two plates of our special for the day on his way to another table. I note Kimberly's eyes light up as she sees the chicken croquettes and takes in the faint scent they leave behind. "Has your appetite returned? Would you like to hear the Raynell/ Gregory story over some lunch?"

Kimberly smiles. "Now that you mention it."

"And shouldn't you get back to work?" I ask Wavonne. "Go put in a croquette order for Kimberly, would you?"

"All right, all right," Wavonne says, and gets up from the table.

Kimberly and I watch her leisurely meander toward one of the POS stations to put the order in, and I can tell we are both thinking the same thing: *slow, slow, and slow.*

CHAPTER 29

So, here I am back at Rebirth Christian Church, but, as it's a weekday, the parking lots are mostly empty. After nabbing a space close to the entrance and walking into the massive building, I follow the instructions Alvetta gave me for finding her office. We spoke on the phone earlier, and I told her I had an errand to run in the neighborhood and wanted to check in with her and see how she's doing following the loss of Raynell.

I make a left down a wide hall to an elevator, which promptly deposits me on the third floor. I stride past a large office with "Pastor Michael Marshall" displayed on the open door. I take a quick peek inside and see a spacious executive suite fit for the CEO of a *Fortune* 500 company . . . and given the amount of revenue this place brings in, I guess it shouldn't be surprising.

When I reach Alvetta's office I find her on the phone. She smiles and waves me in. While it's not quite as grandiose as Michael's space, I'd still be surprised if Michelle Obama had a more lavish office in the White House. I step onto the thick cream-colored carpet and sit down in a beige leather chair across from Alvetta. She's seated behind an imposing wraparound wooden desk that sits in front of a bank of floor-to-ceiling windows that overlook the church grounds and some of the few remaining acres of farmland in Prince George's County.

"Hello, Halia," she says to me after hanging up the phone. "The work of a minister's wife is never done. I'm trying to make final arrangements for Raynell's service, and my phone won't stop ringing. Three couples want the chapel for their weddings the first week in October, and they are all trying to sidestep the process and get me to work it out for them."

"Chapel?"

"Yes, it's on the other side of the building. It's a smaller space than the main sanctuary . . . only holds five hundred people. Parishioners often prefer to have their ceremonies in a more intimate setting. And some like that the chapel has the feel of a traditional church with wooden pews and stained glass windows."

"I love that a space that seats five hundred people is considered an *intimate* setting."

Alvetta laughs. "It's all relative I guess. Welcome to the megachurch world. Very little is done on a small scale here."

"Hey . . . whatever works." I take a slow look at her face. "So, are you okay? You and Raynell were so close. How are you coping?"

"How I always cope—by staying busy. Raynell

and I talked almost every day. I would fill her in on church gossip, and she would tell me I looked tired and needed a new moisturizer, or that my hair was going limp, and she'd heard about a new balm that would help."

I smile. "God bless her. She was no stranger to offering criticism."

"That was just her way. Somehow it made her feel better about herself. I never took it to heart." I notice Alvetta's eyes start to well up. "She was really the sister I never had. Yes, she was bossy and sometimes . . . well, much of the time she built herself up by tearing other people down, but she always looked out for me."

She pauses for a moment to keep the lonely tear lingering just outside her right eye from erupting into a full-fledged sob and grabs a tissue to delicately wipe it away. "She even introduced me to my husband."

Your husband, whom she was having an affair with, I think to myself.

Her affection for Raynell and angst over her death does *seem* sincere. If she knows about Raynell's affair with Michael or had anything to do with her untimely demise, she's hiding it well.

"Sorry." She lifts her shoulders and raises her head, determined to fight off further tears. "I'm still grieving I guess, but I don't like to get emotional in front of other people."

"There's no shame in crying over a loved one who's passed."

"I know, but as First Lady of this church, I've gotten used to not letting my emotions take over. I've been to more funerals than you can count, and it's my job to be strong and keep it together so I can comfort others. I guess it's just habit." She gives her eyes one more dab with the tissue. "And speaking of funerals, I've got a meeting with the choir director to go over the music for Raynell's service in a few minutes, so I do need to run shortly, but it really was nice of you to drop by, Halia."

"Sure. I'll let you get back to work, but before I go, do you mind if I ask you a few questions?"

"Not at all."

"When we talked the other day you said Gregory and Raynell had a secret romance in high school and had recently reconnected. Did you ever find out who reached out to whom to start working together? Do you know if he initially contacted Raynell, or if she reached out to him about her real estate services?"

"I asked Christy about it, and she said Gregory originally called Raynell. He claimed he had heard she was the best and wanted her help in scouting restaurant locations and a home in the area."

"A home? He was looking to move here as well?"

"I guess . . . or at least spend enough time here to warrant owning a house."

"Interesting."

"What do you mean?"

"I just can't get past the idea of Gregory reaching out for help from someone who wronged him so badly. Raynell probably stood to make a lot of money off any sales she facilitated for him. Why would he want to reward someone who did nothing but use him—even if it was a long time ago?"

"You're not back to that whole murder thing?

The police met with Terrence yesterday and assured him it was an accident. Besides, you don't really think a successful restaurant entrepreneur like Gregory would risk everything and kill someone over some petty high school shenanigans, do you?"

"I normally wouldn't, but I have it on good authority that Gregory was at Raynell's house the night she died."

"How do you know that?"

"I really can't say, but someone saw him approach her house late Saturday night."

Alvetta hesitates for a moment. "Well . . ." She takes a breath and looks down at her desk. "That's really not surprising. Terrence was out of town, and Raynell and Gregory . . . well . . ."

"They had a thing going?"

"I shouldn't be sharing this. Wow . . . I feel like I'm violating Raynell's confidence, but, yes, Gregory and Raynell shared more than just a business relationship."

"Wow" just falls from my lips as I try to make sense of him flirting with me at the reunion and my date with him on Monday night. *Why is he showing a romantic interest in me if he had a relationship with Raynell?*

"Yes. I loved Raynell, but, like all of us, she was imperfect and didn't always make the best choices. Apparently they started working together and . . . you know . . . one thing led to another."

"Did Terrence know?"

"No. At least I don't think so. Raynell's work involved all sorts of odd hours, so I doubt Terrence would have gotten suspicious if she wasn't home some evenings. And she and Gregory had the perfect excuse to spend time together. I think she worked it out so Christy handled many of the business outings with Gregory—that way Raynell's time with him could be more . . . shall we say *social*."

"Really?"

"Yes. It was mostly Christy who showed Gregory commercial properties and multimillion-dollar homes. She scheduled the appointments and did the research . . . and answered his calls."

"Multimillion-dollar homes? Gregory's restaurant chain must really be doing well."

"It would appear that it is. And what you said earlier about Raynell standing to make a lot of money is very true. Commissions on commercial leasing are steep, and whoever sells him a home now will probably net tens of thousands of dollars from that commission alone, and—"

Alvetta's interrupted by a buzzing sound. She looks at the screen on the phone. "That's the choir director. I really do need to meet with her."

"Sure, sure."

"Thanks again for stopping by."

"Of course. I hope you and Michael will come by the restaurant some time soon."

I get up from the chair and try to give Alvetta a hug, but the desk is too wide. Instead, I take her hand in mine. "Please call me if I can do anything for you. I'm sure this a rough time."

I exit Alvetta's office with my mind aflutter. She has given me so much to think about. Despite her apparent grief, I still wonder if she knows about Raynell's affair with Michael. Your supposed best friend sleeping with your husband is certainly motive for murder. I also wonder if Terrence knew about Raynell's affairs with Michael . . . and/or Gregory. (Sister *got around.* That's for sure.) Another motive for murder. Then I consider whether or not an old high school wound is enough motive for Gregory—or Kimberly—to kill Raynell. And, as I make my way to my van, I can't help but think about what Alvetta said . . . how, with Raynell out of the picture, whoever helps Gregory close some real estate deals stands to make out like a bandit. If Christy has been Gregory's go-to girl all along, wouldn't she be his logical choice to assist him now that Raynell is dead? Is being positioned as the next in line to a hefty real estate commission enough reason for Christy to kill Raynell?

Alvetta, Terrence, Gregory, Kimberly, Christy—they all had reasons to do away with Raynell. I guess it's now up to me to figure out if any of them actually acted upon those reasons.

CHAPTER 30

When the elevator opens on the main level of the church I quickly scurry down the hall toward the exit. I'm in a rush to get back to Sweet Tea so, as I hasten toward the door, I almost miss her. But, as I pass the reception counter, my eyes take note of a familiar petite figure talking to the security guard. She's holding a large cardboard box with both hands.

"Christy?"

"Halia. What are you doing here?" Christy asks and steps toward me.

"I just came to check on Alvetta. What brings you this way?"

"Alvetta asked me to pick up some photo albums from Raynell's house and bring them over. She's working on a tribute for Raynell's service. I e-mailed her a bunch of electronic ones, but she wanted some of the older prints as well."

"Why didn't she ask Terrence?"

"Because Terrence probably wouldn't have known where to find them."

"But you did?"

"Please. I know where everything is in that house. When you work . . . *worked* for Raynell, you have a very loosely defined job description. I did much more than just assist her with her real estate business. When you pick up and put away someone's dry cleaning, organize her closets, and oversee the installation of her new hardwood floors, you learn where things are."

"I guess so. Sounds like Raynell kept you very busy. Alvetta was just telling me that you were the one who did most of the work to help Gregory scout locations for his restaurant and find a home in the area."

"I guess that's true, but he's a nice person . . . easy to work with."

"So will you continue to work with him now that Raynell has passed?" I'm hoping it doesn't sound too obvious that I'm fishing for information. "Sounds like you deserved whatever commissions were to come from the deal anyway."

"Maybe so, but unfortunately I'm not a licensed agent, so I'm not eligible for commissions. Technically, I shouldn't have even been showing Gregory properties without a license, but Raynell wasn't exactly one for always following rules."

Well, that blows my theory that Christy offed Raynell to get her hands on some real estate commissions. "I guess Gregory will have to find a new agent." I almost add "and another mistress," but keep those words to myself as I have no idea if Christy is aware of Raynell's proclivity for extramarital affairs. No wonder she needed Christy to do all of her work. She was too busy swinging from the chandeliers with Gregory and her best friend's husband, and God knows who else, to sell real estate.

"Terrence has asked me to stay on for a few weeks to help field Raynell's phone calls and settle some affairs, so I'm a little swamped, but I'll give Gregory a call this week and set him up with another agent in Raynell's office."

"That's nice that you're helping Terrence. I'm sure it's a difficult time for him . . . and for you. How are you doing?"

"I'm okay. Raynell was a hard ass and not the most respectful person in the world, but . . . I don't know . . . I sort of miss her. She was like one of those yippy little dogs that growls and tries to nip everyone, but you sort of get used to having them around . . . and they leave a void when they're no longer there."

"So you miss her like you might miss a mean Chihuahua? I hope you're not writing the eulogy," I say with a smile.

Christy laughs. "No. I'm not sure who is . . . probably Alvetta or Terrence."

"How is Terrence?"

"He's hanging in there. I haven't seen him in a few days."

"He wasn't at the house when you went to pick up the albums?"

"No. I think he had some errands to run."

I want to ask her how she got in the house if Terrence wasn't there, but I think I've asked enough nosy questions for the time being. And, besides, it's probably safe to assume she has a key to the

Rollinses' house given all the personal work she did for Raynell.

"Well, give him my best next time you see him."

"Sure. I'll probably be helping him out for another week or two, and then I need to start searching for a new job."

"I'm sure you won't have any trouble on that front. What's it they say about New York? 'If you can make it there you can make it anywhere.' I think the same thing goes for working with Raynell. If you can work for her, you can work for anyone."

"I hope you're right," Christy says. "I guess I had better get these albums to Alvetta."

"Okay. It was nice to run into you. Best of luck on your job search."

Christy and I part company, and, on my way to the parking lot, I visualize my suspect list in my head. I'm about to draw a line through Christy's name—if she's not eligible to receive any real estate commissions, that strips her of a key motive for killing Raynell. In fact, if she didn't stand to make any financial gain from Raynell's death, it's unlikely she'd kill the person who signs her paychecks and makes it possible for her to earn a living. I picture a line going through her name, but I'm not quite ready to cross her off the list entirely. Maybe she didn't get rich off Raynell's demise and is facing unemployment as a result of her death. But, much like everyone else Raynell came into contact with, she treated Christy pretty badly. From what I saw she mostly just barked orders at her all day. And that's how Raynell treated her in public—who knows how bad it was in private. Maybe Christy had enough, was going to quit anyway, but, before she did, figured she'd kill Raynell for no other reason than Raynell being an insufferable witch.

RECIPE FROM HALIA'S KITCHEN

Halia's All-Natural Margaritas

Ingredients

¾ cup tequila
¼ cup triple sec
⅓ cup honey
1 large orange, peeled and de-seeded
1 lime, peeled and de-seeded
1 lemon, peeled and de-seeded
6 cups ice

Combine all ingredients in blender. Blend on high until smooth. Salt rims of glasses if desired.

Four Servings

Note: If blender is not large enough to add 6 cups of ice at once, start with 4 cups, blend until smooth, then add remaining cups, and blend again.

CHAPTER 31

"Why don't you run home and change clothes before you meet him?" Wavonne asks. It's three o'clock. The last lunch customers have just left, and we're starting our midday closure. Gregory called this morning and asked if I'd give him my opinion on a property he's looking at, and I'm about to leave to meet him. "Khakis and a knit shirt ain't exactly date clothes."

"Forgive me, Wavonne, but I can't very well run a restaurant in stilettos and a miniskirt. Besides, there's no point. I told you. I'm not sure what Gregory is up to—why he was flirting with me at the reunion and kissed me the other night when he'd been having an affair with Raynell up until the night she died. Maybe he's just playing me for some free advice about the local restaurant scene. I don't think he's really interested in me."

"Halia, you say that like a brotha can't be interested in two women at the same time. That ain't true. If Raynell was doin' the freaky deeky with him and Michael . . . and, God forbid, maybe her actual *husband,* too, then surely Gregory could be interested in you even if he had somethin' brewin' with Raynell. And let me assure you, you got the leg up over Raynell in this situation—considerin' you still have a pulse."

"Whatever. I'm not really interested in getting involved with someone who was fooling around with a married woman anyway."

"Oh blah blah whatevah. Who says you have to get *involved* with him anyway. For once in your life just have some fun, Halia. Ride the wave."

"Did you *just* meet me? I'm not exactly a 'ride the wave' type of person. The only reason I'm meeting him at all is to ask him some questions and nose around a bit . . . see if he might have had a hand in Raynell ending up in a pool of blood on her bathroom floor." I pull my keys from my purse and sling it over my shoulder. "I've got to get going. I should be back before we reopen at five."

"Fine. Go lookin' like that. Oh well . . . who knows . . . maybe Gregory's into the 'high school gym teacher' look. Stranger stuff has happened."

I ignore Wavonne's final comments before heading for the door. Evening rush hour is already starting, so traffic is heavy as I drive over to the Boulevard at the Capital Centre, an expansive shopping complex in Largo. It was built on the site that once housed the Capital Centre, an arena that, before it was torn down about fifteen years ago, was home to the Washington Bullets (now the Wizards), the Washington Capitols, and hosted all the big name concerts that came to the D.C. metro area back in the day. I think half of my high school went to see Lionel Richie there back in the eighties.

The Boulevard started off with a bang when it opened in 2003 and brought some much needed retail outlets and restaurants to the area. Unfortunately, it all quickly went downhill thanks to several of its major tenants going out of business (anyone remember Circuit City, Linens 'n Things, Borders?), rowdy teens causing mayhem . . . and . . . well . . . three men being gunned down at the Uno Chicago Grill back in 2008 didn't exactly help an already damaged image.

Gregory mentioned via text that he wanted my opinion on a location he was scouting by the Magic Johnson theater, so I find a space on the east end of the parking lot and head toward a vacant storefront a few doors down from the theater.

"Hey there," Gregory says when I find him standing outside the property. When he leans in and gives me a hug I feel the firm contours of his chest. Suddenly, I wish I had taken Wavonne's advice and spruced myself up a bit before meeting him.

"Hi." *Do I really look like a high school gym teacher?* "Sorry, I'm a mess. It was a busy day. But I guess I don't need to tell you about life running a restaurant. How many do you run now? Seven?"

"Twelve. Six in Florida, three in Georgia, one in South Carolina, and two in North Carolina. And hopefully my first location in Maryland very soon." The proud smile on his face and jovial demeanor seem out of place for a man who just lost his mistress. Come to think of it, he didn't seem terribly bothered or distracted by Raynell's death when we had our date earlier in the week, either.

"Impressive. I can barely keep up with one restaurant."

"From what I hear, you are keeping up just fine." Gregory opens the door to the vacant space and gestures for me to follow him.

I look around me at the concrete floors and unpainted drywall. "It's a good-sized space."

"Yes. I've already got the floor plan mapped out, found a local contractor, and I've been doing some research on the shopping center."

"Research on the shopping center? So you're aware it has a precarious history?"

Gregory smiles. "Yes, but the landlord has really started to turn things around and is eager to attract new tenants."

"That's nice to hear. I noticed when I drove in that a lot of the empty retail spaces have been filled."

"They've lured several new shops and restaurants and really improved security. I think now is a good time to get in. The owners are offering a rent abatement while I do the build out and will even chip in on some of the construction costs."

"That's great. I didn't get any such concessions when I opened Sweet Tea so many years ago. But, at the time, I didn't really know to ask for them. Live and learn."

"That's for sure. I learn so many new things with every restaurant I open. For instance, I really appreciate the big lots here. I made the mistake of opening a location just outside Atlanta with only street parking. I think the lack of convenient parking is the reason sales at that location have been soft."

"Yes. Easily accessible parking was a must when I opened Sweet Tea . . . and lots of street lights for safety . . . that was important, too. There's good lighting in the lot here—that's definitely a plus."

"I also love that this space is right next to the movie theater. I can really take advantage of people going to and from the movies with an appetite."

I turn around and give the space another look. "If the price is right, and the square footage meets your needs, maybe you really did find a great site for the next South Beach Burgers. Shall I plan to be the first in line for a Miami Deluxe in a few months?"

"How do you know about the Miami Deluxe?"

"A third pound of Certified Angus Beef on a brioche bun with Muenster cheese, avocado, crispy onion rings, and Russian dressing," I say. "I gave your Web site a quick look before I came. It's very nicely done."

"Thanks. I have a great designer. If you have any advice about the Web site . . . or about anything really, I'd love to hear it."

"I'm sure you've got general restaurant management down to a science at this point, but I bet I can give you pointers on all the local regs you'll need to deal with—the permits and licenses, the signage restrictions, the building codes . . . all that jazz. I would have loved for someone with my current experience to walk me through all those hoops when I got Sweet Tea up and running. So many ridiculous rules and fees—it almost made me wonder if the county wanted any new businesses to open at all."

"I hear you. I think it's all designed to make lawyers money. I have to hire a local attorney for each area that I expand into."

"And their services are expensive. At least it sounds like you're getting a good deal on this place."

"I think I am. Raynell . . . well, Christy mostly, showed me several properties and this one really seemed to be the best of the bunch."

"Speaking of Raynell . . ." I'm assuming this is the best opportunity I'll have to move the conversation toward the topic of her demise. "Are you holding up okay following her passing?"

Gregory looks at me as if I've just asked him an odd question. "Sure. I'm fine. It's very sad for her family and friends, though."

"Sad for her family and friends? No one else?"

"What do you mean?"

"It's not sad for you?"

"Of course it's sad for me, but we were not exactly close. I guess we had been working together for several weeks scouting restaurant locations, but it was really just a business arrangement."

I narrow my eyebrows at Gregory. "Is that what the kids are calling it these days? A *business arrangement?*"

"What are you getting at, Halia?" He's trying not to show it, but I can sense that my questions have unearthed some anxiety.

I don't say anything for a moment or two, but

when it's clear that he is not going to come clean I speak. "Alvetta told me about your affair with Raynell."

Gregory's jaw drops. "How did Alvetta know?"

"Those two told each other everything. They've been a pair of cackling hens for almost thirty years."

Gregory stares at me, clearly embarrassed that I know about his indiscretion. Then he looks down at the ground and then back at me again. "There wasn't anything between us."

"Oh?"

"Really. I didn't feel anything for Raynell . . ." He seems to stumble for words. "The whole thing with her was just . . . just complicated. I didn't even like her. You, Halia . . . *you,* I like."

"Apparently, you liked her enough to show up on her doorstep after the reunion Saturday night."

I see that familiar jaw drop again, and with it, Gregory knows he's already shown his guilt. There is no point in denying that he was there.

"Yes. I know you were at her house the night she died."

"Okay . . . you've got me . . . I was there, but I didn't even see her."

"What do you mean?"

"Terrence was out of town, so we made plans to get together after the party, but by the time I got there, she must have been out cold. She didn't answer the door. And, honestly, I was relieved." Gregory steps closer to me. "We . . . you and me had spent such a nice evening together. You were on my mind. Not Raynell."

"Then why the late-night rendezvous with her?"

"Like I said, it was complicated. I had my reasons, but none of them involved any affection for Raynell Rollins."

"I think you'd better share those reasons with me, Gregory. Not everyone is convinced that Raynell's death was an accident. And, honestly, you being seen late at night at her house hours before she's found dead might sound very suspicious to some people."

Gregory cocks his head at me and laughs nervously. "You don't seriously think I had something to do with Raynell's death?"

I actually take a moment to really ponder the thought before responding. "You know, I guess I don't. At least I don't think the Gregory I knew in high school was a killer. But unless you can shed some light on what was going on with you and Raynell, I'm going to have to tell the police about your whereabouts the night she died."

Gregory takes a long slow breath and lets it out. "I'm not sure where to begin."

"I suspect it all started sometime in the eighties."

Gregory laughs nervously again. "You would suspect right." He pauses and then looks me in the eye. "That woman . . . Raynell . . . she really hurt me. Yeah, it was more than twenty years ago, but some scars never heal."

"That woman . . . Raynell . . . hurt a lot of people."

"Maybe so, but she led me to believe she cared about me. You remember me in high school—I was skinny and gawky . . . and shy. When Raynell took an interest in me I started to feel like I was *somebody*. I trusted her and even agreed to keep our relationship quiet. From the outside I'm sure it seems like I should have known she was only using me for help with her studies, but . . . I don't know . . . sometimes we believe what we want to believe. It nearly killed me when she dumped me after I took the freaking SATs for her. She had been so nice to me, and I thought we really had a good time together. But when she turned on me, boy did she *turn* on me. The last words I remember her saying to me before we reconnected this year . . . the last words I remember the girl I was in love with saying to me were: 'If you tell anyone about us, I'll make your life a living hell.' "

"And anyone who knew Raynell was well aware that she could and would make that happen."

"I was dumbstruck by her behavior . . . and man, was I hurt, but I was smart enough not to cross her. She could be as mean as a rattlesnake, and I knew better than to end up on the other end of a strike attack."

It's been decades, but as Gregory talks about her, I can see the pain in his eyes that Raynell inflicted on him. It makes me sad for him.

"So life went on. I slowly got over it I guess . . . and let it go. At least, I thought I had, but then . . ."

"Then what?"

"Facebook. That's what."

"What do you mean?"

"I was late to the Facebook party, but when my team started putting together a Facebook page for South Beach Burgers I decided to go ahead and put up a personal page as well. I had barely had a profile up there for a day when friend requests from old classmates started coming in like crazy. I just accepted them without much thought. Then one day, I clicked on that little "you have a friend request" icon, and a photo of Raynell popped up. I tell you, my heart sank to the floor all over again just from seeing her face. I accepted her request and, stupid me, thought she might actually send me an apology for how she behaved in high school."

"I take it she didn't do that?"

"Of course not, but she did e-mail me . . . multiple times. She told me how 'fine' I looked now, and how she wished she wasn't married so she could get 'all up in that.' From there her e-mails got even more suggestive. I'll admit I enjoyed the attention I was receiving from her, but getting back in touch with her also showed me that she hadn't changed. She would e-mail with hateful gossip about classmates, and I'd see condescending comments she'd write on other people's posts. Chatting with her via Facebook and seeing how she was still the same old Raynell stirred something in me. That feeling of inadequacy began to rear its head all over again. I'd dealt with her using me and then dumping me once I'd served my purpose so many years ago. I think I let *that* go. But the fact that she threatened to ruin me if I told anyone about our relationship was too much to ever let go. It made me feel like I was such a nothing—less than a nothing—that I was so awful Raynell didn't want anyone to know we'd had a relationship."

Gregory goes quiet as his head hangs with his face toward the floor. Then he inhales slowly and looks at me. "I'm a success now. I'm rich. I look good. I should have been above revenge. . . ." He lets his voice trail off.

"But?"

"Word of the reunion was all over Facebook. I thought it would be fun to attend, and I really am looking to expand South Beach Burgers into Maryland. I figured if I was going to make the trip anyway I may as well give Raynell a taste of her own medicine."

"You're starting to scare me a little bit," I say. "Your taste for revenge didn't end up with Raynell dead on her bathroom floor, did it?"

"Of course not. I would never kill anyone. But all I could think about after getting back in touch with her was how, back in high school, she said she would ruin me if I told anyone about us. So, you know what?" Gregory is silent for a second or two as he rolls his shoulders back and lifts his head. "I decided I would ruin her."

"Ruin her? How?"

"She made it clear in our online chats that she was attracted to me and had no problem being unfaithful to her husband. That gave me an idea. What if . . . what if I took advantage of her loose morals and lured her into an affair, made her fall in love with me the way I fell for her . . . and then . . . and then made sure her husband caught us. After Terrence found out and threatened divorce, I planned to agree to be there for her when she left him . . . and then . . ." There's a wicked twinkle in Gregory's eye. "Ditch her the same way she ditched me in high school. I was all set to make sure she was left without me, without Terrence . . . and without any money when Terrence divorced her ass for cheating on him."

I can't help but look at Gregory with startled eyes as I take all of this in. "So, did Terrence ever find out about your affair with Raynell?"

"I don't know. I left a monogrammed men's T-shirt just under his side of the bed when I was there last, and I always made sure to wear heavy cologne when I met her at their house, so the scent would linger on the sheets when Terrence got home. If she had let me in after the reunion I was going to leave this ring. . . ." Gregory holds up his hand. "This *man's* ring behind . . . make it look like it had fallen between the bed and the nightstand."

As I continue to listen to him speak I try not to let my facial expression show what I'm feeling, but he can read me anyway.

"You think I'm pathetic, don't you? Hell, *I* think I'm pathetic. That *woman* just had such an effect on me."

"I don't think you're pathetic, Gregory," I say, even though I guess I sort of do. "But why was it so important to get back at her? You got yours—like you said, you're successful, you look great, you're rich . . ."

"I don't know, but so many years after high school, she was still able to get under my skin. But I assure you, Halia, I never would have killed her and I—" Gregory gasps as if he's just been hit with a revelation. "Oh my God! What if I did play a role in her death?"

"What are you talking about?"

Gregory leans against the wall and puts his hands on his forehead. "My goal was to have Terrence find out about us and kick Raynell to the curb, but what if . . . *what if* he found out she was cheating on him and went to a much further extreme?"

I think about what Gregory has just said and consider telling him that he was not the only one Hottie McHot Pants was cheating on her husband with, but I don't think telling Gregory about Raynell's affair with Michael Marshall would serve any purpose, so I keep it to myself.

"But you don't know if Terrence found out about your affair with Raynell?"

"No, I can't say for sure. But what I can say for sure is that I did *not* kill Raynell Rollins. If you have to tell the police about me being at her house the night she died, then so be it. But I wish you wouldn't." He steps in closer to me and lightly grasps my hand. "It's just an intrusion in my life I really don't need at the moment. I'm busy . . . really busy expanding my restaurant, and, honestly, I'd love to find some time to reconnect with you, Halia."

I look at his big brown eyes staring down on me, and I can see what a handsome man he is, but he just isn't attractive to me anymore. The bizarre revenge game he was playing with Raynell . . . his unhealthy obsession with settling the score over something that happened decades ago . . . that he would be intimate with a woman he hated . . . it's all just too creepy.

"I'm really busy, too, Gregory, and I imagine you'll have to be getting back to Florida soon."

He looks away from me. "I'm assuming that's a nice way of saying you're not interested."

I don't respond. I just look at him, try to smile, and clumsily remove my hand from his grasp. It seems nicer than verbally confirming his assumption, but it doesn't make the situation any less uncomfortable.

"I've really got to get back to Sweet Tea." I can hear the awkward tone in my voice as the words come out. "We reopen for dinner soon."

"Okay," he responds, a defeated look on his face. "Thanks for coming by."

"You're welcome." I turn to leave. "This really is a nice space. I think you'll have a lot of success with it."

"I hope so."

As I walk toward the door I wonder if Gregory is worth keeping on my suspect list. I wonder if Terrence killed Raynell over one or more of her affairs. I wonder about Alvetta and Christy. But mostly, when I see Gregory's reflection in the glass door on my way out—his attractive face, his full lips, his solid stature—I wonder if I just made a huge mistake by turning down his romantic advance.

CHAPTER 32

"Wouldn't it be easier to just chop all this meat with a knife?" Wavonne asks me as we stand next to the counter hand-tearing chicken breasts.

"I suppose, but hand-torn chicken just tastes better than chopped chicken. I don't know why. It just does."

And I really don't know why hand-shredded chicken tastes better than chopped, but we only use shredded chicken in our chicken salad, our chicken and dumplings, and the chicken potpies we are preparing now. We always start with roasted bone-in skin-on chicken breasts. The bone adds flavor to the chicken, and the skin left intact adds a little fat and moisture to the meat as it cooks.

Farther down the counter, Tacy is rolling out the crusts for the potpies. We've already prepared the batter based on Grandmommy's simple recipe—flour, sugar, salt, butter, butter-flavored shortening, ice water, and a pinch of baking powder. But I must confess, unlike Grandmommy, we no longer mix the recipe by hand. We use my commercial food processor to save time and labor and, fortunately, it produces a pie crust just as light and flaky as the one Grandmommy made. Once she perfected the recipe Grandmommy used the same one for all her pies whether she was preparing a savory pie like the chicken potpies we are making now or sweet creations like apple or peach tarts.

"So, do I get to wait on them when they get here?"

"Who?"

"Alvetta and Michael."

"No. I asked Darius to take care of them."

"Why does he always get all the good tables?"

"Because I can count on him to consistently provide a high level of service."

"*I* provide a high level of service."

"Of course you do . . . when the mood strikes you."

"Well, the mood is strikin' me tonight," Wavonne says. "I know they ain't comin' here for a leisurely dinner. You've got an angle for invitin' them, and I wanna know what it is."

"I don't have an *angle,* Wavonne. I just thought having them as my guests would give me a chance to talk to Michael."

"Michael?"

"Yes. He was with Terrence at the retreat in Williamsburg. If Terrence knew about Raynell's affair . . . *affairs,* and decided he wanted her dead . . . well, Williamsburg is not that far from here . . . barely three hours if there's no traffic. He could have easily slipped out of his hotel room, driven up here, pulled Raynell from a drunken slumber, bashed her head against the porcelain tub, and been back at the hotel before daybreak."

"What do you think Michael's gonna be able to tell you?"

"All sorts of things. He can tell me how late it was when he last saw Terrence on Saturday night . . . and when he first saw him on Sunday morning. Terrence would have needed at least six hours to pull the whole thing off. Michael might also be able to tell me something about Terrence's demeanor Sunday morning. He was bound to have been edgy and unsettled if he'd just killed his wife hours earlier."

"Instead of Michael and Alvetta, I think you . . . *we* should talk to Terrence directly . . . get his side of the story. And if he happens to offer to hook a sista up with a wealthy Redskin, then so be it. I've been—"

Laura cuts Wavonne off when she pokes her head through the kitchen door. "Halia, your guests are here. Mr. and Mrs. Marshall. They're at table four by the window."

"Thank you, Laura." I put the chicken I was handling back on the counter and step over to the sink and wash my hands. "Wavonne, can you finish up the chicken, please? We need to get those pies in the oven." Fortunately, we just need to add the meat to the filling, which we've already prepared, and then pour the mixture into the pie crusts Tacy is about to wrap up. Everything in the pies is already cooked, so we only need to brown the crust and heat the contents. Then they will be ready to serve to the dinner rush that is beginning to gather outside the kitchen door.

"Hey!" I smile after I step outside the kitchen and greet Michael and Alvetta. "Welcome."

They stand up. Michael shakes my hand, and Alvetta gives me a hug. I've actually grown to like her during the last few days. Her close association with Raynell is not exactly a selling point, but aside from that, she's seems to have matured into an affable person.

"Please, please. Have a seat," I say as I take one myself next to Alvetta. "I'm so sorry I couldn't make Raynell's funeral this morning. I've been running my assistant manager ragged lately. She was scheduled to be off today, and I just couldn't ask her to cover for me again. I hope it went well . . . as well as can be expected, at least."

"It was a lovely service . . . very sad of course, but I think it helped to give her friends and family closure and say our good-byes," Alvetta says, trying to not get emotional as she speaks of the funeral, but I can see the grief in her eyes.

"Alvetta worked day and night to make it special. She put together a very touching tribute," Michael says and directs his eyes from me to Alvetta. "You did a wonderful job, honey. You did Raynell proud," he adds as Darius appears at the table.

"Welcome to Sweet Tea. My name is Darius, and I'll be taking care of you this . . ." Darius lets his voice trail off as he notices that he may have interrupted a sensitive moment. "Should I come back?"

Alvetta adjusts herself in her seat. "No . . . no. We're fine. Thank you," she says, and takes in a long breath. "Actually, I would love a drink."

"I can certainly help with that. Just for the summer we are featuring crushed-ice margaritas. No syrups or mixers. We make them with fresh oranges, lemons, and limes."

"That sounds lovely," Alvetta says.

"Just a draft beer for me," comes from Michael. "Michelob Ultra if you have it."

"We only have that in the bottle."

"That's fine."

"One margarita and one Michelob Ultra," Darius confirms. He's about to step away from the table when he notes my raised eyebrows. He grins at me, pulls out his pad, and writes down their drink order. I'm not a fan of waiters failing to write down orders, even very simple ones. It's a pet peeve of mine. A good server like Darius can generally gauge when he needs to write an order on his pad rather than commit it to memory, but even he can get tripped up if something distracts him on the way to inputting the order into the computer system. Customers get testy enough if their order comes to the table without the sauce on the side as they requested or with the onions they asked to be left out when a server *has* written the order down. If we mess up (yes, it happens on occasion, even at Sweet Tea ☺), and their server didn't write the order down, people get *really* annoyed. Even if one of my servers had some sort of extraordinary memory skills and never forgot anything, I'd still require that he or she write orders down. Some customers might be impressed that a server can remember the most lengthy and complex of orders, but the mere act of a waiter not recording their order makes them anxious that their meal will not come to the table exactly as they requested. That's not how I want my customers to feel. I want a night out at Sweet Tea to be a relaxed, positive experience in every way.

"Are you having anything?" Alvetta asks as Darius departs from the table.

"I'm sure Darius will bring me an iced tea."

"Aw. Don't make a girl drink alone. Have a margarita with me."

"I wish I could. I have a long night ahead of me. The dinner rush is just starting. I need to keep a clear head. I thought I'd just sit with you for a bit and say hi and then let you two enjoy your evening. I'm sure you could use a relaxing night out after . . . well . . . you know . . . events of late."

"That's very thoughtful of you, Halia. It has been a challenging time."

"I don't know if a few drinks and some good food can even put a dent in the grief I'm sure you're feeling, but maybe it can help you take a little break from it for a few hours."

"Truthfully, it would be nice to not think of Raynell's death for a little while," Alvetta says. "Wow, that sounded really selfish, didn't it?"

Michael reaches for Alvetta's hand across the table. "Not at all," he says. "You were the best friend anyone could have been to Raynell. And let's be honest, Raynell was not the easiest person to love. But you did love her, and you were a good friend to her." He holds her hand for another moment or two before letting it go. "Now, let's talk about something else."

"Yes," I say. "How about the retreat last weekend, Michael? How was it?"

"It was very nice . . . until we got the news about Raynell." Michael pauses. "No. We said we would take a break from talking about Raynell." He straightens himself in his chair. "It was actually very productive. If our church is going to continue to thrive, we need a strong online presence. We developed a strategy during the conference that I think will be quite effective."

"That's great," I say. "Terrence was at the conference, too, wasn't he? Was he involved in the discussions? I guess I don't think of a former football player being a technical guru."

Michael laughs. "No. Terrence is not terribly computer savvy, but I always ask him to attend our conferences. If churchgoers know Terrence Rollins is attending an event, we always get a sizable turnout. Terrence is professional sports royalty, and people just like to be around him. Like Saturday night at the hotel, he held court in the lounge until after two a.m."

"Really?" I ask. "Two a.m.? That must make getting up for morning service a bit tricky."

"Not for Terrence. That man has a lot of energy. I passed him on the way to the gym at six a.m. when I was going to help set up the hospitality room."

"Raynell always complained about Terrence being a morning person," Alvetta says. "Raynell would sleep until noon every day if she could."

"I suppose I would, too, but that pesky need to earn a living is a bit of an obstacle," I respond, grateful that I didn't have to find a way to tactfully grill Michael about Terrence's whereabouts the night Raynell died. If Terrence was hanging out at the hotel bar until after two a.m. and was later seen at six a.m., then he couldn't have killed Raynell. There simply wasn't time for him to drive back to Maryland, do the deed, and get back to Williamsburg by six a.m.

"Why don't I go check on Darius and see what's keeping those drinks."

I mentally cross Terrence off my suspect list as I hop up from the table and head toward the bar.

"What's the holdup?" I ask Darius.

"Word has gotten out about our margaritas. Everyone is ordering them. The blenders are backed up."

"I guess I'll need to order another one to get us through the summer."

"I'll bring the drinks to the table as soon as they're ready if you want to get back to your guests."

"Thanks! I'll give them some time alone."

"Found out what you wanted to know already?" Darius asks, a sly smile on his face.

"What do you mean?" I feign innocence.

"He means did you find out from Michael if Terrence had time to get back from Williamsburg Saturday night and lay waste to his cheatin' ho-bag of a wife?" Wavonne says, seemingly appearing out of nowhere.

I sigh, annoyed that Wavonne has been discussing Raynell's death and my little informal investigation with Darius. "If you must know, yes, I did get the information I was after. According to Michael, Terrence was in the hotel lounge until after two a.m. and was seen again on the way to the gym at six a.m., so I guess he's in the clear."

"What makes you think Terrence would want to kill Raynell anyway?" Darius asks.

"Because she was cheating on him all over God's creation—not only with an old high school classmate, but also with Michael Rollins," I say, and direct my eyes toward Michael.

"Yeah," Wavonne says. "We found this note in Raynell's house. It's from Michael. It's signed *M*, and it's his handwriting." Wavonne pulls the infamous note from her pocket.

"What are you doing with that?" I ask as Darius reads the letter.

"I just thought it might come in handy . . . be useful sometime. A certain someone"—Wavonne diverts her eyes across the room toward Michael—"might be willing to pay a sista a little something to keep his wife from seein' it."

I shake my head in exasperation. "That's called *extortion,* Wavonne, and could land you in jail."

I grab the letter when Darius is done reading it to keep it from getting back in Wavonne's hands.

"You know," Darius says. "This letter isn't *necessarily* for Raynell."

"What do you mean?"

"Look"—Darius points to the top of the note—"It just says 'hey, good-lookin'.' "

"What are you getting at?"

"You found the note at the Rollinses' home, right? Raynell is not the only one who lives there."

"But the note was in her office." Wavonne says.

"Actually, we really don't know if it was *her* office where we found the note," I counter. "Yes, her real estate paraphernalia was scattered about, but she had that stuff stored all over the house."

"Did it ever occur to you that the note could have been for Terrence?" Darius asks.

"From Michael to Terrence? But that would mean—"

Wavonne cuts me off. "What are you sayin'? That Terrence likes his bread buttered on both sides?"

"He's been rumored to be one of 'my people' since he was an active player back in the nineties. I have friends that swear he was a regular at The Bachelor's Mill back in the day . . . before everyone had cameras on their phones to snap photos of a closeted football player."

"The Bachelor's Mill?"

"It's a gay bar in D.C. Before he married Raynell, whenever reporters asked him about a girlfriend he always said he was too busy to date, or just hadn't found the right girl. When his engagement was announced everyone 'in the know' assumed it was just an arrangement. Besides, from what I've heard, why else would anyone marry Raynell Rollins?"

"So what you're saying is that Michael may have been having an affair with Terrence? Not Raynell?"

"Word on the street has always been that Terrence's marriage to Raynell was just for convenience. She got access to his wealth and status, and he got a beard to have on his arm at the ESPYs."

"Wow. This just gets more and more complicated." I stop to think for a moment. "But Michael is married to Alvetta. I just can't believe it. They are so good together. If what you're saying is true, then Michael must also . . ."

"Get the hots for the brothas?" Wavonne says. "Well, I know how we can find out for sure. Look, Alvetta's goin' to the ladies room." We watch as Alvetta heads toward the back of the restaurant. "I'm gonna saunter over there with my girls on display." Wavonne looks down at her chest, loosens her tie, and unbuttons her blouse. "If he's straight, you know he's gonna wanna get down with all *this*."

Darius and I observe from the bar as Wavonne sashays toward the table where Michael is looking at his phone. I can tell she's asking about changing out the salt and pepper as she jiggles her bazoombas in front of his face while she reaches for the shakers. Michael barely looks up from his phone and can't be bothered to stare at all when Wavonne drops her pen and bends over right next to him to pick it up.

"Gay as a pink feather boa," Wavonne says once she's back at the bar.

"Maybe you're just not his type," I protest.

"Of course I'm not his type. I don't have a—"

I look at Darius and break in before Wavonne has a chance to finish her tirade. "Why don't you try it?"

"Me?" Darius asks.

"Yeah," Wavonne says. "Go over there and strut your stuff. See if he bites."

Darius lets out a quick laugh. "All right. I'll

play along. Looks like their drinks are ready anyway." He places Alvetta's margarita and Michael's beer on a tray.

"Serve the drinks and then turn around, put your hands in your pockets on the way back, and pull your slacks forward," Wavonne instructs as Darius walks toward Michael. "Show off what your momma gave you."

Darius reaches the table and sets the drinks down. Wavonne and I discreetly observe as Michael looks up from his phone and steals a quick look at Darius's chest. When Darius *accidentally* drops the tray on way back to the bar and bends over to pick it up, Michael's eyes follow and linger on Darius's backside way longer than any straight man's should.

"So Michael is having an affair with *Terrence,*" I say to Wavonne as we see the spectacle unfold in front of us. "This changes everything."

CHAPTER 33

"I think I've stepped foot in this building more than most tithing members during the last several days," I say to Wavonne as we walk down the main hall of Rebirth Christian Church. I didn't want to be away from the restaurant too long, so we timed our visit to coincide with the end of the eleven a.m. service.

"I don't know why you made me come," Wavonne says. "That fool never called me . . . never texted me . . . nothin'," she adds about Rick Stevens, the gentleman we chatted with two weeks ago at the retreat table who tried to recruit Wavonne for the event in Williamsburg. "Now you want me to try and wrangle some information out of him."

"Who knows why he didn't call you, Wavonne. It hasn't been that long. Maybe he still plans to."

"Fine. But I'm gonna play it cool with him this time. I think I came off too eager when we were here last. Maybe that's why he didn't call."

"Just do whatever seems to make him comfortable. Whether he's called you or not, I could tell he was attracted to you. I figure you're my best bet for getting his version of what happened at the hotel in Williamsburg the night Raynell died. Surely, we can't trust Michael's version, knowing what we do now about his relationship with Terrence."

"Raynell was bangin' Gregory. Michael and Terrence are hookin' up. The rate these thots are goin' at it, I wonder if there was a retreat at all. Maybe it was just a big swinger's convention."

I snicker. "It doesn't seem to be a very righteous group, does it?" I comment as my eyes catch sight of Rick looking dapper as ever in a beige suit, light blue shirt, and a patterned silk tie. Once again he's staffing the Church Retreat Ministry table.

"Well, hello, so good to see you again. . . ." He's clearly struggling to remember our names.

"Halia," I say, coming to his rescue. "And this is—"

"Wavonne," he says before I have a chance to. I guess he at least remembered Wavonne's name. "I owe you a phone call."

"Do you?" Wavonne asks, acting as though she hasn't been checking her phone every hour on the hour for more than a week. "So what goods are you peddlin' this week, Rick?" she continues, feigning disinterest.

"We have another retreat scheduled for September . . . this one's in Baltimore. It's called 'Journey to Reinvention.' It will focus on transforming our lesser qualities into strengths through focused self-improvement."

"Hmm . . . wonder if a certain gay minister can reinvent himself as a straight man," Wavonne says under her breath to me.

"What was that?" Rick asks.

"Nothing." I turn to Wavonne. "'Journey to Reinvention.' That sounds like something you might be interested in."

"Me? I ain't got no lesser qualities I want to change."

I give Wavonne a look that asks her to drop the attitude and play along. When you spend as much time together for as long as Wavonne and I have, sometimes a look is all you need.

She reluctantly changes her disposition. "Okay . . . well, maybe a weekend in Baltimore wouldn't be such a bad thing. I could get me some crab cakes and some of them Berger Cookies . . . you know, those shortbread cookies with the chocolate frosting on top."

"Yes. We do like our retreats to be all about the available local food options," Rick jokes.

"I've heard good things about the retreat last weekend in Williamsburg. If the Baltimore retreat is half as good, maybe Wavonne should check it out." I take my best stab at turning the conversation in the direction I want it to go.

"Really?"

"Yes. Pastor Marshall was at my restaurant the other night. He said the sessions during the day were very effective, and everyone enjoyed the social time afterward. I think he even mentioned some attendees mingling in the hotel lounge until the wee hours."

"We probably did stay up a bit too late Saturday night."

"So you were part of the after-hours crowd?" Wavonne asks.

"Guilty as charged. The day was intense. So it was nice to relax with friends."

"How late did the evening go?"

"I packed it in about two a.m."

"So I guess you didn't outlast Michael and Terrence Rollins . . . you know Terrence, right? The football—"

"The football player. Of course. Everyone knows Terrence. He's one of our celebrity members. Great guy. And what a career! But no, I think I outlasted him and Michael. Terrence isn't much of a partier. Michael, either."

"So how late did they hang out with you and the others in the lounge?"

"They didn't. I think they both retired to their rooms early. I'm sure they were tired. It was a busy day for them."

"So they weren't in the lounge on Saturday night? At all?"

"No. Why?"

"No reason," I say. "When Michael mentioned people gathering until very late, I assumed he, and probably Terrence, were part of the group."

Wavonne and I exchange looks . . . looks that say the same thing: *so Michael was not only lying about Terrence's whereabouts the night of Raynell's demise, he was lying about his own.*

All three of us are quiet for a moment, before I

take an obvious look at my watch. "Look at the time," I say. "Wavonne, we really need to get going. Why don't you take some of the promotional materials and give some thought to the retreat in September."

"Yeah . . . okay." Wavonne haphazardly grabs a brochure and a couple of flyers.

"Let me know if I can answer any other questions . . . and I still owe you a phone call," Rick says to Wavonne. "You were going to give me some ideas about the church's Web site."

"Sure . . . whateveh," Wavonne says.

"Thanks again for the information," I offer before Wavonne and I begin to walk away from the table.

"He was lying," I quietly say to Wavonne.

"I know he was. He ain't gonna call me."

"Not Rick! Michael. Michael was lying about him and Terrence partying in the lounge until two a.m. From the sound of it, they went missing after dinner. You know what that means?"

"You think I played it okay with Rick . . . you know . . . actin' all indifferent?"

"Are you listening to me at all!? Michael lied about his and Terrence's whereabouts. They were not seen after dinner on Saturday night, which would have given one or both of them plenty of time to drive back to Maryland, furnish Raynell with a one-way ticket to being facedown on her bathroom floor, and be back at the hotel in Williamsburg in time for breakfast."

"So you think they both could've had somethin' to do with Raynell buyin' the farm?"

"They are both wealthy men. If they really

wanted to be together, they would need to get divorces—divorces that might cost them half or more of their fortunes." As I say this, my eyes catch sight of Alvetta several yards down the long hall in front of us. Earlier, I was hoping to avoid her and figured it wouldn't be hard given that a few thousand people are milling about, but now I'm glad to run into her. When her eyes meet mine, and she waves in our direction, it occurs to me that if Michael and Terrence want to be a real couple and avoid messy divorces, getting rid of Raynell only solved half the problem. As the other half of the problem is walking toward me in a smart gray pantsuit with a familiar smile on her face, all I can think is *ticktock . . . ticktock.*

CHAPTER 34

"So good to see you back here," Alvetta says after she gives both Wavonne and I a quick hug. "You should have told me you were coming. I could have arranged for you to sit with me in the Pastor's Circle. Did you enjoy the service?"

"Um . . . we didn't actually make it to the service."

"Oh . . . no worries. What brings you by then?"

"Well . . ." I try to come up with some words. How do you tell someone that not only is her husband cheating on her . . . he's cheating on her with a *man* . . . and not only is he cheating on her with a man, but he and said other man may be plotting to kill her? It's not the sort of thing you just blurt out in the middle of a crowded church hallway. "Do you think we could talk to you in private, Alvetta? Maybe in your office?"

"Sure," she says, a curious expression on her face. "I'm due at a choir meeting. Let me just text the director and let her know I'll be a few minutes late."

Alvetta sends the text and leads us toward the elevators, which whisk up to the third level. When we reach her office, she takes a seat on the long sofa by the window rather than behind her desk. Wavonne and I sit down next to her.

"Lawd." Wavonne takes in the office. "Cookie Lyon don't have an office this nice on *Empire.*"

Alvetta laughs. "It is a nice space. Took me months to furnish and decorate it. I wanted everything 'just so.' " She looks around the room as if to remind her how lovely it is. "I'm very blessed."

I want to say, "I'm not so sure about that." Instead I remain quiet, and there is a lengthy and awkward silence among the three of us.

"So?" Alvetta eventually asks. "What can I help you with?"

I clear my throat. "Gosh. I'm trying to figure out how to say this . . ."

"Say what? You're starting to make me nervous. Is something wrong?"

"Possibly," I say. "Possibly *very* wrong. Your husband . . . Michael . . ." I struggle for words. "He . . . well, he and Terrence. How do I put this—"

"Vetta, girl," Wavonne says. "Michael and Terrence are doin' the nasty, and Halia here thinks they may have teamed up to ice Raynell. And your bougie ass might be next."

"Very *tactful,* Wavonne." I glare at her while Alvetta does the same. She seems to be letting Wavonne's words settle in. "What Wavonne was trying to say is—"

"I know what she was trying to say, Halia. I may

be a minister's wife, but I don't live in a bunker. I'm aware of what 'doin the nasty' means. But that's silly. I mean . . . *really* . . . where did you ever get such an idea?"

Though she claims to think the idea of her husband having an affair with Terrence is ridiculous, the look in her eyes and slight tremor in her voice betray her. Clearly, we've unsettled her.

"We came upon this note at the Rollinses' residence." I hand the incriminating love note to Alvetta. "I recognized Michael's handwriting from his column in the church bulletin. At first I thought it was from him to Raynell, but given some recent events, I'm quite certain it was from Michael to Terrence." I spare Alvetta the details about the little experiment we conducted at Sweet Tea that established that Michael was clearly more interested in the goods Darius was peddling than the ones Wavonne put on display in front of him.

Alvetta takes the note from my hand and begins to read it.

"And it's not just the note." I take a breath. "Wavonne and I did a little checking today with Rick Stevens at the retreat table in the main hall. That's really why we came by today—to see him. According to him, Michael was not being truthful about his and Terrence's whereabouts the night Raynell died. Rick said neither one of them socialized in the lounge that night. In fact, he didn't see them at all after dinner."

Alvetta puts the note down on the table in front of the sofa and stands up. "Wow. Not much gets past you, Halia, does it?" She walks toward her desk.

"I'm sorry we had to be the ones to tell you this, but if you're in danger you need to know."

"Know?" Her back is toward us, and her hands are lightly resting on her desk. "Know? Oh, Halia, I've *known* for years. I knew before I married Michael."

"Sista, say what?!" Wavonne asks.

Alvetta turns around and leans against the desk, more looking at the floor than at us. "As with most things nefarious, it all started with Raynell—that woman could scheme a fat kid out of cake." She lifts her head and looks at us. "I don't follow sports, so I knew nothing about Terrence, football player extraordinaire, back in the day. But apparently, in the nineties, when Terrence was at his height with the Redskins, rumors were swirling that he . . . that he . . ."

"Prefers hot dogs to taco shells?" Wavonne says.

Alvetta nods. "This was almost twenty years ago. Professional football isn't exactly welcoming to gay men now, but back then, it was absolutely unthinkable for the truth about Terrence's sexual orientation to get out. His career would have been over. The rumors had to be squelched, and Raynell signed on to do the squelching. In exchange for helping Terrence keep up appearances, Raynell gained the celebrity of being a star football player's wife and, more important, access to his millions."

"So what does this have to do with you and Michael?"

"It wasn't long after Terrence married Raynell that he met a deacon with a gift for public speaking at a small Baptist church in Camp Springs."

"Michael."

"Yes. I guess one thing led to another, and Terrence and Michael became an item—an item that had to be kept on the down low. As Michael became more and more successful and moved to progressively larger congregations, he found himself in the same position Terrence had years earlier—he was also a star in his career field. But, unfortunately, much like Terrence, he chose a career that, at the time . . . maybe even now, could have been ruined by gay rumors. Thankfully this was before TMZ and Perez Hilton, but apparently a tabloid photographer had begun snooping around and noticing the extensive amount of time Terrence and Michael were spending together with no women on their arms. The attention was not good for either of them. So, once again, it was Raynell to the rescue.

"I was trying to make it as a model at the time, but I was spending more time waiting tables than booking photo shoots. Raynell recruited me to silence the rumors about Michael just like she had for Terrence. I was broke, and my mother was sick . . . and my modeling career was going nowhere fast. It was the right offer at the right time. Rebirth was not in this mammoth building back then, but it had already become a force to be reckoned with, and Michael had amassed a tidy fortune. And I liked him . . . I *still* like him. We're good friends . . . we enjoy each other's company . . . I enjoy my work here . . . and, yes, I'd be lying if I said I didn't revel in the status of being the First Lady of one of the largest churches on the East Coast. It's a mutually beneficial relationship for both of us."

"I guess I'm a little relieved you already knew about Michael and Terrence. I wasn't thrilled about having to be the one to break the news to you. But isn't it still possible that maybe they've decided they wanted to be together in a more . . . I don't know . . . *official* or *open* manner and could have killed Raynell to avoid a costly divorce?"

"No," Alvetta says without hesitation. "Both Raynell and I signed airtight prenuptials. Under the terms of the agreement, Raynell wouldn't have ended up destitute in the event of the divorce, but Terrence would have held on to the bulk of his fortune. The same goes for me and Michael. I would get a little something if we divorced, but definitely nowhere near enough to keep me living in the manner to which I've become accustomed. And, in reality, the legal agreement between Raynell and Terrence is irrelevant at this point. Raynell kept it a closely guarded secret, but several years ago she and Terrence made a series of bad investments and lost the bulk of Terrence's fortune. Terrence does pretty well doing local television, but he's certainly not making millions. That's why Raynell got into selling real estate and was so rabid for new clients in the market for expensive homes. They needed to supplement Terrence's earnings if they were going to keep up the same lifestyle they had before they lost most of their savings."

"So, even if you take money out of the picture, do you think Terrence and Michael's relationship could have had something to do with Raynell's death?"

"No. I can assure you Terrence and Michael have no plans of going public with their relationship. I know things have changed over the years. But Terrence is involved in the world of professional sports, which can still be a rough place for gay men. And Michael . . . well, you can't exactly be an out gay man and also lead a church with an Out of the Darkness ministry."

"What's that?"

Alvetta rifles through some brochures on the table, picks one up, and begins reading. "Out of the Darkness provides healing for individuals suffering from same-sex attraction with the goal of releasing these men and women from the bondage of these feelings."

Alvetta continues reading for another moment or two while Wavonne and I sit there speechless. And, honestly, the deceit and manipulation . . . Raynell and Alvetta marrying gay men for the fringe benefits . . . Michael running a ministry to rid people of same-sex attraction when he's, as Wavonne would say, "gettin' some" on the side with Terrence. It's all making my stomach turn.

When Alvetta is done reading aloud she sets the brochure back on the table only to have Wavonne pick it up and shove it in her purse. "For Darius."

"I don't think Darius is interested in changing anything about himself."

"I know. I'm just trying to hook a brotha up. He's been complainin' about a dry spell—sounds like a good place for a gay man to get a date."

"Have at it. I've never been terribly comfortable with the ministry, and given the way the tide is turning, I suspect its days are numbered," Alvetta says, and looks at me. "So you see, Halia, you're chasing a dead end if you think Terrence and

Michael killed Raynell. The four of us had a good thing going, and it worked for all parties. Michael and Terrence were free to pretty much do whatever they wanted. There was no reason to take Raynell out of the picture."

"So, if Michael and Terrence were free to do whatever they wanted, does that mean Raynell was free to do whatever—"

Wavonne interrupts. "And *whoever* she wanted?"

"Yes, she was. Raynell had no shortage of her own affairs and, believe me, Terrence couldn't have cared less."

I let out a sigh. "I can honestly say this is not what I expected to hear when we asked to talk with you."

"It is a tangled web. I know. But you do what you have to do."

"Of course your relationship with Michael . . . Raynell's relationship with Terrence—they are really none of my business. I really just wanted to make sure you were not in danger."

"Michael is my best friend. He would never hurt me." She pauses for a moment. "At least not in that way." The look in her eyes tells me that perhaps she is *his* best friend, but he is a bit more than that to her . . . and that maybe this arrangement doesn't work quite as well as she was trying to have us to believe . . . at least not for her.

CHAPTER 35

"So, what have you got for me?" I ask Momma after I walk into the kitchen at Sweet Tea. Yesterday, I asked her if she'd whip up something special for me to take to Terrence. I wanted something especially yummy—something so good he'll be distracted by the taste and let his guard down while I discreetly pump him for information.

I've talked at length with Alvetta, Michael, Gregory, and Kimberly—Terrence is really the only one on my suspect list who I haven't had a real conversation with. Given Alvetta's insistence that he wouldn't have been bothered by Raynell's affair with Gregory and had no interest in a divorce, maybe it's unlikely that he's to blame for Raynell's death. But if he doesn't offer any information to incriminate himself, maybe he can provide some new leads.

Momma turns to the counter and lifts the top

from a cake caddie to reveal a decadent yellow cake with a sugar glaze trickling down the sides and thinly sliced candied lemon slices on top. "Ta da. My brown-butter lemon pound cake."

"Aunt Celia, please tell me you made two of those? I need to have me some of that," Wavonne calls. She was completely engrossed in whatever trashy magazine she was reading on the other side of the counter. But now that the lid is off Momma's creation, Wavonne is taking a break from the latest celebrity gossip to eye the pound cake.

"Stop looking at it that way, Wavonne," I say. "There is only one, and it's for Terrence."

"Why does Terrence get *my* cake?"

"Because I need an excuse to go over to his house. I figure dropping off some delicious baked goods is a nice gesture while he's mourning the loss of his wife."

"Halia, I wish you wouldn't get involved. If that Rollins girl died as the result of foul play, let the police deal with it," Momma says. "Besides, you should be spending time with that nice Gregory fellow. Why don't you take him a cake?"

"Seriously, Momma? I told you about his antics with Raynell. And he's not off my suspect list just yet. You really want me dating a possible murderer?"

"I don't think that nice boy killed anyone. And if he did kill that Rollins girl it's only because she made him mad. Just don't make him mad, Halia, and he won't kill you . . . and I'll get my grandbabies."

I shake my head and roll my eyes. "Just give me the cake, Momma."

Momma snaps the lid back on the caddie and hands it to me.

"I should be back before we open."

As I start to walk out of the kitchen, I hear the hurried clicking of heels on the tile floor behind me. If I didn't know better I'd think the sound was coming from Wavonne, who hasn't changed into her work shoes yet. But "hurried" and Wavonne don't exactly intermingle. I'm through to the dining room and almost at the front door when I turnaround to find it is, indeed, Wavonne tailing me. Apparently, I *don't* know better.

"I'm comin' with you," she says. "If you won't let me have some of that cake, maybe Terrence will."

"Wavonne, I need you to stay here and wait on customers."

"You said you'd be back before we open."

I sigh. She's got me there. "I guess I did. Do you promise you'll behave yourself and not go anywhere near Raynell's closet?"

"Promise."

"Fine. But let me do the talking."

When we arrive at the Rollins residence Terrence is outside watering some shrubs with a hose. He waves to us as I park the van on the street in front of the house. I phoned him this morning before I left the house, so he's expecting us.

"Hello," I call to him as Wavonne and I get out of the van, cake in hand.

"Hello, ladies," he says as we approach him. "What do you have there?"

"My mother makes all the desserts at Sweet Tea, and I asked her to bake a little something special for you. It's not much, but I enjoyed reconnecting with Raynell, and Wavonne and I just wanted to stop by and pay our respects since we couldn't make the funeral."

"Thank you. That's very nice."

Terrence accepts the cake from me with a perplexed look on his face, as if he's surprised anyone would enjoy reconnecting with Raynell. "Please, come in for a few minutes. I'm about done out here. It's been so dry this summer. The gardener isn't due until Friday, so I wanted to give the bushes a little water."

Terrence leads us into the house and down the hall to the kitchen where he sets the cake on the counter. "Please have a seat." He points toward the kitchen table. "What can I get you to drink? I still have some coffee on if you'd like a cup."

"Yes. That would be nice."

Terrence grabs a few mugs from one of the cabinets, fills them with coffee, and brings them over to the table with a small carton of half-and-half. "There's some sugar right there." He points to a ceramic bowl on the table.

"You know what would go really well with the coffee?" Wavonne says. "Some of my Aunt Celia's lemon pound cake."

"Wavonne, the cake is for Terrence. He may want to save it for later."

"No, no. Let's cut it up." Terrence walks back to the counter and pulls a knife from a wooden block. "Wow," he says when he lifts the lid. "It looks so good. I hate to slice into it."

"Then let me do it." Wavonne gets up from her chair and takes the knife from Terrence. "You get us some plates."

Terrence does as he's instructed, and moments later the three of us are seated at the table about to get fat and happy on coffee and pound cake.

Terrence takes a bite. "This is some good cake."

"Yes. Momma is the Queen of Desserts." I help myself to a forkful as well. "So, how are you holding up, Terrence?"

"I'm hanging in there. There's been so much to do since Raynell passed. Keeping busy has helped me cope. I'll start back to work on Monday. I think that will be good for me."

"You must really be going through a lot."

"I guess so, but I'm not sure it's registered that Raynell's really gone. It's so quiet around here without her shouting orders all day," he says with a laugh.

"Girlfriend did like to tell people what to do," Wavonne says.

"That she did," Terrence agrees. "She knew what she wanted and wasn't afraid to ask for it . . . *demand* it. Actually, I kind of liked that about her. She wasn't always the most pleasant person, but, let me tell you, life with Raynell Rollins was never boring."

"I'm sure of that." I shift around in my chair. "Can I ask you something, Terrence?"

"Sure."

"There's been some talk . . . some talk that maybe Raynell's death was not an accident. I guess I'm just wondering what you think about that."

"I think that's just gossip. I've talked with the police and, though we're waiting on the autopsy results, they are all but certain it was an accident. There was no sign of anyone breaking into the house, nothing was missing, and there was nothing to indicate that she struggled with anyone. Raynell liked her cocktails, and sometimes she indulged a bit too much . . . *way* too much. I've seen her unsteady on her feet before from too much vodka. It's not that surprising that she lost her footing and fell hard. I just wish I had been here when it happened. I could have gotten her help."

His eyes start to tear up, and I can tell he's trying to keep his composure and prevent some full-fledged waterworks from starting. "If I had been here instead of at that stupid conference, I could have helped her . . . if she didn't die immediately from the fall, I could have gotten help, and she might still be here." He takes a long breath and lifts a napkin to his eye to catch a stray tear. "I know she could be difficult, but I don't think she ever did anything so bad that someone would want to kill her. And Raynell had another side that most people didn't see—she raised huge amounts of money for her foundation. She really did care about helping those kids. She was always sending money to her family in Roanoke . . . she even foot the bill for some crazy expensive surgery her 'what do I need health insurance for?' brother required. There was a lot to like about Raynell—she was full of energy, smart as a whip, and she knew how to make things happen. Honestly, I'm going to be a bit lost without her."

He may be gay, and there may not have been a romantic connection between them, but I can tell from the tone in his voice that he did have a certain fondness for Raynell, which makes me think it's highly unlikely that he killed her. In fact, I'm beginning to wonder if she was killed at all. Maybe she really did just slip in the bathroom and hit her head on the side of the tub.

"You'll be okay." I reach for his hand on the table and place mine over it. "In time, you'll be okay."

He smiles at me, and the three of us sit quietly until Wavonne breaks the silence. "Who's up for some more cake?"

"None for me," I say.

"Me either," Terrence adds.

"Guess it's just me then." Wavonne gets up from the table and starts to cut herself another slice.

"Can you take that to go, Wavonne? We really need to get back to Sweet Tea." I get up from the table.

"There's some foil and Cling Wrap in the drawer right in front of you," Terrence says.

As Wavonne shamelessly packs up a piece of cake for herself, I'm just about to let my little amateur investigation of Raynell's death go when I look past Wavonne into the family room that adjoins the kitchen. My eyes catch sight of the painting of Sarah Vaughan that I noticed when I was here to pick up the antique desk more than a week ago.

"That painting . . . the one of Sarah Vaughan. Raynell told me a little about it when I was here before the reunion. It's such a lovely piece. Do you mind if I take another look at it?"

"Of course not. Raynell sure was disappointed to find out it's not a real Keckley, but I think she took a bit of liking to it anyway. I can't say I was terribly fond of it, though. I wish she would have donated it to the silent auction at her reunion."

Something looked slightly off about the painting from the kitchen, and, as I get closer to it, the image appears faintly different from how I remembered it. The colors somehow seem richer . . . or more vibrant than I remember. It doesn't have the same worn look it did the last time I was here.

"Wavonne? Are you about ready with the cake?" I call to the kitchen.

"Yep," Wavonne says, and appears in the family room.

"Good. We need to let Terrence get back to his day."

"It was nice of you to stop by. I've been getting a lot of visitors. I'm sure there will be more, and they'll love the cake."

"What's left of it," I say, my eyes shifting toward Wavonne and her doggie bag before I look back at Terrence and lean in and give him a hug. "If there's anything we can do, please let us know."

Terrence hugs Wavonne as well, and as we start toward the door, I immediately reopen the investigation I was about to close. I could be wrong, but I'm pretty certain the painting I saw of Sarah Vaughan the day of the reunion is not the same one leaning against the wall in Terrence's family room now. What if the one I saw earlier really was an original Keckley? Could someone who knew it was an original have switched it out with a reproduction?

I stop and think before I open the van door and get inside. *Who would know enough about art to determine the authenticity of the painting and have the skill to make an imitation?*

Only one person comes to mind: Kimberly Butler.

CHAPTER 36

"I don't think it was the same painting. I think someone switched it out," I vent to Wavonne as we head to the restaurant in my van.

"What painting?"

"The one in the family room. The one I was asking Terrence about . . . of Sarah Vaughan."

"Who?"

"Sarah Vaughan. She was a jazz singer long before your time. Apparently there was an artist . . . what was his name?" I think for a moment. "Keckley. Arthur Keckley. He painted portraits of famous singers who performed at the Lincoln Theater on U Street back in its heyday. Raynell said she thought the painting might be one of his creations. She bought it from a real estate client. Supposedly, if it's genuine, it's worth thousands of dollars . . . maybe hundreds of thousands."

"Get out!?"

"But Raynell said she had the painting assessed,

and the art appraiser told her it wasn't a genuine Keckley."

"So if it ain't real, then why would someone swap it out?"

"I don't know. Maybe it *is* real, and Raynell's appraiser was wrong. Maybe Raynell told Kimberly just enough about the painting at the reunion to pique Kimberly's interest."

"You think Kimberly may've killed Raynell? Over a painting?"

"Maybe I do." My mind starts running through some scenarios. "Perhaps Raynell was actually awake when Kimberly came by after the reunion. What if she showed Kimberly the painting, Kimberly figured out it was the real deal, decided to knock off Raynell, and nab the painting for herself? She would have had just enough time to make a sloppy reproduction and bring it back the next day. Perhaps her whole story about coming back to switch out the shampoo bottle the day after Raynell was killed was just a ruse. Maybe she was really there to replace the legitimate painting with her imitation."

"Terrence didn't seem to think the painting looked any different."

"Weren't you the one who said earlier that men don't notice anything unless it involves a basketball or a pair of titties?"

"A *football* or a pair of titties, but same difference. And knowin' what we now know about Terrence, I guess the 'pair of titties' don't apply no more."

"Either way, Terrence probably never paid enough attention to the painting to notice, and he even said he didn't particularly care for it. If I hadn't found it so striking when I first saw it, I probably wouldn't have noticed it was different, either."

"You *sure* it's not the same painting you saw the first time you were there?"

"Yes . . . well . . . I think so. It really did have a different . . . a different *look* . . . I think."

"I don't know, Halia. You're not soundin' so sure anymore."

"Now you've got me questioning whether it really did look different." I'm frustrated with my lack of certainty. "I need to see the painting again and give it a closer look."

"So we gonna turn around and go back to Terrence's house?"

"Possibly." I hand Wavonne my phone. "Look up Terrence in my contacts, would you?"

Wavonne does as I ask and hands the phone to me. "He said he wasn't a fan of the painting, so maybe he'd be willing to sell it to me."

"You want to buy it?"

"I'm not against the idea, but if I pretend I want to buy it, it gives me an excuse to take a second look at it and really give it a good once over."

I hit the call button on my phone and wait for Terrence to pick up.

"Hello."

"Terrence. It's Halia. I'm sorry to bother you. I know we just left a few minutes ago, but we're on the way back to the restaurant, and I got to thinking about that painting of Sarah Vaughan in your family room."

"Really?"

"You mentioned you didn't exactly love it. And . . . well . . . I actually do like it. I thought maybe I could take the painting off your hands . . . for a fair price of course."

"Um . . . I guess . . . maybe."

"Can we set up a time for me to take a second look at it, and then we can talk about payment? Or Wavonne and I could come back now."

"I have to leave for a meeting shortly, so now is not good. Maybe we can set it up another time," he says. "And as far as payment goes, I really have no idea what the painting is worth. I know Raynell had hoped it was some long lost painting from the Lincoln Theater or something. It turned out not to be, but I guess it's still worth a few hundred bucks or so . . . maybe more."

"Yes. Raynell did mention to me that she had it appraised." Suddenly, I have an idea. It's almost impossible for me to be one hundred percent sure the painting was replaced with an imitation. But if anyone could conclude if the painting I saw today is different from the one I saw almost two weeks ago, it would be the appraiser. "Why don't we ask the appraiser to take a second look and find out what he or she thinks it's worth?"

"I guess we could do that. I'd need to check with Christy. She set that up for Raynell."

"I've got Christy's number. Why don't I give her a call?"

"Sure. She'll be over here later this afternoon sorting through some of Raynell's things for me."

"Okay. I'll be in touch. Thanks, Terrence."

I hang up with Terrence and hand my phone to Wavonne, so she can pull up Christy's info while

I'm driving. As Wavonne pecks on my phone with a lone red fingernail, I begin to draft plans in my head for the next day or two. I'll need to make arrangements with Christy to get the appraiser to take another look at the portrait. If he confirms it's not the same piece of artwork he examined for Raynell, then I need to figure out how to prove that Kimberly is the guilty party—that she killed Raynell . . . and not over some petty high school vendetta, but for the reason people have been killing each other for centuries—greed!

RECIPE FROM HALIA'S KITCHEN

Halia's Country Grits and Sausage Casserole

Layer 1 Ingredients

1⅓ cups water
1⅓ cups half-and-half
1 garlic clove, minced
2 tablespoons butter
1 teaspoon salt
½ teaspoon black pepper
⅔ cup quick-cooking grits
½ cup mixed Mexican shredded cheese
(Monterey Jack, Cheddar, Queso Quesadilla, and Asadero)
3 eggs lightly beaten

- Preheat oven to 350 Fahrenheit.

- Bring water and half-and-half to a boil in large saucepan. Stir in garlic, butter, salt, pepper, and grits. Lower heat to simmer mixture and continue to stir for 6 minutes. Remove from heat, stir in cheese, and let set for 10 minutes.

- Stir beaten eggs into grits mixture until well combined. Transfer to well-greased, 12-inch cast-iron skillet and spread evenly.

- Bake for 20 minutes. Remove from oven. Use a spatula to lightly flatten any bubbles. Set aside.

Layer 2 Ingredients

½ pound mild ground pork sausage
1 cup mixed Mexican shredded cheese
4½ tablespoons all purpose flour
7 eggs
1½ cups sour cream
1½ cups whole milk
1 teaspoon salt
½ teaspoon black pepper
⅛ teaspoon ground Cayenne/red pepper
1 tablespoon chopped fresh parsley
1 tablespoon chopped fresh sage

- Brown sausage in a large skillet until crumbled. Drain and blot with paper towels.

- Sprinkle sausage and cheese over grit cake.

- Mix eggs and flour on medium speed until mostly smooth (about 20 seconds). Some small lumps will remain. Add sour cream, milk, salt, black pepper, and red pepper. Continue to mix on medium speed until well combined. Strain mixture through a sieve to remove any lumps.

Stir in parsley and sage before pouring over grit cake.

- Bake at 350 degrees Fahrenheit for 30–35 minutes until firm.

- Cool for 20 minutes prior to serving.

Eight Servings

CHAPTER 37

It's been officially two weeks since Wavonne and I stumbled upon Raynell's dead body. We've just opened for Sunday brunch and the kitchen at Sweet Tea is busier than a tree full of Keebler elves. My prep staff is chopping fruit and making batter for pancakes and waffles, and the deep fryers are fired up for those first batches of fried chicken. Laura has enough home fries going on the grill to feed a small country, and, just now, the first sausage, egg, and grits casseroles are coming out of the oven . . . and they do smell heavenly. We start off with a base of grits, garlic, and cheese and top the mixture with some freshly browned sausage, eggs, and, yes, more cheese. It's one of our brunch specials for the day along with Grandmommy's brown sugar banana pancakes.

"Mmmmm!" Wavonne eyes the casseroles as Tacy lays them on the counter. "Those babies sure look good."

"That they do."

We'll sell out of the ones coming out of the oven by noon, so, just as Tacy finishes removing the last of the cooked casseroles, I move behind him and put in the reinforcements.

"Wavonne, why are you standing here? We're starting to seat customers. Get to work."

"I was hoping to get me a slice of one of these casseroles before I start my shift."

I barely have a chance to give Wavonne one of my signature glares when Saundra sticks her head through the kitchen door. "Halia, there's a young lady here to see you. She said her name is Christy. She has a painting with her."

"Thanks, Saundra. I'll be right out."

I take my apron off, hang it on a hook, and head out to the hostess stand. I called Christy a few days ago and explained that I was interested in purchasing the Sarah Vaughan painting. I asked her if she would connect me with the person who appraised it to help Terrence and me settle on a fair price. She told me the appraiser's name was James Barnett and gave me his number. We originally agreed that I would come by the Rollinses' house while she was there doing some work for Terrence to take a second look at the portrait and meet with James. But while I was chatting with her she mentioned how much she enjoyed her lunch at Sweet Tea a few weeks ago, so I suggested we all meet here. It would give her a chance to enjoy a nice meal and saves me the trouble of having to duck out of the restaurant on a busy Sunday morning.

"Christy. Hi. Thanks so much for coming."

"Sure," she says, grasping the painting with both hands.

"Can I help you with that?"

The painting isn't exactly *huge*—maybe four feet long and about three feet wide—but it's a bit much for Christy's petite frame.

"Yes. Please."

"Let's take it in the back." I grab the painting from her, and she follows me to two tables in the rear of the restaurant. I lay the artwork on one of the tables and signal for her to sit at the other. I give the painting a quick once-over. I'm still fairly convinced it's not the same one I saw at the Rollins house before the reunion.

"What can I get you to drink? A mimosa? Bloody Mary?"

"Just coffee, please."

"Sure. And I'll fetch some menus," I say. "Should I keep an eye out for Mr. Barnett? What's he look like?"

"Actually, I'm not sure. I haven't met him in person. I found him for Raynell on the Internet, and he met with her at the house several weeks ago."

"Okay. I'm sure Saundra will bring him back when he checks in."

I return to the front of the restaurant and pick up a few menus. I'm just about to head to the drink station to get some coffee for Christy when a slight black man walks into the restaurant. He's only about five and a half feet tall and maybe a hundred and thirty pounds. He looks a little lost as he hovers near the door.

"James?" I ask. "James Barnett?"

"Yes."

"Hi. I'm Halia. I'm so glad you agreed to come by."

"No problem. Thank you for having me. I don't get too many offers for a complimentary brunch."

"You're quite welcome. Christy, Raynell's assistant . . . *former* assistant is here already. She brought the painting. Let me show you to the table."

I lead James through the restaurant to the table in the back where Christy is already seated. She stands up when she sees us approaching.

"You must be James," she says when we reach the table. "Christy. So nice to meet you in person."

"You too. I appreciate you connecting me with Ms. Rollins. I had hoped to do more work for her in the future. I was so sorry to hear that she passed. She was such a nice lady."

Christy and I exchange looks. Clearly we are biting our tongues over the "nice lady" comment.

"I understand you want me to take a second look at the Sarah Vaughan portrait."

"Yes. It's right over there." I point to the adjacent table. "But let me treat you to brunch first." I motion for Wavonne.

"What up, boss?"

"You remember Christy."

"Yeah," Wavonne says. "Hey, sista girl."

"Hi, Wavonne."

"Can you bring Christy and me some coffee?" I turn to James. "And what would you like to drink?"

"Coffee is good for me, too."

"I'll give you a few minutes to look over the menu, but keep in mind we have brown sugar banana pancakes and a sausage eggs and grits casserole on special. I highly recommend both of them."

"The casserole is delish!" Wavonne says. "It comes with a blueberry muffin and fresh fruit."

"Sounds good to me," Christy says. "Bring it on."

"Make it two," James says.

"Two sausage, egg, and grits casseroles comin' up."

"Should I look at the painting now while we wait?" James asks after Wavonne walks away to put the order in.

"Sure."

The three of us get up from the table and gather around the painting.

"While not a genuine Keckley, it is a nice portrait, and likely produced around the same time as the original." James leans in closely toward the portrait. "It's a striking piece of work and captures the essence of Ms. Vaughan. It definitely has what we call 'wall power' and, given its age and great condition, I'd say it could fetch anywhere from one to two thousand dollars . . . maybe a bit more if someone really took a liking to it."

"Oh my. That's probably a bit too much for me to spend on artwork. Terrence and I were thinking it was only worth a few hundred dollars. I guess I'll need to think about it," I say. "So, I'm just curious. How can you tell it's not an original Keckley?"

"Right here." James points to the artist's signature on the painting. "Arthur Keckley always signed his paintings A. Keckley at the bottom right-hand side. The signature on this painting is signed Arthur Keckley, and it's on the bottom left side."

I lean in close to the painting to take a look at the signature, and, as I do, I get a whiff of a familiar scent. I can't quite place it, but I know I have smelled it before.

"Well, I guess that's that. It *is* a very nice painting," I say, even though I don't mean it. It must be the same painting I saw before the reunion. If anyone would notice it's different, it would be James. But I just don't find it anywhere near as alluring as I did when Raynell first showed it to me. And I definitely don't care for it enough to spend a thousand dollars on it.

"So, Christy," I say after we've moved back over to the other table to have our coffee, which Wavonne just delivered. "Terrence mentioned you were helping him with some of Raynell's things. How is that going?"

"Yeah, how is that going?" Wavonne slides into the seat next to me. "What's Terrence doin' with all those fab purses and shoes?"

"You forgot the jewelry, Wavonne. And what about the belts? And maybe the furniture?" I chide. "Honestly, the woman's body is barely cold, and you're already making a play for her wardrobe."

Christy smiles. "That's okay. Raynell did have quite the designer collection. Actually, I'm working with Alvetta to set up an auction for many of her things at Rebirth. All the proceeds will go to Raynell's foundation."

"Auction? When?" Wavonne asks.

"We haven't set a date yet, but I'll be sure to keep you in the loop."

"Satisfied?" I ask Wavonne. "Now would you get back to work, and go see if Christy's and James's entreés are ready?"

Wavonne lets out a huff and gets up from the table only to return a few minutes later with two loaded plates for my guests. She puts their dishes down on the table, and they look at them eagerly.

"Thanks, Wavonne," I say. "Can you bring us some more coffee, please?"

"And some ketchup if you don't mind," Christy asks.

Wavonne looks at me to see if I'm keeping a poker face. She knows I have a pet peeve with ketchup, and she's checking to see if my expression shows it. To me, ketchup is for one thing and one thing only—French fries.

Wavonne grabs a bottle of Heinz from a nearby, recently vacated table, and, as she heads off to get us some more coffee, I try not to grimace while James squirts out a long ribbon of ketchup on to his slice of my casserole. I just hate to see food that was perfected to be eaten a certain way ruined. I know it shouldn't—my customers pay for the meals and should be able to eat them however they choose—but it just bugs me when customers sprinkle excessive amounts of salt on carefully seasoned meals, drown a tenderly aged steak with A.1.

sauce, or in this case, drench my Grandmommy's casserole in freakin' ketchup.

"You're not having any breakfast?" Ketchup Man asks me.

"No. Just coffee for me this morning. How do you like the casserole?"

"It's *very* nice," Christy says.

"Yes, very," I hear from James.

We chat for a while longer, and Christy shares some preliminary details about the planned church auction with me, how she's almost done wrapping up Raynell's business dealings, and how she'll be in the market for a new job soon. James is not much of a talker, but he does comment a bit on the painting and suggests that Christy talk to Terrence about including it as part of the church auction.

"Even if it's not the real deal, it is an antique, and could raise a nice little sum for Ms. Rollins's foundation."

"I think that's a great idea. I'll talk to Terrence about it when I take the painting back," Christy says. "Speaking of which, I guess it's time for me to get back over to the Rollins house. I have to start cataloging items for the auction. Thanks so much for a lovely brunch. I hope to come back again soon."

"You're so welcome. I appreciate you saving me the trouble of having to leave Sweet Tea to give the portrait another look. I'm sorry I wasn't able to make an offer on it, but I think it's just too expensive for my blood. I hope Terrence agrees to add it to the auction."

"I'm sure he will." Christy gets up from her chair and walks over to the next table.

"Why don't I help you with that?" James says as she's about to reach for the painting. He walks over and lifts the painting from the table. "Thank you, Ms. Watkins. Breakfast was quite a treat."

I nod and smile, and he begins to walk ahead of us toward the door.

"Can I ask you something, Christy?" I inquire as we linger back.

"Of course."

"You spent a lot of time with Raynell. What do you think—do you think her death was really an accident?"

"I suppose I do. You know as well as me that Raynell was no saint, but I can't think of anything that she ever did to anyone that was so horrible they would want to kill her."

"You're probably right. I guess it's time for me to just let it go."

I continue to walk Christy out, and we find James waiting by her car with the painting.

"Thanks for carrying the painting out for me," Christy says, and presses a button on her keychain to pop the trunk open. She's already got the back-seat folded down, so James slides the painting in the trunk.

I watch Christy get in her car, and James climb into a small pickup truck a few spaces away.

I guess it's about time for me to let it go, I think, recalling how I just said that to Christy as they drive off, but, in reality, I'm not quite ready to do that. Before I'll really be ready to move on, there is one more thing I'd like to do . . . one more visit I'd like to make.

I grab my phone from my pocket and hit the screen a few times. "Hey, Kimberly. It's Halia. I was just wondering . . . if you're still in town, mind if I come by for a quick visit?"

CHAPTER 38

"Hello. I'm Halia Watkins, and this is my cousin, Wavonne. We're here to see Kimberly. You must be Mrs. Butler."

"Yes. She said you'd be stopping by," comes from the elderly woman at the front door of a modest split-level house in Clinton. "You're one of her classmates from high school, right?"

"Yes."

"She's in the garage. It was her makeshift studio when she still lived at home, and we never changed it. I guess her father and I were afraid she may not come back to visit if she didn't have somewhere to paint while she was here."

She waves for me to follow her down the steps.

"Those weren't good days for Kim . . . her high school days I mean," Mrs. Butler says. "Kim told me that horrible girl who caused her to lose her hair died a couple of weeks ago. I supposed it's sad for her friends and family who lost her, but I can't say I'm sorry."

"It was an awful thing to do. Even by high school 'mean girl' standards," I agree.

We follow Mrs. Butler through a quaint family room to a side door. "I'm not sure my Kim ever fully recovered from the incident. But I guess some good came of it. Being so out of place in school left her a lot of time to focus on her art, and now she's doing so well. She's been trying to move Mr. Butler and me to some grand new house for years, but this is home . . . we don't really want to leave."

Mrs. Butler opens the door, and the three of us step into the garage, where we find Kimberly screwing a spray nozzle on a metal can.

"Kim, your guests are here."

Kimberly turns to us and lowers the mask she had covering her nose and mouth. "Hi, Halia. Wavonne."

"I'll leave you three alone. Can I get you anything? A glass of water or a soda?"

"I'd love a Diet Dr Pepper and if—"

"No thank you, Mrs. Butler." I cut Wavonne off. "Nothing for us. We just want to chat with Kimberly for a bit."

"Okay. It was nice to meet you."

"So what can I do for you?" Kimberly asks me as the door shuts behind Mrs. Butler.

"You could start by telling me a little bit about this piece you are working on." I figure there's no need to dive right into questioning her, and I really am curious about her art.

"It's nothing. I've just started experimenting with spray art. I thought it might be an area I could get into, but I'm finding it's too messy, and the fumes from the paint are a bit much. I don't particularly like wearing a mask while I work. But since I started this project I figure I may as well finish it."

"You ever make T-shirts with the spray art? Like they do at the beach?" Wavonne asks.

Kimberly looks momentarily horrified by the question. "Umm . . . no."

I take a closer look at the piece she is working on. "It looks like you're off to a great start."

"Thank you, Halia, but somehow I doubt you came over here to discuss my art."

"Well . . . no . . . no, I didn't," is all I manage to get out. I can't quite figure out how to delve into the subject of the Sarah Vaughan painting, but, as I look around at the extensive studio Kimberly has set up in her parents' garage, it's clear she definitely had the means to quickly create a replica of the original painting and hurriedly switch it out with a copy the morning after Raynell's demise.

Kimberly looks at me quietly as I try to find some words. "What is it, Halia? I assume this has to do with Raynell's death?"

"Yes . . ."

"Did you follow up on the lead I gave you about Gregory being outside Raynell's house the night she died?"

"As a matter of fact, I did."

"And?"

"It's a long story." I think of Gregory's affair with Raynell, and how it was all a pointless ploy to eventually leave her with no husband and no money . . . laughable, actually, considering her husband wouldn't have really cared and the money was mostly Raynell's earnings these days . . . but I decide it's more detail than I want to share with Kimberly. "I mean a *really* long story. But the jist of it is I don't think Gregory killed her."

"What about me, Halia? Do you think I killed her? She was a wicked toad of a woman, and I can't say I'm shedding any tears over her death, but I *did not* kill her."

"I never said you did, Kimberly, but . . . well . . . if I were to . . . to imply that you played a role in her death, there are some things that would support that conclusion."

"Like?"

"Raynell mentioned a painting to you at the reunion—a painting she thought might be an original by Arthur Keckley. He painted—"

"I know who Arthur Keckley was, Halia. And, yes, I remember Raynell mentioning the painting to me. As I told you earlier, I was going to use the painting as an excuse to pay her a visit—I had planned to tell her I was there to take a look at it, and let her know what I thought of it."

"And what *did* you think of the painting?"

"Honestly, I never saw it. When I got there and found her asleep upstairs, I made the shampoo switch and was on my way. There was no need to bring the painting into it."

"You would understand, though, if someone might think you actually did see the painting and used your knowledge of art to determine it was, in fact, a genuine Keckley."

"Um . . . okay. And so what if I did?"

"Well, you must know Keckleys are worth huge amounts of money. It wouldn't be unreasonable to think that you decided to steal the original, quickly paint a facsimile to replace it, and kill the one person who would know the difference—a person you really couldn't stand anyway."

Kimberly laughs. "Wow. You have quite the imagination, Halia, but there's a flaw in your reasoning."

"Oh?"

"Yes. You seem to think I would have stolen Raynell's painting, and killed Raynell, to make a fast buck."

"People have killed for far less reasons."

"I'm sure they have, but did you see the Tesla in the driveway when you came in? It stands out like a sore thumb in this working-class neighborhood."

"Actually, I didn't notice it."

"Girl, I noticed it," Wavonne says. "That is a *nice* ride."

"Well, it cost me about a hundred thousand dollars. The dress I had on the night of the reunion, it was J. Mendel—it cost me over six thousand dollars. And if you must know, I rent a loft in Manhattan for twelve thousand dollars a month . . . and I have another house in the Hamptons that even I'm embarrassed to say how much I paid for it. Do you get what I'm saying here?"

I just look at her as I try to wrap my brain around someone renting an apartment for twelve thousand dollars a month. *Twelve thousand dollars!*

"What I'm saying, Halia, is that I don't need to

steal paintings that would sell for a few hundred thousand dollars—I *create* paintings that sell for almost that much. You're barking up the wrong tree if you're looking at me as someone who killed Raynell for money."

I look down at the floor, embarrassed that Kimberly has shot holes through my accusations. Then I lift my head and sigh. "I've got no one left on my suspect list. Maybe she really did just fall in the bathroom in a drunken stupor."

"She was pretty wrecked when she left the reunion."

"Yes, she was," I agree. "I'm sorry I came over here pointing fingers." I feel like a puppy with its tail between its legs.

"I appreciate the apology. It's fine, really. But I'd like to get back to my work here."

"Of course. We'll show ourselves out."

I turn to leave as Kimberly lifts the mask back over her face, turns a knob on her canister, and aims it at the canvas in front of her. I'm about to step away when the smell of the streaming paint reaches my nose—the fumes Kimberly mentioned earlier that caused her to wear a mask. They have the same smell that I noticed when I got close to the painting when it was laying on the table at Sweet Tea. This little piece of insight gets the gears in my brain spinning and prompts me to turn around and walk back over to Kimberly as she carefully applies paint to her canvas. She sees me hovering next to her and shuts off the sprayer.

"Was there something else?"

"Yes. Just one thing. Would you mind lowering your mask for me . . . just for a sec?"

Kimberly lowers the mask from her face as if she's willing to do anything if it will get rid of me and my prying questions. With the mask lowered, I study her face for a moment while she looks at me, bemused.

"Thank you," I say. "You've no idea how helpful you've just been."

"How so?"

"I think you've just helped me figure out who actually did kill Raynell."

"By spraying paint on a canvas?"

"Yes."

"So who . . . who did it?"

"Why don't you come with us, and I'll show you."

CHAPTER 39

"I'm a busy man, Ms. Watkins," Detective Hutchins says to me as Wavonne and I step out of my van with Kimberly following. He must have arrived a few minutes before us. "I've got a few men here as well." He points toward two patrol cars also parked in the lot of Christy's apartment building. "We're spending taxpayers' dollars. This had better not be some wild-goose chase."

I called Detective Hutchins after leaving Kimberly's parents' house and asked him to meet us at Christy's home. I assured him that I can prove that Raynell's death was not an accident and, after much prodding, he finally agreed.

I lead us toward Christy's apartment. On the way, we pass by Christy's car and see that the painting is still on the folded-down backseat. James Barnett's truck is parked next to it.

We walk up the steps to her unit, and, when I knock on the door, we hear some scurrying around inside. Sometime later, Christy opens the door just enough to poke her head through.

"Hi, Christy. Can we speak with you for a few minutes?" I ask.

"Now is really not a good time."

"That's okay. We'll just be a minute." Wavonne pushes the door open and walks into Christy's apartment, with the rest of us following. We've barely entered the living room when we hear a door close down the hall.

"You can come out, James," I call. "I know you're here. I saw your truck in the parking lot."

James opens a door down the hall from the living room and steps out. He tries to smile as if he has nothing to hide, but he's not a good actor.

"Christy invited me back after lunch at your lovely restaurant," he says. "To . . . um . . . to . . ."

"I thought you said you'd never met James before today?" I ask Christy, interrupting James's stammering. "Do you always invite men you've just met back to your place?" I do the air quotes thing with my fingers when I say "just met."

"I'm not sure that's really any of your business, Halia. Is there something I can help you with?"

"Yes. We'd just like to ask you some questions." I point to my left. "You remember Wavonne and Kimberly . . . and this is Detective Hutchins with the Prince George's County Police Department."

Christy and James were clearly unnerved by our intrusion, but even more worry comes across their faces when they hear the word "police."

"Like I said, Halia, my bringing a man I've just met back to my place is really not any of your business."

"Man you've just met? You'd never met James prior to this morning? Really?" I don't wait for an answer. "Then how, pray tell, did you know he liked ketchup on his eggs?"

Christy looks at me with an inquisitive expression.

"You asked for ketchup after your entreés arrived at brunch today. You never used it, but James was certainly a fan. My momma used to do that for Daddy. He'd always forget to ask for Tabasco sauce before the waiter left the table, so Momma got in the habit of asking for it for him. That's what people who've been together for a long time do. They think for the other person."

"That proves that I knew James before today? Because I asked for ketchup? You've got to be kidding me."

"That's not all. James agreed to carry the painting for you when you were leaving Sweet Tea. He walked ahead of us while you and I chatted. And, when we caught up with him, he was waiting by your car. Funny how he didn't need any instruction on which car was yours."

Clearly flustered, she responds. "That's just a coincidence. He was just . . . he was just waiting for us and happened to be near my car."

"Hmm. Maybe." I switch gears. "So, we saw Raynell's painting out in your car."

"So? I plan to take it back over to Terrence later. You aren't accusing me of stealing it, are you? You asked me to retrieve it for James to reassess it at your restaurant. We all know it doesn't have any major value anyway . . . at least not enough to make it worth stealing."

"No, the *one* in the car doesn't have any significant value, but I suspect *that* one does." I point to some edges of a frame sticking out from underneath the sofa. "When you rushed to hide it from us when we knocked on the door, you should have made sure it was entirely out of sight."

"Ooh . . . it's about to go *down!*" Wavonne steps over to the sofa and slides the painting out from underneath.

I take a quick look at it. "Yes, that's the one I remember seeing at Raynell's weeks ago. It definitely has a more weathered look than the poor imitation out in the car. You know what else I noticed when I leaned in close to examine the imitation on the table at Sweet Tea?"

"What did you notice, Halia?" James asks, irritation in his voice.

"It had a certain smell—a smell that I just figured out over at Kimberly's studio earlier today was the scent of fresh paint. You'll notice this one"—I point toward the painting on the floor—"doesn't have a smell, which is how I knew James was lying when he said the copy he viewed at Sweet Tea, the copy that's down in your car as we speak, was painted about the same time as the original. Portraits that are decades old don't smell of paint, but newly made reproductions do. Any real art appraiser would have noticed the smell and immediately concluded that the portrait viewed at Sweet Tea was painted recently. But James isn't a real art appraiser, is he?"

No one answers my question.

"You arranged for James, who I'm guessing is your boyfriend, to pretend to be an appraiser so he could tell Raynell that the painting was worthless. You—"

Christy interrupts me. "I have no idea what you're talking about."

"Oh, I think you know a lot . . . about a lot of things, Christy. Let's take art for instance. Who would have guessed that an assistant to a real estate agent would have a master's degree in art history?"

"How did you know that?"

"I had Wavonne do a little digging on her phone on the way over here. You shouldn't keep things on your LinkedIn profile that you don't want others to see." I pause for a moment. "My guess is there are not a lot of jobs out there these days for art history majors, so you had to settle for what you hoped would be a temporary gig with Raynell."

"Having an art degree is hardly a crime."

"No, but it does give you the credentials to determine the worth of art or at least have an idea if a piece might be worth something. My guess is you knew the value of the Keckley as soon as you saw it, and you immediately began scheming about how to keep Raynell in the dark about it. I guess that's where James came in. You two conspired for James to pose as an art expert and tell Raynell her painting had no value, when you knew that it was worth hundreds of thousands of dollars. I'm thinking you even had him tell her that her antique desk was worth a few thousand bucks to throw her a bone and keep her from getting suspicious."

"Pure fiction," James says.

"Real life is always more interesting than fiction, James. I bet killing Raynell was not part of the original plan. You probably just planned to switch out the painting with a better reproduction at some later date, but suddenly you needed to act fast when you heard Raynell asking Kimberly to take a look at the painting at the reunion. You decided to kill Raynell before Kimberly could tell her how much the painting was really worth, which would have led Raynell to investigate the two of you. Then not only would you have lost your chance at making some serious cash, but you may very well have found yourself in jail on conspiracy charges."

"This is silly," James says. "Okay, so you caught us with the real painting. Maybe we did switch it out. But you can't prove we killed Raynell. Besides, from what I've heard, all indications lead to her death being an accident. Word is there was no sign of forced entry or struggle."

"Of course there was no forced entry. Christy has a key to her house and, even if she didn't, she was the last one to see Raynell alive when she put her to bed the night of the reunion. She could have left the door unlocked for reentry later."

"That doesn't explain why there were no signs of struggle," Detective Hutchins says. "And these two"—he gestures toward Christy and James—"are not big people. Even together I doubt they could have killed Ms. Rollins without her putting up a good fight . . . a struggle."

"There were no signs of struggle because . . . well, because Raynell was already dead . . . or at least unconscious when Christy and James slammed her head against the bath tub."

Christy visibly tenses up. "That's ridiculous!"

"No, I'm afraid it isn't. And I'll tell you why. Word on the street is that someone stole Raynell's Escalade the day after she died—"

"Yeah . . . some hood rats must've heard Raynell croaked and figured they'll steal her car while there was no one home," Wavonne interrupts.

I eye Wavonne in such a way that tells her to cool it and let me do the talking. "But whoever stole the vehicle abandoned it on the side of the road when it ran out of gas only a few miles from her home."

"So?"

"That always struck me as odd. Raynell was very detailed-oriented and on top of things . . . and, like a Boy Scout, she was always prepared. She earned her living in her car and was hardly the kind of person who would let her gas tank get so low that her car would run out of gas before she could get to the nearest filling station."

"What does that have to do with anything? It means nothing," Christy says.

"It means we look for an explanation of why her gas tank was near empty the day she's found dead. Perhaps it was because *someone*"—I look at Christy as I say this—"left the car running all night with the garage door closed. Perhaps *someone* brought her home from the reunion and put her to bed. Then went into the garage and started the car, knowing that Raynell was so drunk she'd likely sleep through the carbon monoxide fumes coming into her house until they killed her or at least rendered her immobile."

"And not that anyone did, but let's just say that

someone else entered the house shortly after you left." I move my gaze from Christy to Kimberly. "And let's just say this someone was there to . . . I don't know . . . switch out shampoo with hair removal cream. The running car in the garage would also explain why this person left Raynell's feeling light-headed and was so loopy that she had to pull over and get some rest in a parking lot. The house would have likely just started to fill up with fumes when she came to settle an old high school vendetta. While she wouldn't have been there long enough for the fumes to kill her, they could have made her feel unwell on the way home and caused the lingering headache she might have reported for days afterward."

"If you really think someone left the car running all night, what makes you think it was me?" Christy asks. "There were tons of people in town with motive to kill Raynell. From what I understand, half her former classmates hated her. Why not Gregory Simms . . . or her." Christy directs a finger toward Kimberly.

"Interesting that you're pointing to Kimberly. I went to see her today, and she was working with some spray paints. Did you know people wear masks when they work with spray paints? Funny thing, when she took the mask off, the straps that go behind her ears left some marks on her face—the same kind of marks you had on your face when I came to get my check from you the morning after the reunion. I thought they were sleep lines from a wrinkly pillowcase, but now I'm quite certain they were from a mask—a mask you wore when you went back to Raynell's after filling her house with carbon monoxide all night. It would have been necessary to wear one when you went around opening all the windows to let the fumes out.

"I thought it was odd that all the windows were open the morning we found Raynell. She was always complaining about how much she hated the heat—"

"Girl was a bigger sweater than Whitney Houston during her crack days."

I nod in agreement with Wavonne. "And why would she have all the windows in her house open when she was home alone? Let's face it, Christy, you went back to Raynell's the morning after the reunion, opened all the windows to clear the house of car exhaust. And, at some point, James joined you, and the two of you dragged Raynell's dead body out of bed into the bathroom and slammed her head against the tub. Shortly after you hastily created a bad reproduction of the Keckley painting and replaced it with the original, hoping it would go unnoticed."

"That's all speculation," James says.

Christy looks at him, and it seems that the stress of her actions and the lies to cover them have taken their toll. "So what if we did kill her? The bitch had it coming."

"Christy!" James calls, trying to get her to shut up.

"They've already got us on the stolen painting, James. It's over," she says to him, and then turns to the rest of us. "She was a horrible person. All she did was scream at me all day and complain about everything I did. She wouldn't have sold a single house if it wasn't for all of my work. But do you think that miser ever shared so much as a penny of one of her commissions with me? When she made a big sale, do you know what she would do? She'd give me some of her designer hand-me-downs in a plastic trash bag as some sort of warped thank-you. Like I was supposed to have undying gratitude for her leftover Manolos. Yeah, we killed her to keep her from finding out we tried to dupe her out of a hefty sum of money and to make sure we got the painting, but just ridding the world of Raynell Rollins was reason enough."

As Christy continues to unravel, I see Detective Hutchins approach the living room window and signal to the officers outside. Neither Christy nor James appears braced to make a run for it, so I'm surprised when Detective Hutchins flips his jacket back to reveal his gun. "I'm placing both of you under arrest," he says. "Don't make me take this out of its holster."

The words have barely left his mouth when two armed police officers open the front door, and quickly step inside with their guns drawn. Detective Hutchins directs them to cuff Christy and James and take them outside to read them their rights.

"I have to hand it to you, Halia, you did it again," Detective Hutchins says to me with a look of surprise. "But maybe from now on you should leave the detective work to the professionals. Or one of these days you may end up getting hurt yourself."

"I'll do my best."

While Wavonne and I watch him walk outside the apartment to check on his underlings, she leans toward me. "Think you can keep them distracted while I take a quick peek in Christy's closet for some of those hand-me-down Manolos?"

EPILOGUE

It's a crisp fall day, and I'm thankful to have a break from the heat we've dealt with all summer as Wavonne and I step out of my van and make our way to one of the event rooms in good old Rebirth Christian Church. I wasn't that eager to come, but Wavonne, for once in her life, has actually saved up money for the opportunity to bid on some of Raynell's things that are going to be auctioned off today, so I agreed to bring her.

It's been almost two months since Raynell's untimely death. I'm not sure if Terrence wanted to allow for a respectable amount of time to pass before putting Raynell's finer things up for sale, or if the lag time was due to Christy, the original curator, who was tagging everything and getting it ready for event, being hauled off to jail on murder charges.

I've been to Rebirth enough times now that I

sort of know the lay of the land at this point; accordingly, it doesn't take Wavonne and me long to find the room reserved for the auction.

"I think I've died and gone to heaven," Wavonne says as we enter the space.

"They really didn't spare any expense, did they?" I take a look around. I guess I shouldn't be surprised by how grand the displays are. I should know by now that Rebirth does nothing on a small scale. Many of Raynell's outfits are displayed on actual mannequins just like you'd see in a department store. Some of her shoes and handbags are displayed in groups on long tables draped in silk fabric while others are displayed solo on individual pedestals. Jewelry, wallets, and scarves are displayed in glass cases.

"I wonder if Tiffany & Co. is as well-appointed as this place," I say to Wavonne as we begin to peruse the displays.

"I wonder if Tiffany is as expensive as this place." Wavonne looks at the bidding form for a pair of T-strap Valentino pumps. "The bidding starts at five hundred dollars. And they want at least four hundred for those Fendi beaded sandals." She sighs. "There're no bargains to be had here. I saved two hundred and fifty dollars for nothin'."

"Let's keep looking. I'm sure there is something you can afford."

I pick up a glossy color booklet from one of the tables and begin to thumb through it. It has a complete description of all the items up for auction, a brief bio about Raynell with her photo, and some information about her foundation. Once again I should not be surprised, but I find myself taken aback when I read the fine print at the bottom of one of the pages. It reads: "A portion of the proceeds from the event will go to the Raynell Rollins Foundation for Children in Need." *A portion?* I think to myself. The idea that *all* the proceeds will not go to the foundation seems a little shady, not to mention tacky, considering the auction has been heavily promoted as an event to benefit charity. But given that Raynell was likely the major bread winner in the Rollinses' household, Terrence may be hoarding earnings from her estate auction to meet the shortfalls he's bound to face without her income coming in.

"Halia and Wavonne," I hear come from behind as we move toward the jewelry display cases.

"Alvetta," I say. "How are you? Clearly you've been very busy," I add, looking around me.

She gives Wavonne and me a quick hug. "I'm fine," she says. "Yes, I've been busy getting everything ready for tonight. We've attracted a good crowd. I think we'll raise a lot of money for Raynell's foundation. It's a great way to honor her memory."

I'm tempted to ask exactly how much of the money made tonight is actually going to charity, but I decide to let it go. I'd rather just assume that most of it is slated for people in need.

"Yes. It looks like lots of people are placing bids." I take another look around and notice a few somber-looking people seated in the rows of chairs positioned in the middle of the room. "I guess those folks have already placed all their bids?"

"No." Alvetta laughs. "Those are the *serious* bidders. I doubt they are taking part in the silent auction at all. They are here for the live auction."

"Live auction?"

"Yes. For the Sarah Vaughan painting. It's been officially authenticated as an Arthur Keckley original." Alvetta points to the far side of the room, and I see the painting on display. Wavonne had me so caught up in Raynell's clothes and accessories I hadn't looked in the direction of the portrait.

"It really is stunning," I say as the three of us begin to approach the portrait. "It looks even more exquisite now that it's displayed with the appropriate lighting."

"And what do we have here?" Wavonne says when we reach the painting, and she takes note of a nicely built armed security guard standing next to it. "Mm-hmm," she adds, looking him up and down.

"We're here to look at the *painting,* Wavonne."

"Speak for yourself," she replies as the guard cracks a smile.

"Is an armed guard really necessary?" I ask Alvetta.

"We're starting the bidding at a hundred thousand dollars, so yes, I'd say so," she replies. "Sotheby's did the valuation, and they are handling the live auction. It should be starting soon. We're about to close the silent auction, so you two should get any final bids in."

"I guess we should. It was nice to see you, Alvetta."

"You too," she says. "I hope you'll come to service again sometime soon." She gives us each a quick peck on the cheek and darts off to speak with a gentleman near the podium, the auctioneer, I assume.

Wavonne and I continue to walk the room, and it's not long before we are both thoroughly frustrated at the starting bids on most of the items.

"There's nothin' here for me," Wavonne says, defeated.

"They really did price things quite high." As I say this I try to think of some of the less expensive items we've seen tonight. There was a very small Coach wallet that started with a bid of two hundred dollars, but it was a simple leather piece and way too conservative for Wavonne. Some of the scarves and belts had starting bids under one hundred dollars, but I think Wavonne really had her heart set on a purse or a pair of shoes.

"What about those Fendi pink sandals we saw when we first came in?" I ask. I'm sure they have a smaller heel than Wavonne would like, but they are florescent pink with a wide beaded toe strap. I don't think Wavonne has ever turned down a florescent anything.

"Those started at four hundred."

"If no one has placed a bid on them, and they are still going for four hundred, I'll throw in the other one fifty," I offer, hating the idea of Wavonne having actually behaved like a mature adult and saving some money amounting to her leaving empty-handed.

"You would?" Wavonne's face lights up, and she leads us back over to the sandal display. Fortunately, no other bids have been placed, and with the silent auction about to close, I think it's safe to say Wavonne will be the winner.

"Looks like I'll be leaving with these babies."

"I think they have to reconcile everything tonight. You'll probably have to come back and pick them up tomorrow or another time."

Only slightly deflated, Wavonne writes down her bid, while, from the corner of my eye, I see someone approaching carrying a flat package wrapped in brown paper. I turn my head to bring the individual into full view.

"Kimberly!"

"Hi, Halia," she says while Wavonne is still distracted by the shoes. "I just came back for a quick visit to see my parents and to give you this." She nods toward the package. "I went by Sweet Tea to surprise you, and they said you'd be here."

"What is it?" I ask, intrigued.

"You'll see."

I take the package from her and set it on one of the display tables, so I can unwrap it. My excitement builds as I gently remove the packing paper, and it becomes clear that Kimberly's gift is a portrait—*the* portrait that we discussed her painting of my grandmother.

"I have no words," I say, smiling from ear to ear as I take in the painting of my hero and mentor and namesake . . . and all around special lady, Mrs. Mahalia Hix. "I love it!"

"Girl can throw down with a paint brush," I hear Wavonne say behind me as she takes in the painting.

"Hi, Wavonne," Kimberly says.

"Hey, girl. That painting's dope!"

Kimberly laughs. "Thank you," she says to Wavonne, and then turns to me. "I figured I owed you one. If you hadn't put all the pieces together and figured out who killed Raynell, I could have been in a lot of trouble if the police figured out I was there the night she was murdered. It's the least I could do."

"Well, I still insist on paying you."

Kimberly lifts her hand at me. "I won't hear of it. How about just the occasional complimentary meal at Sweet Tea when I come to town?"

"You've got yourself a deal."

"Perfect."

"I can't wait to take this back to Sweet Tea and get it on the wall."

I'm still gushing over the painting when Alvetta steps to the microphone and announces that the bidding has closed on the silent auction items, and that the live auction for the Keckley painting is about to begin.

"Can I entice you with one of those complimentary meals now?" I ask Kimberly. "You can help me hang the painting and see how perfect it looks at Sweet Tea."

"You don't want to stay and see how much the Sarah Vaughan painting goes for?" Wavonne asks.

I look past her at the portrait, and, while it is lovely, I can't help but think how it ultimately played a role in the death of Raynell and the incarceration of Christy. In my mind it's hard to separate the beauty of the artwork with the dreadful series of events that unfolded because of it.

"You know," I say to Wavonne as I pick up the painting of Grandmommy and gesture for her and Kimberly to follow me out the door, "the only painting I really have any interest in at the moment is this one. Let's get it back to Sweet Tea and admire it over a tall glass of iced tea and a few slices of whatever Momma has whipped up for dessert."

Mahalia's Sweet Tea boasts the most flavorful soul food in all of Prince George's County, Maryland. But as events at the beauty industry's leading trade show turn ugly, owner Halia Watkins needs to bite into an unsavory new item on the menu—murder!

When the chicest hair convention of the year gets cooking in town, so does business at Mahalia's Sweet Tea. Halia can barely handle the influx of customers looking to satisfy their appetites after spending the day surrounded by outrageous runway styles. As buzz builds around beauty mogul and pop culture icon Monique Dupree, collard greens start moving out of the kitchen faster than models strutting down the catwalk . . .

But the glitz fades the moment Monique is found shot to death. Turns out, the glamorous entrepreneur's vanity empire was stained by bitter rivalries, explosive affairs, and backstabbers scheming for fame and fortune. With more suspects than ingredients listed on a bottle of deep conditioner, Halia and her cousin Wavonne rush to discover who pulled the trigger—before the conniving culprit dishes another deadly surprise . . .

Please turn the page for an exciting sneak peek of the next Mahalia Watkins Soul Food mystery MURDER WITH COLLARD GREENS AND HOT SAUCE coming soon wherever print and e-books are sold!

"I thought we could start at Macy's," I say after I've parked the van in the parking garage of the Fashion Centre at Pentagon City, a multi-level mall just across the bridge from Maryland in Arlington, Virginia.

"Macy's?!" Maurice bemoans as if I just suggested we shop for outfits at a flea market. "You may enjoy sorting through heaps of marked-down clothing flung all over the place, but I prefer stores that don't look like the Tasmanian Devil had a sudden need for a tunic and a discounted pair of leggings."

"Yeah . . . Macy's all ghetto these days," Wavonne says as the three of us step out of the van and walk toward the entrance. "Can't never find anyone to wait on you, and they all funky-monkey about their returns. I tried to take back that Michael Kors dress I bought there a few months ago—you know, the green sheath dress with the studs on the sleeves . . . the one I wore to Melva's wedding . . . and to Linda's birthday party . . . and my date with that cheap-ass brotha that took me to that nasty Cici's pizza buffet—although I will say macaroni and cheese on pizza crust is not the *worst* idea in the world. *Anyway,* the heifer behind the register wouldn't take the dress back . . . .somethin' about how the tags had been removed and it had clearly been worn. It was a *hundred* dollars. I can't afford a hundred dollar dress."

"Well then, maybe you shouldn't have purchased it in the first place."

"Save the lecture, Halia," Wavonne replies as we approach the mall directory. "At least I was able to sell it on eBay . . . got forty bucks for it. So I'm only out sixty, but I'm done with Macy's for the time bein'."

"Everyone at Macy's will be so hurt that you've taken your 'buy, wear, and return' routine to their competitors."

Maurice ignores our bickering as he eyes the map and sighs. "What kind of place is this? No Neimans, no Saks . . . no Prada, no Burberry . . . no Chanel. We may as well be at one of those outlet malls where women shop in sneakers and sweatpants," he laments about what I always thought of as at least a *semi*-upscale mall. There may not be a Tiffany & Co. or Cartier, but there's a Banana Republic, and a Zara, and a Hugo Boss . . . and Coach and Kate Spade . . . it's way nicer than any of the malls we have on the other side of the river in Prince George's County.

"At least there's a Nordstrom." There's a sound of resignation in Maurice's voice. "I guess it will have to do."

Wavonne and I follow Maurice through the

busy mall corridor, and, when we cross the threshold into Nordstrom he stops to speak to the first sales person we encounter.

"May I help you?" the young man asks.

"Yes." Maurice looks Wavonne and me up and down then back at the sales associate. "Where's the Encore section?"

"Encore?" I ask Wavonne as the sales guy directs Maurice.

"It's Nordstrom's fat lady section."

The sales clerk overhears Wavonne. "Not at all. It's our department for plus . . . um . . . *full-figured* women."

"Well that's me. I'm definitely full-figured." Wavonne looks down at her ample bosom. "My girls ain't gonna fit in nothin' petite—that's for sure. Oprah and Gayle," she says, looking at her left breast and then her right, "need room to breathe."

"I'm sure you'll find some great fashions over there with plenty of room for . . . um . . . Oprah and Gayle."

Maurice thanks the young man and the three of us set off for, as Wavonne put it, "the fat lady section."

"Hello," a smartly dressed middle-aged woman asks when we reach our destination. "What can I help you with?"

"I need to find something suitable for these two . . . for an exclusive event . . . a white party," Maurice says. "What's your name, dear?"

"Susan."

"Okay, Susan. Well she's looks to be about a fourteen." Maurice points to me. "And she's a sixteen," he adds with a finger toward Wavonne.

"Sixteen?" Wavonne scoffs "I'm a fourteen too."

"Wavonne, sweetie," Maurice replies while waving his hand from her neck down to her feet "just because, with a little vigor and a lot of Vaseline, you can finagle all that into a size fourteen, doesn't mean you *are* a size fourteen."

"I've been telling her that for years."

"Don't be hatin' on all my jelly. I like a fitted look."

"There's *fitted*, and then there's buttons hanging on for dear life," Maurice says. "Let's just plan to go for a . . . um . . . a *less fitted* look for the white party. Trust me. I'm highly experienced at dressing generously-proportioned women. I've been styling Monique for years." Maurice turns back to Susan. "I want something formal for both of them, but still fun and stylish." He points to me again. "Let's go a bit more conservative for this one . . . maybe something from Alex Evenings or Adrianna Papel . . . or Eileen Fisher." Then he looks at Wavonne. "This one . . . she's more Mac Duggal or City Chic."

"Sure . . . sure," Susan says. "Why don't I get you both set up in the fitting rooms, and I'll bring some selections to you."

Susan is about to lead us to the dressing area when Maurice speaks up again. "They'll need some Spanx too . . . and not just the tummy ones . . . tummy *and* thigh."

Over the next thirty minutes or so, Susan helps Wavonne and me into these sort of torture devices called Spanx to smooth out our curves and begins bringing dresses to us. We try them on while Maurice sits on a stool just outside the stalls and provides commentary.

"No," he says to Susan, exasperation in his voice, as I model a Pisarro Nights beaded gown trimmed with something Susan calls "sheer-illusion lace." "Why didn't you tell me that dress had a drop waist? Anyone can see she's a pear!"

"A pear? What does that mean?" I ask.

"It means you have small titties and a fat ass," Wavonne says. She's standing next to me admiring herself as we share a mirror. "*I*, on the other hand, am an hourglass."

I give her a quick look. "More like an hour and a half glass."

Wavonne scowls at me in the mirror as Maurice looks me over once again.

"Dear God," he grumbles to Susan. "If the dress was purple, she'd look like that slow-witted creature in the McDonald's kiddie commercials."

"He's talkin' about Grimace."

"I *know* who he's talking about, Wavonne," I respond as Susan unzips the back of the dress, and I head back into the dressing room.

"Bring me something flowy with a softly fitted waistline," Maurice commands before I have a chance to close the curtain and finish getting out of the dress. "Something sparkly above the waist and plain below . . . we need party on the top," he says, gesturing toward my upper half before lowering his finger in the direction of my waist and thighs, "and all business on the bottom."

"He's trying to draw attention away from your big behind," Wavonne quips, paying me back for my "hour and a half" comment.

I close the dressing room curtain without bothering to respond. As I step out of the dress, I hear Maurice make a few comments about the outfit Wavonne is modeling before sending her back into the changing room for another round as well.

A few minutes later, Susan brings me yet another frock. I try it on and dare to think that we may have finally found a keeper. It's an ivory-colored knee-length dress by Adrianna Papel with a slightly lower hem in the back than in the front, a scoop neck, and something Susan called "flutter sleeves." It ties loosely at the waist and is actually quite flattering.

"Now we're getting somewhere," Maurice says as I step out of the fitting room. He walks a complete circle around me, adjusts the neckline, and redoes the tie so the bow sits more to the right of my waist than the middle.

His eyes meet mine in the mirror and he smiles. "Lovely! I think we have a winner."

I smile back at him and decide that maybe he's not quite as snarky and irritating as I originally thought.

"*Very* nice." Wavonne gives me a long look as she steps out of her stall in Susan's latest selection. "Girl, they better turn off the detectors, cause you smokin'!"

I laugh. "Thank you, Wavonne. You look very nice yourself."

"Hmmm," Maurice says, scrutinizing her dress, a floor-length white gown with silver sequins dotted throughout. "It just sort of pours down your body, doesn't it?" He circles her like he did me a few minutes ago. "I'm not sure about the plunging neckline. That's a lot of décolletage for a party that starts early in the evening."

"Décolletage?" Wavonne asks.

"I think he's talking about your cleavage."

"It's not awful, but I don't think this is it. Maybe we need to go in another direction." Maurice turns his neck. "Susan," he calls out toward the main shopping area, prompting her to appear. "I saw a red jumper on one of the mannequins. Do you know which one I'm talking about? That might be a good look for Wavonne if you have it in white."

"Yes. That's by Marina. I think we do have it white. Let me check."

As Susan returns to the racks I see Maurice look at his watch. "Let's try the jumper. If it's not *you*, we'll go with this one. We're getting short on time. I've got to get Monique dressed, and only God knows what sort of drama will be going on in that house by the time I get to there."

"Drama?" Wavonne asks. "What sort of drama?"

"Oh nothing . . . let's just say I may be her stylist, but half the time I feel more like her psychiatrist. There's always something going on between her and Nathan that I have to hear about and help her process. The man is a total sleaze."

"Can't say I'm surprised to hear that." I say. "I don't particularly care for him based on what little interaction I've had with him."

"You're not the only one. He's always up to no good."

"What sort of 'no good' we talkin' about here?" Wavonne asks.

"I'm not one to gossip," Maurice replies in that

way people who love to gossip speak right before they're about to start gossiping. "You name it. Drinking. Women. And, lately, gambling. Monique will not even tell me how much of their fortune he's lost over at MGM." Maurice is referring to the swanky Las Vegas-style casino that opened to great fanfare a few years ago in National Harbor, a multi-use waterfront development that has become Prince George's County's haughtiest neighborhood. "He's a regular in the high limit room. I've heard rumors of him losing more than a hundred thousand dollars in a single day."

"A hundred thousand dollars!?" I bellow. "Oh my."

"Why doesn't she get rid of him if he's gambling away all her money?"

"Your guess is as good as mine. Monique is a smart beautiful woman, but when it comes to relationships, she makes bad decision after bad decision."

"Speaking of relationships, what is up with her and Odessa?"

"Those two." Maurice shakes his head. "They've had a . . . shall we say *tenuous* relationship since I've known them. They started out in the cosmetology trenches together . . . low paid styling jobs at chain beauty shops . . . and, while Odessa has certainly had some success with her salon, Monique just surpassed her by leaps and bounds and became this nationwide phenomena. I don't think Odessa can handle it. She's jealous."

"So why did Monique invite her to dinner last night if they don't get along?"

"I don't know. Their whole deal is complicated. They go way back, and they have a mutually beneficial relationship. From what I know, Odessa sells more of Monique's products than any hair salon in the country, so Monique gives her some discounts on the wholesale prices. They are both making a lot of money for each other."

Maurice pokes his head outside the dressing area. "Where is that sales girl?"

"I'm not sure we need her," Wavonne says. "The longer I wear this, the more it grows on me."

"It's okay, but it would need a little tailoring to make it a perfect fit, and it might be a little too glittery . . . with the silver sequins and all."

"There is no such thing as too glittery when it comes to Wavonne."

"Not for *Wavonne,*" Maurice says. "For *Monique.* She'll get testy if she knows I helped Wavonne select something that, even for half a second, takes any attention away from her."

"Is that even possible? For someone to take attention away from Monique," I ask, although I guess, if anyone was going to do such a thing, it would be Wavonne. "Monique would be the belle of the ball in a potato sack. And I'm sure whatever she's wearing to the party will be in a league all its own."

"Oh, it will be. Monique would settle for nothing less," Maurice says. "She's had a custom-made gown in the works for months . . . mermaid silhouette . . . Bateau neckline . . . hand-sewn beads . . . it's gorgeous . . . just *gorgeous* . . . worth every penny of the four thousand dollars she's paying for it."

"Four thousand dollars?!" Wavonne shrieks.

"Wow. That must be some white dress," I say.

"*White?*" Maurice responds. "Aren't you cute." He's talking to me as if I'm a naive child. "Now how do you expect Monique to be the undeniable center of attention in a *white* dress at a *white* party?"

Wavonne and I stare back at him, perplexed.

"That's Monique's *thing*. . . every year she throws a white party and insists that all her guests wear white . . . then she makes a grand entrance in a bold-colored dress. This year she is wearing a vivid Larimar blue evening gown."

"Sounds like it will be quite something."

"Yes, and if I don't get over to her house and help her get into it soon, I'll never hear the end of it." Maurice looks at his watch once again. "I'm going to go find Susan. We need to get a move on."

"Larimar?" I ask Wavonne as Maurice steps away. "Must be one of those trendy designers my unfashionable pear-shaped self has never heard of."

"How can you not have heard of him, Halia? He's dressed Halle Berry and like a million other celebrities."

"Really? That's —"

"Here we are," Susan says, interrupting me and handing a white jumper to Wavonne.

"Try it on and let's see how it looks," Maurice instructs. "We are out of time, so if this is not a good look for you, we'll just go with the dress you have on. I've got to get over to Casa Monique and help her get ready . . . and help her deal with whatever antics that husband of hers has been up to."

"Wow, it sounds like working for Monique is quite the roller coaster ride," I say as Wavonne steps into the dressing stall and closes the curtain.

"It's certainly never boring," Maurice says. "Never ever boring."